ELLIE AND THE HARPMAKER

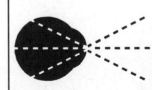

This Large Print Book carries the
Seal of Approval of N.A.V.H.

ELLIE AND THE HARPMAKER

HAZEL PRIOR

THORNDIKE PRESS
A part of Gale, a Cengage Company

GALE
A Cengage Company

Farmington Hills, Mich • San Francisco • New York • Waterville, Maine
Meriden, Conn • Mason, Ohio • Chicago

LIBRARY OF CONGRESS CIP DATA ON FILE.
CATALOGUING IN PUBLICATION FOR THIS BOOK
IS AVAILABLE FROM THE LIBRARY OF CONGRESS

ISBN-13: 978-1-4328-7186-4 (hardcover alk. paper)

Published in 2019 by arrangement with Berkley, an imprint of Penguin Publishing Group, a division of Penguin Random House, LLC

Printed in Mexico
1 2 3 4 5 6 7 23 22 21 20 19

To my dear parents,
who loved music, the countryside
and fun

A thought:
*Some things are easier to hide
than others.*

A fact:
*Harps come under the "others" category.
So do small boys.*

A quote from Shakespeare:
If music be the food of love, play on.

1
DAN

A woman came to the barn today. Her hair was the color of walnut wood. Her eyes were the color of bracken in October. Her socks were the color of cherries, which was noticeable because all the rest of her clothes were sad colors. She carried an enormous shoulder bag, canvas. It had a big buckle (square), but it was hanging open. The woman's mouth was open too. She was shifting from one foot to the other by the door so I told her to come in. The words came out a bit mangled due to the fact that I was wearing my mask. She asked what I'd said, so I took it off and also took off my earmuffs and I said it again. She came in. Her socks were very red indeed. So was her face.

"I'm sorry to be so rude, but I'm gobsmacked." She did look it, to be honest. "Did you . . . you didn't, did you . . . make all these?"

I told her yes.

9

"Wow! I just can't believe it!" she said, looking round.

I asked her why not.

"Well, it's not exactly what you expect to find in the middle of nowhere! I've been past the end of your lane so many times and I just had no idea that all this was here!"

I put my earmuffs and mask on the workbench and informed her that indeed, all this *was* here. Perhaps I should have pointed out as well that this is not the middle of nowhere. Not at all. Exmoor is the most somewhere place that I know and my workshop is an extremely somewhere part of it. I did not say this, though. It would have been rude to contradict her.

Morning light was pouring in on us from the three windows. It outlined the sloping rafters. It floodlit the curls of wood shavings. It silvered the edges of the curves and arcs all around us and made strung shadows on the floor.

The woman was shaking her head so that the walnut-colored hair bounced around her face. "How lovely! They're beautiful, so beautiful! It is like a scene from a fairy tale. And how strange that I've stumbled across this place today of all days!"

Today is Saturday, September 9, 2017. Is that a particularly strange day to stumble across a Harp Barn? I smiled politely. I wasn't sure if she wanted me to ask why it was strange. Lots of people find things strange that I don't find strange at all, and lots of people don't find strange the things that I find very strange indeed.

The woman kept looking at me and then gazing around the barn and then back at me again. Then she pulled on the strap of her canvas bag to rearrange it in a different way over her shoulder and said: "Do you mind my asking, have you been here long?"

I informed her that I'd been here for one hour and forty-three minutes. Before that I was out in the woods, having my walk. She smiled and said: "No, I mean, have you had this place a long time? As a workshop?"

I told her I came here when I was ten years old and I was now thirty-three years old, so that meant (I explained in case her math was not very good) that I'd been here for twenty-three years.

"No! I just can't believe it!" she said again. She seemed to have a problem believing things. She shook her head slowly. "I think I must be in a dream."

I offered to pinch her.

She laughed. Her laugh was interesting: explosive and a little bit snorty.

The next thing that happened was I went

across and shook her hand because that is what you are supposed to do. You are not supposed to do pinching. I knew that really. "My name is Dan Hollis, the Exmoor Harp-maker," I said.

"Pleased to meet you. I'm Ellie Jacobs, the Exmoor . . . housewife."

"Housewife" does not mean you are married to a house. It means you are a woman who is married to a husband and your husband goes off to work every day and *you* don't go off to work at all but embark on house dusting, house hoovering and various ironing and washing duties and other things that happen in a house, and in fact you aren't really expected to go out of the house at all except to get yourself to a supermarket and then you go up and down the aisles with a trolley and a list looking sad. What a lot of things are embedded in that housewife word.

"It's funny," she mused, her eyes wandering around the barn again. "Harp playing was on my list."

I asked if she meant her shopping list.

She paused and looked at me with arched eyebrows. "No, my before-forty list. Lots of people have them, apparently. You know — the list of things to do before you reach the age of forty. Like swimming with dolphins and seeing the Great Wall of China."

I asked if she had swum with dolphins and she said no. I asked if she had seen the Great Wall of China and she said no. Then she added that she had a few years to go yet. I asked her how many, but she didn't answer. Perhaps I shouldn't have asked her that. There are lots of things you are not supposed to ask, and I fear that might be one of them. So I changed my question and asked her what would happen if she didn't manage to swim with dolphins or see the Great Wall of China or play the harp before she reached the age of forty. She said, "Nothing."

We were silent for a bit.

"It smells lovely in here," she commented finally. "I love the smell of wood."

I was glad she had noticed it because most people don't, and I was glad that she appreciated it because most people don't. Then she gestured toward the harps. "They're utterly exquisite," she said. "Will you tell me something about them?"

I told her yes. I informed her that they are Celtic-style traditional harps and they would have been fairly widespread in Britain during the Middle Ages, especially in the north and west. I told her I had carved the *Elfin* from my own design out of the sycamore tree that had fallen by the brook four years ago. I mentioned that I had made the *Sylvan* from ancient beech and the *Linnet* from rosewood. I showed her the drawers of strings and explained about the red ones being Cs, the black ones being Fs and the white ones being As, Bs, Ds, Es and Gs. I told her about each one being a different thickness and the importance of tension. I showed her the holes in the back and how they were anchored inside. I explained the use of the levers for sharpening the note. I told her about the pebbles. I gave her a couple of pieces of wood so that she could hold them and compare the weight. I expanded on the different resonances of different woods.

Then I realized that I had not asked very much about her, so I stopped telling her things and I asked the following eight questions: How are you? Do you have any pets? What is in your enormous shoulder bag? What is your favorite color? What is your favorite tree? Where do you live? Do you enjoy being the Exmoor Housewife? Would you like a sandwich?

She answered me the following answers: fine, thank you; no; a big camera and a notepad and a thermos with soup; red; birch; about five miles southwest of here; um; that would be very nice.

I made twelve sandwiches using six slices of bread and substantial quantities of cream cheese. I cut them into triangles because I reckoned she was a lady.

I've noticed that the act of cutting always helps me think. I do some good thinking when I cut up wood to make harps too. That might have been why, over the triangles of the sandwiches, I came to a decision.

2
ELLIE

"He *gave* you one?"

"Yes."

"Just like that?"

"Well, pretty much."

Clive lowered the motoring magazine and transferred his full attention to my face. His eyebrows drew together and two deep vertical creases appeared between them.

"I presume you're having me on?"

"No," I said, and added a "Not" to underline it.

"So he offered, and you just took it?"

"Well, it was . . . it was hard to say no."

This was going to be tricky. I couldn't explain it to myself, let alone offer an explanation to anyone else. Which was why I'd been driving around Exmoor for the last half hour — with frequent stops to look in the back of the car and check that it was true — before I finally headed homeward.

Our nice but nosy neighbor Pauline was

out in her garden, so I had gone straight in. I had launched myself into the kitchen. I'd swept a brief kiss into my husband's receding hairline. I'd sought out the kettle, filled it to the brim, spurted myself with water in the process and abandoned it. Then I'd blurted out a tangle of sentences that sounded frothy and ridiculous. I'd blushed, become aware of it, and blushed some more. Now I stood limply grinning by the fridge.

Clive closed the magazine and tugged at the neck of his sweatshirt. "Sorry, El, but I have to ask: Exactly *how* long have you known this man?"

My mind traveled back to the strange encounter of earlier: the huge open door of the barn that had enticed me in, the warm scent of wood, the light falling on the myriad harps, and there, in the center of them all, the lone figure. There had been some sort of tool in his hand, but already my memory was playing tricks on me and I couldn't say what it was. He had initially appeared to be an alien. His lower face was covered by some sort of blue mask and he was wearing earmuffs, presumably protection from sawdust and machinery noise. But the minute he'd taken them off, I was struck by the beauty of the man. He was tall and

17

sinewy with dark, disheveled hair. Although his skin looked weather-beaten, there was a strange translucent quality about it. His face was classically sculpted, as if a great deal of thought had gone into every line and curve. But it was his huge, dark eyes that really claimed my curiosity. I'd never seen eyes like that before.

"I only met him the first time this morning."

Clive was as nonplussed as I'd been an hour earlier. He leaned forward, his expression wavering between amusement and disbelief. "I don't get it."

I laughed manically. Explanations swam round in my head, but not one of them was managing to formulate itself into words.

Clive was clearly preparing to escort me to the nearest asylum.

"Come and look," I tried. Once he saw it, surely he would be as enthusiastic as I was?

I led him outside into the bright chill of the September air. Pauline, I gratefully noticed, had disappeared. The car was still unlocked. I flung open the rear door. Clive's eyes nearly popped out of his head.

"Ah!" I cried in a voice that was half irony, half relief. "So I wasn't hallucinating!"

It's a good thing we have a hatchback and seats that go down. I stood back to allow

18

my husband a thorough examination.

The harp was carved out of red-gold wood (cherry, Dan had told me, to go with my socks). It had a lovely soft sheen and there was a marbled swirl in the graining at the joint where it would rest against my shoulder. A light Celtic pattern was carved along the sweep of the neck, and embedded in the wood at the crest was a shiny blue-black pebble. Apparently Dan always puts an Exmoor pebble into his harps. Each pebble is carefully chosen to complement the style and character of the instrument. This harp — *my* harp — was a lovely size, just as high as my waistline when it was standing. Now it was lying on one side, nestled cozily on the tartan rug in the back of the car.

Clive knocked at the wood of the soundboard with his knuckles as if to check it was real. "But this is quality craftsmanship!"

"I know," I said, smug now, almost proud of Dan. "He's been making them all his life."

"This would cost — what — two thousand pounds? Three? More, even, if it's all handmade. Look at the carving along the top."

"The neck. It's called the neck. Apparently."

Clive was scrutinizing as only Clive can scrutinize. "It's — well, I have to say it's pretty cool! But, honeybun, there's no way you can keep it. You do know that, don't you?"

The voice of logic. It came hurtling through my haze of surreal, heady joy, and it stung. "Of course I do," I mumbled.

Clive straightened and shook his head. "The guy must be insane."

I sprang to his defense. "He's definitely not insane. But he's a little . . . unusual."

"That's a cert! What could have possessed him? A woman he doesn't know from Adam comes waltzing into his workshop one day and, on the spur of the moment, he decides to give her — to *give* her — nothing less than a *harp*. A handmade harp that took him God knows how long to construct. *Sell,* fair enough, I could understand *sell,* but *give?* Even the materials must have set him back a bit. Come on, hon, get real! You must have misunderstood. He must have meant you to pay."

"No, he didn't. He made that quite clear."

Clive frowned, unable to comprehend such a concept. "Well then, I guess he gave it to you to try out, hoping for a sale, and you completely got the wrong end of the stick."

"I didn't! Look, I told him about fifteen times I couldn't possibly accept it. He just

20

didn't get it. He kept asking why not — and he was so . . . I don't know, so open, so well-meaning, that I felt stupid and couldn't think of an answer. Then he said, 'Don't you like the harp?' He sounded really hurt."

"He sounded *hurt*? El, I think you're pushing it a bit."

"No, I swear it's true! And then he started pacing through the barn, hunting for another, better one to give me! So I had to tell him it was a lovely harp. I had to tell him I loved the harp. And it's true. How could I not? But I said again and again I'd never be able to play it and it would be wasted on me, and I kept on protesting." I leaned over and gazed lovingly at my gift. "While I was protesting he just carried it to the car and put it in."

My mind leaped back again. I had felt so touched by the man's extraordinary gesture. I had not been able to resist plucking a few strings, as the harp lay there on its side in my car. I did it badly, of course, never having done such a thing in my life before, but the sound was rich, wild and resonant. It had a strange effect, like a shower of golden sparks soaring inside me.

"Good," Dan had said. "You can cross it off your list now." He had walked quickly back into the barn and shut the door behind him.

I had stared at the door for a long time.

Today, of all days. After all my wandering and crying and remembering.

Clive's voice jolted me back to the present. "Look, El, I'm afraid it's going to have to go back."

The words bore down on me with their dull weight of common sense. Of course he hadn't realized what day it was today, and what that meant for me. I probably should have reminded him, but my stubborn streak wouldn't let me.

"I know. You're right," I said, trying to sound as if I didn't care.

He was rubbing a hand over his brow. "I'd love to buy it for you, hon, really I would. But it would be way too pricey. And you'd get bored of it pretty soon anyway. You've never shown any interest in playing a musical instrument before, after all."

"I suppose not."

"And we can't be in this man's debt. It would be taking advantage."

I put my hand on his arm. "I know it would. I never should have accepted. I'm sorry I was so stupid. It was one of those crazy moments. I don't know what came over me."

"I don't either!" he said.

Then I made myself say: "Well, do you want to come with me to return it? I think you'd be interested to see the place. It's a converted barn at the end of a long lane, right out in the wilds, and it's full, totally full of harps — and bits of harps. You can see them at every stage in their creation. It's really fascinating."

Clive scanned my face as if there was something there he didn't recognize. "How did you find it?"

"I just discovered it by chance. It's not signposted or anything, but I thought I'd go up the lane and see where it led. I had an idea there might be a nice view or something. I never expected to find a harp workshop. I certainly never dreamed I'd come back home with a harp."

"The guy's a nutter!" Clive declared. "Or else he fancies the pants off you. Either way, it would be wrong to keep the thing."

I promptly removed my hand from his arm. All that remained of the magic had now been shattered.

"I don't think my pants come into it!" I snapped. "But you're right, I should return it." I slammed the rear hatch shut. Clive is a big man and I am used to him towering over me, but at that moment I was feeling exceptionally small. "I'll take it back now. There's no point in even getting it out of the car really, is there?" I was struggling to control the bitter twang in my voice. "Are you coming?"

He shook his head again. Sometimes his lack of curiosity amazes me.

"No, I think I'll leave it to you. If I go with you, it might look as if I forced you to take it back. It'll make me look like the wicked ogre. You go, hon, and don't forget to make it clear it's your choice, and you'll have nothing more to do with it. OK, love?"

The "OK, love" did not make it any easier. I was in no mood to be OK-loved. But I got into the car and I drove up the hill and back the way I'd come, to the Harp Barn.

3
DAN

She brought it back. I was sad. I guess giving away a harp is one of those many, many things you are not supposed to do.

Why can't I give her the harp? She likes the harp. She wants the harp. Isn't it my harp to give? I made it with my own hands, with my own wood, with the help of my own saws and glue and plane and sander. I want to give her the harp. She seems to think I must want money for the harp and says she is so sorry, but, much as she'd love to, she really isn't in a position to buy it. I don't want money for the harp. Not at all. If she gave me money for the harp it wouldn't be a gift, would it? She would not value it as much. I want it to be valued. I want it to be valued by her, the Exmoor Housewife, because she has harp playing on her before-forty list and what's the point in having a list if you don't do the things written on it? It is a good harp, made of cherrywood.

Cherry is not her favorite tree, birch is her favorite tree, but I do not have any harps made of birch. Still, I think she likes cherry too. It is a warm and friendly wood. And she was still wearing those cherry-colored socks.

"Thank you, Dan . . . for your *incredible* kindness. I'm really sorry. I've been so stupid, so unreasonable."

I wished she would stop shuffling her feet about.

"I'm sorry to mess you around and change my mind. I'm sorry I took the harp in the first place."

I wished she would stop saying she was sorry.

"It was very wrong of me."

It wasn't. It wasn't. It wasn't wrong. No. But what could I do?

I carried the harp back to the barn from the back of her car. She followed me in. I placed the harp on the floor, in the middle patch of the three patches of light cast by the three windows, in the center of everything. She put herself beside it, sniffing and shuffling. The other harps stood around, hushed and pale.

"I only took it because my head isn't working properly," she told me.

26

I glanced at her head. It looked all right to me.

"You see, it's an important anniversary today."

I wished her a happy anniversary.

"No, not that sort of anniversary. It's actually, well . . . my father died a year ago today."

I said I was sorry about that. It is a sad thing when your father dies. I should know.

She cleared her throat. "I still miss him so much."

I asked if she'd like another sandwich.

She shook her head. "We were very close," she said. "Even closer when he got ill. I used to sit and read to him when he couldn't get out of bed anymore, and I remember him lying there, listening and looking into my face. Then one day, toward the end, he said something to me that I just keep on thinking about."

It was hard for me to look at her face so I focused on the socks. But out of the corner of my eye I could see her left hand. Her palm was creeping up the back of the harp, stroking it with the lightest touch. Then it moved away slightly and floated in the air. Her fingers hovered beside the strings like a restless butterfly.

It seemed to me that the thing her father

had said must be very important or she would not be acting so strangely. But I didn't need to ask what it was because that was exactly what she told me next.

"He said I sometimes gave him the impression I was drifting, just drifting along. And he said that wasn't surprising, as he'd done a good bit of drifting and dreaming himself. But it might be an idea to clarify and think about what I wanted. I should pick a dream, any dream, any one of the hundreds, and just try and see if I could make it come true. Just one. Realistically, one could be possible, if I tried hard enough. Because he didn't want me to come to the end of my life full of regrets. And I shouldn't leave it too long, because you never knew when . . . He was talking about himself, you see . . . So after that I made my before-forty list because I had a whole load of dreams and needed to narrow them down a bit. I was remembering and pondering it this morning, and then, just as I was thinking about the list and how I hadn't done a single thing on it . . . I stumbled across your lovely barn."

Her voice sounded odd, as if she had stuffed rags down her throat. "I probably won't call in again," she said.

Sometimes I do the things I am not supposed to do. Sometimes I say the things I am not supposed to say, even when I realize.

I pointed at the harp. "Play it," I said.

"I can't," she murmured. But her hand stayed hovering by the strings.

Harps each have their own unique voice and I knew that this one was a powerful one. It could charm and enthrall, it could plead and it could command. People say that certain sounds can melt a heart of stone. If there is anyone who has that sort of a heart — which I doubt (as far as I am aware hearts are made of fibrous materials, fluid sacs and pumping mechanisms) — if anyone *does* have a heart composed of granite or flint and therefore not at all prone to melting but just conceivably meltable when exposed to very beautiful sounds, then the sounds made by my cherrywood harp, I am confident, would do it. However, I had a feeling the heart of Ellie the Exmoor Housewife was completely lacking in stony components. I had a feeling it was made of much softer stuff.

"Play it!" I repeated, and I managed another quick glance into her face. Her eyes looked soft and dewy. She stretched out her index finger and ran it across the strings. They rang out with a cry, pure and wild, just as they had done the first time from the back of her car.

I waited. An echo of the notes shimmered in the air between us. But Ellie the Exmoor Housewife still seemed to need persuading. Persuading is not a thing that I normally do, but I set myself the challenge of doing it.

I carefully addressed her socks. I told them that I didn't mind if she went away and came back later because sometimes it takes time to make decisions. But whether she came back or not, the harp belonged to her, Ellie Jacobs the Exmoor Housewife. It was her harp, and always would be. I never took back a gift. The harp would sit here in my barn and wait for her. It would sit and wait until all the cows had come home. This did not sound like a very long time, so I made it longer. The harp would wait, I told her, until the sea dried up (which someday it would if you gave it long enough) and the stars dropped out of the sky (which someday they would if you gave them long enough), but nevertheless this harp would never, ever belong to anyone else. I would never, ever permit another person to play it. So if she did not come back it would sit here un-played until the world ended (which some-day it would, but it was likely to be rather a

30

long wait). Which was a sad thing. However, if she *did* come back and *did* play it, that would be a lot less sad. I added that she could even play it here if she liked, if that was better for her and she did not want to take it home. Perhaps, I reflected, a harp does not fit into the home of an Exmoor Housewife all that well; perhaps it gets in the way of the dusting and hoovering. Harps do that, sometimes.

I have a little room upstairs, which is quite comfortable and warmer than the rest of the barn. I suggested that, if she saw fit, she could use that little room to practice her harp while I was busy making more harps. I would not even hear her from downstairs. I have a few books on learning to play the harp, which I could lend her. I knew a harp teacher and I could lend *her* too. All the right ingredients were there. I had made my choice about giving her the harp. She only had to review *her* choice about accepting it. I hoped she would think again. I would be so happy if she would think again. I had now said what I wanted to say. So I stopped talking.

The socks were very still. I could hear the rumble of a distant tractor and the chattering of swallows as they flew over the roof of the barn. The sun shone through the middle window a little brighter than before. It shone onto the harp, so that the cherrywood glowed.

Finally Ellie Jacobs said: "If the harp stayed here and I came to try it out once in a while . . . there would be no harm in that . . . would there?" It sounded as if she was talking to herself, not to me. So then I did look into her face, properly, to try and work out if she wanted a reply or not. She had little water droplets stuck along her eyelashes. I decided that a reply was possibly required and might even be helpful. I decided to do that thing where you ask a question to which the answer is so obvious nobody needs to give it. Only she'd already done that, really, so all I had to do was repeat certain words, just to make it quite clear.

"Harm?" I said. "In playing a harp?"

She smiled then, and turned, and without another word she walked to her car. She got in and drove away.

But I had a feeling she would be back.

4
ELLIE

The car jolts down the lane. The world reels. I'm all over the place — full of streaming tears one moment and manic bursts of laughter the next. I'm driving completely on autopilot. I probably shouldn't be driving at all.

This isn't the kind of thing that happens to me. I must have fallen through a magical portal into somebody else's life. My existence has somehow transformed itself into something bright and light, filled with frolicking colors. Life was nothing like this when I woke up this morning.

There's no way I can go home yet and face Clive. A walk in the wilds is what I need. Somewhere high up. High places always help me think, which is what I need to do right now. I put my foot on the accelerator and launch into the road that leads up to Dunkery Beacon.

I leave the car in a lay-by and stride up

one of the rocky paths to the cairn at the top. The wind whips my hair and sweeps across the purple tufts of heather. I breathe in cool sea-tang and the fresh, peaty scent of moor.

If I've decided what I think I've decided, how can I possibly explain it to Clive? I love Clive, of course, and Clive loves me, but there are lots of things we don't quite get about each other. I don't get his fascination with football or with finance. He doesn't get why I take myself off onto Exmoor with my notepad and write poems — poems that nobody will ever read — about bark and clouds and spiderwebs and running water.

Clive likes things to be straightforward. Clive likes things to fall within certain guidelines. My poetry doesn't really fall within those guidelines. My current issue — being given a harp by somebody I've just met — is way outside them.

I walk faster and faster, swinging my arms. I reach the summit in record time. The views on every side challenge me with their rugged beauty: green pastures alternating with patches of tawny moorland, stubby hawthorns, distant hills that melt into the sky, jags of coastline that climb, fall and reach out to the sea. Today the sea is slate gray, laced with a thousand dancing threads of blue and silver. It seems to reflect my overwhelming sense that wonderful things are possible in this world after all.

My mind flits from Clive to Dan, from Dan to Clive. Back to Dan, trying to make sense of it all. Dan seems such an innocent, but something I saw in his workshop tells me I should be wary.

I speak his name into the air, trying it out on my tongue: "Dan."

I listen to the sound of the word as it is carried out to sea.

"Dan, the Exmoor Harpmaker!" I assert, a little louder. But the sound echoes back into my skull with an edge of doubt. Slowly, as it continues echoing, I realize it has transmuted itself: *Dan, the Exmoor Heart-Breaker.*

Clive meets me at the door with a concerned kiss. "You took your time. Everything all right?"

"Fine," I reply. "I went up to Dunkery for some fresh air."

"No wonder you're looking so wild."

I prod my hair about.

"So you managed to return the harp?" he asks.

"Yup." I make sure my eyes meet his. This much, at least, is true.

He gives me a pat on the back. "That's my gal! I know you liked the look of it, but it would've been wrong to accept it — you said that yourself!"

I push past him into the kitchen. He follows me.

"And it wasn't exactly practical, was it, hon-bun?"

"No, not really."

"I expect the guy was pretty glad to see it again, once he realized how silly he'd been. Now he'll be able to sell it."

"Mm-hm."

"And he'll get a good price for it, and someone else will appreciate it. Someone who can make the most of it, someone who can actually play the thing. Like a properly trained musician."

I'm not enamored with those last three words.

Can I really see myself playing the harp? If I'm honest it was only on my before-forty list because it was a pleasing idea, an exotic image. One of those dreams that remains hazy and amorphous because you assume it will always stay just that — a dream. But now, if I'm not careful, that dream might just somersault into reality. And I have to say, I really, really don't want to be careful. I'm fed up with being careful.

"You should be careful, you know," Clive comments. "Wandering about on the moor by yourself. Meeting strange men with strange propositions . . ."

"Yeah, I know I'm a bit crazy. But you wouldn't love me if I was normal, would you?"

We've had this conversation before. And I know exactly what comes next.

"I'd love you whatever, El."

"Love you too, hon," I say quickly.

He helps himself to a beer from the fridge and opens it with care, savoring the prospect of pouring it down his throat during the highlights from Bristol City's latest game. I examine his profile; his long, aquiline nose, powerful jawline and sparsity of sandy-brown hair. His shoulders are square, his arms gym toned. His blue sweatshirt strains tightly against the muscles of his chest. He looks younger than his forty-one years. He is an attractive man. There's a determination and strength about him that has always drawn me. He is my rock and I am his . . . well, his limpet . . .

I need to broach the harp thing. Why is it so hard? Why is it that out on the open moor I was fizzing with joy, yet now that I'm at home the whole situation seems fraught with problems? It should be easy to drop it into the conversation now: "Hon, I've decided to go up to the Harp Barn every so often to have a go at playing the harp. The harpmaker's quite OK with it — in fact, he seems to think I *should.*"

But no. The words don't make it to the surface.

The *Telegraph* is lying on the chair by the window. The leading column is all about terrorist attacks. I listlessly pick up today's post that's lying on the table. Bills — I'll leave those to Clive — and a fund-raising letter from a charity. The letter is plastered with pictures of pale children behind bars and horror stories of people-trafficking. I hold it up for Clive to see.

"No, El, I'm sorry. We just can't afford to give to any more charities."

I stuff the letter into the recycling bin, but the terrible images stay with me. Suddenly I'm weary. I switch on the radio for some light relief, only to be regaled by a story about female genital mutilation. Clive makes a face. I switch the radio off again.

All those people suffering in the world. And here I am fretting about an overly generous gift.

I picture the harp, the beautiful harp, *my* harp. Dan was adamant. He said it would sit there unplayed forever.

Unless I came back to play it.

Decisions stress me out. It's much easier when I'm in a situation where I can just mold myself to somebody else's will. But now Clive's will and Dan's will keep pulling me in opposite directions.

I think about my parents, whose iron rule dominated my life for so many years. My mother would have disapproved in the days when she understood such things, there's no doubt about that. She disapproved of pretty much everything. And my father, who died a year ago today? What would he have made of my harp quandary? The earlier version of himself would have been strict and sensible, but the later, iller, more pensive, more lovable version — the version who told me to pick a dream and follow it? I can't be sure.

Perhaps it's not so much the harp as Dan himself who is the issue.

Because Dan is a man. What manner of man? I ask myself. A startlingly handsome one — I could hardly fail to notice that. But what sort of person is he? Certainly not the sort I'm used to.

While Dan was busy making sandwiches, I'd taken the chance to nose around the Harp Barn. As well as the harps themselves, the place was overrun with sawdust —

mounds of it on the floor and little fragments floating around in the air. Bits of lichen, fir cones and feathers also seemed to be scattered around in random places. Shining pennies were laid out on the windowsills in long, snaking lines. Behind them were glass dishes filled with pebbles. The workbench was stacked with tools and finely penciled diagrams. I'd also noticed, hanging above the workbench, a large corkboard covered with photos. Photos of women. They were all attractive and mostly young. Some were posing with harps; all were very much posing. In the center was a blonde with a low-cut top and stunning blue eyes.

"Ellie, look at you! You're miles away! Still fantasizing about becoming a harpist?"

"Not at all," I reply, blushing and springing to action. I start opening cupboards, hunting for ingredients. "I think I'll get straight on with the supper. Spicy Bolognese all right?"

"Yum! That'll be great!"

I manage to find an onion. I cut it in half and start peeling off the skin.

Can it be that Dan is a very clever actor, a man who seduces vulnerable women — by giving them harps? It seems absurd, but perhaps Clive is right. Perhaps I should be careful.

"Ahhh, that's better." Clive sighs, a smile spreading across his face after a long draft from his beer bottle. "Give me a shout if you need a hand, El. I'll be in the sitting room."

He disappears and I hear the sounds of the telly being switched on, followed by a roar from fans. Bristol City must have scored. When Clive's finished with them, it'll be a repeat of *Doctor Who*. After that, spicy Bolognese cooked by the wife. I hope the Bolognese will turn out all right. The wife is finding it extremely hard to concentrate.

5
DAN

I've been thinking about that song. The one that goes on and on about money. Money, the song purports, must be funny in a rich man's world. I am not a rich man but, I have to say, I consider money to be funny anyway. I mention this to Thomas when I see him on Monday morning when he stops off on his rounds. Thomas is a Welsh man, a postman, a tall, thin, lanky man and my friend.

Thomas crosses his long arms in front of him. "Do you mean funny peculiar or funny ha-ha?"

I say, "Both."

He leans against his van. He is wearing blue shorts (he always wears shorts, no matter what the weather is doing; his legs are hairy, very) and a hoodie that is psychedelic green with yellow stripes around the edges.

The day is bright and clear. Thomas is in no hurry to deliver letters.

"Why?" he asks.

I tell him that in my opinion money works in a very upside-down way.

"I still don't get you, boyo," he says. "What do you mean, upside down?"

So I start at the beginning and explain to him in detail. A one-p piece is clearly a thing of beauty, right? He looks unsure, so I explain this to him too. A penny is a highly desirable item. Its size is small, delicate, perfect. Its color is like a setting sun, bronze, bright, burnished. It has a raised rim around the edge, charming. The engraving on the reverse is a portcullis, interesting. Or else the top half of a harp, even more interesting. I never tire of looking at pennies. I keep all my one-p pieces and shine them up with vinegar and put them on the windowsill of the barn, where they catch the light. Each penny is a work of art. No other coin is as beautiful.

Thomas pulls his mouth to one side.

The two-p, I point out, shares the nice coppery brightness of the penny but is not as satisfactory sizewise. The other coins (surely he must agree?) are not nearly as good colorwise. Pound coins and two-pound coins are always trying to be flashy but failing. Pennies outshine them all. Pennies are by far the best. Yet nobody seems to appreciate them.

Thomas looks at his watch. I go on.

Five- and ten- and twenty-pound notes are ridiculous. How can they be worth hundreds of times more than coins? I like paper, of course — paper is great, made from trees, and who can question the greatness of trees? But paper money is only in very thin strips and is not good quality. And the new notes are made of vile and slippery stuff. Why on earth are they considered more important than the strong and shining coin?

Thomas opens the door of his van and gets in. His dogs, who are Alsatians, very large and drooly, start barking from the back of the van. I carry on explaining to Thomas through the open window.

Even more ludicrous than paper money is the small card made of the ugliest substance known to man: plastic. People seem to value it above almost everything else.

Here Thomas shakes his head at me out of the van window. "The credit card," he says, "is a fabulous invention!"

I ask him why.

"Well, mate," he says, "basically because you can use it to buy fabulous things."

I ask him what fabulous things.

"Like fabulous big houses, and, er, fabu-

44

lous holidays abroad."

But why, I ask him, would I want a big house? Big houses are difficult to clean and difficult to heat and difficult to find your way around. If I had a big house I'd spend far too much of my life walking from one end of it to the other and I don't want to walk inside, we have outside for walking. And why would I want a holiday abroad? Holidays abroad produce hassle, jet lag, sunburn and diarrhea. So much more fun is to be had from staying at home in a barn, making harps and polishing pennies.

"Whatever makes you happy, mate," is what Thomas replies, and he turns his van around and drives off down the lane.

My sister Jo says that I should worry about money. She says everyone worries about money, especially people who don't have any. She says I make her scream and tear her hair out, although I do not think this is true; her hair looks perfectly intact to me. Jo has big ideas about what I am supposed to (and not supposed to) do. She has taken over where my mother left off.

Still, Jo is kind. Jo has put a website in the computer for me. I saw it once, when she brought over her laptop. My website is called "The Exmoor Harpmaker" and it begins with the sentence: "Welcome to the

Harp Barn." There are twenty-five pictures of my harps, which Jo has taken with her very good and very large camera, and each picture has a price written beside it. There is also a picture of me in profile bending over a half-made harp with a lathe in my hands. And there is another of me with a sheepish expression all over my face, which she insisted on putting in there because she said I look dead good and that will make women buy my harps. Women, apparently, like harps made by a sheepish-looking harp-maker.

Jo said initially that I should make a wooden notice to hang at the end of the lane that said: *The Harp Barn. Exmoor Harpmaker. Harps of distinction and quality, locally made.* So that is what I did. I made it out of pinewood and I carved the letters in fine, curling script.

The next day seven people came and stopped in at the barn. They bought four harps off me. This was a good thing, I thought. But Jo said later that she saw two of the harps for sale on eBay. Jo then said if I didn't know how to charge proper money it would be better that people didn't know I was here. She said I had to take the sign down again. So that is what I did. There's no point in arguing with Jo.

I can't remember how much money I got for those four harps. I wasn't that interested. I make harps because I love making harps, not because I love making money. Jo does not understand this. She has put her email address into my website so that people who want to buy harps will have to do it through her. I don't mind. Not at all. So long as I am allowed to make harps.

I haven't told my sister Jo about giving a harp to a cherry-socked woman I have only just met. I have a feeling my sister Jo would not appreciate that.

Today I went to the woods and counted toadstools. I was out for some time and counted a sum total of three hundred and seventeen. They were mostly whitish, flesh colored or inky. Some were like saucers and some were like pudding bowls. It was a damp day, but they didn't mind that and neither did I. After I'd finished counting them I sat on a mossy stump and listened to Exmoor sounds for a while. The sounds I heard were these: a squirrel rustling, a woodpecker pecking, an acorn dropping to the ground, a wood pigeon cooing, a buzzard mewing, a bee humming, the distant bleating of a sheep, the distant rumble of a combine, the not-so-distant rumble of my tummy.

When I came back to the Harp Barn, the cherry-sock woman, who is the Housewife of Exmoor and who is called Ellie Jacobs, was there. She was standing motionless outside the door. When she turned round and saw me her face said lots of things, but her voice said, "Ah, hello, Mr. Hollis! Good to see you again. I was just about to go home. I'm sorry to intrude. I wasn't sure if you meant what you said about the harp . . . when you said it was OK if I came here to practice?"

I always mean what I say. I told her this.

"Oh, good! What a relief! May I come in? If it's not too inconvenient right now?"

I told her it was never too inconvenient. I got out my keys and unlocked the Harp Barn. You are supposed to always keep a building locked when there are thirty-seven precious harps inside and you go out to count toadstools for an hour or two.

"It's so lovely to be here again!" she cried. Her socks were not cherry colored today. They were blue. She had on a blue scarf to match, cotton. It fluttered as she walked around. I watched it flutter as she walked from harp to harp for a bit, then she stopped in front of my corkboard with the photos

48

and took a good look at it. I thought she was about to ask a question, but she didn't. I waited.

Eventually she turned round and said: "So, er . . . the harp that I took home the other day . . . ? Um . . . where is it?"

I said I had moved it to the little upstairs room, which is now her practice room, and would she like me to accompany her upstairs to visit it?

"Yes, please," is what she said.

I led her up the wooden staircase (seventeen stairs) to her new practice room, which used to be my storeroom. If you go through it you get to my bedroom and next to that is my bathroom. Next to the practice room on the other side is my kitchen, where I make sandwiches and other things. It is all up the seventeen steps of the wooden staircase. I asked her if she minded going up the seventeen steps and she said no. Then she said she was worried that she'd never played a harp before and she would never be able to do justice to such a beautiful instrument. I told her balderdash, she'd played the harp six days ago when she first came to the Harp Barn. She said yes, but that was only plucking a couple of notes and she really had no idea how it was supposed to be done. I understand all about having no idea how things are supposed to be done so I felt sympathetic and told her so. Then she said she felt that, as harp playing had been on her list and I'd been so kind as to offer her this opportunity, it was only fair to herself and to me to at least give it a try. I said I absolutely agreed with her. And she replied that if she never made it as a harpist, she hoped I would not be devastated. I assured her that I would not be devastated at all, so long as she would come here sometimes and pluck strings. By this time we had reached the top of the seventeen steps.

"Oh, Dan!" is what she said. She added, "I may call you Dan, may I?"

I said that she may and she said, "Oh, Dan!" again, and, "It's more beautiful than ever!"

She was talking about the harp. I'd placed it by the window on a little cherrywood harp stool so that it would be the right height when she sat and played it.

Then she turned and saw the books I'd put on the table. She picked them up one by one and looked at the titles: *How to Play the Celtic Harp: A Step-by-Step Guide; Easy Tunes for New Harpists; The Harper's Manual;* and, finally, *Have You Got the Pluck?*

After this she ventured toward the harp

50

and touched a finger on a string so gently that it scarcely whispered.

I said she must play it now. I added that when I said play I meant play not as in the thing professional musicians do when they are working but as in the thing children do when they are having fun. She nodded and her blue scarf fluttered.

I went downstairs and left her to it.

6
ELLIE

"Met any more strange men offering you harps?"

I grant him a faint chuckle. Clive's convinced that Exmoor is infested with eccentrics, which has perhaps worked in my favor.

"Nope. Pity, really." I'm impressed with my acting. It's just the right balance between regret, irony and nonchalance.

He shakes his head and rolls his eyes. "It could only happen on Exmoor!"

Clive has no idea. No idea that the minute he's disappeared off to work every day I set off on my own trip to indulge in my own clandestine venture.

When I arrive at the barn Dan is normally working on his current project, a medieval-style harp made of sycamore wood. He welcomes me with enthusiasm, but we don't exchange many words before I head upstairs. I pluck strings for a bit, propping one of the harp books up against a block of wood where I can see it, frowning at the notes on the page. Sometimes hammering or the noise of machinery from below will cut through my tentative playing.

Just before twelve Dan comes in with sandwiches. Always sandwiches, always cut into triangles and geometrically arranged on the plate. He never offers me a hot drink, although the scent of coffee often wafts through from the kitchen. Dan seems to follow certain patterns of behavior, yet he's still a mystery to me. I have no idea what goes on in his head and his odd comments often take me by surprise. But I've realized my initial suspicions were completely unjustified. Dan is without guile. I'm sure those pictures on his corkboard are just photos of people he's sold harps to because he likes to think of each of his harps being played. The fact that the players are all women and all attractive (especially that one in the middle) is hardly his fault.

It's been a couple of weeks since I started harp playing and there's only one person I've told about it: my dearest friend, Christina. Christina is one of the people Clive would classify as eccentric. She dresses in long flowing garments that are usually tie-dyed or organic or made from yak's wool.

She owns a little shop in Porlock selling earrings, pendants and other trinkets she's made herself. Her home is a tiny, creaking cottage in a village about five miles away. I visit as often as I can because, despite her cheerfulness, I know she is lonely.

"Ellie, thank God you're here!" she cried, pressing me with a cup of tea and a flapjack the minute I arrived on Wednesday. "I'm suffering from Alex-withdrawal symptoms."

Christina got herself pregnant at sixteen. The result was the charming but rather irresponsible Alex. After Alex's birth Christina got through two husbands, neither of whom particularly wanted to be his father. Alex is now a hefty eighteen-year-old and has recently gone to Exeter to sample the joys of university life.

"How's he getting on?" I asked.

"Rude to his tutors and can't abide essay writing."

I listened to her grumbles, ate flapjacks, drank tea, stroked her cat and tried to imagine what it was like to have an eighteen-year-old son. How different life would be if I had a mother's role to play. I always assumed I'd have children, but they just didn't materialize and, as it's not happened so far, it's unlikely to happen now that I'm nearly thirty-six. Clive doesn't seem to mind ("So long as you're happy, hon-bun"). Neither of us is keen to seek medical help, so I suppose that's that. My sister tells me that children are painful but satisfying. I do feel a raw hole in my life sometimes when I play with my little nephews and nieces. But my dad once told me it's not helpful pondering what might have been, because you can't change that. You can only change what will be.

I shook the sad thoughts from my head and told Christina my news about the harp.

"Good on you, Ellie! I always knew you were a closet creative."

The cat (who I suspect understands more than she lets on) looked up at me, green eyes glowing.

"What do *you* think, Meow?"

A big, lazy tortoiseshell, Christina's cat is called Meow because Christina says it's only fair that animals should be able to pronounce their own names. Meow twitched the end of her tail and said her name twice, which was not particularly useful.

"Christina, I'm totally in love," I confided. "With the harp. So much it scares me. I don't get a single word of the how-to-play-harp books and I've no idea what I'm doing, but the sound of the instrument! It's like a breath of fresh mountain air . . . or a shaft of sunlight rippling on water. It's like green things growing in a forest glen. Even if all I do is run my fingers up and down the strings, it's just . . . whoooooa!"

My hands wove through the air, trying to get it across to her.

"Ellie, I'm over the moon for you!" Christina grinned. "You needed something like this. The creative stuff is bloody essential. Whenever I'm missing Alex I make myself start a new project and it helps to no end."

"Yes, it's great you've got your jewelry." She was wearing a pair of her own homemade earrings now. They glinted a pale, pearly green against her dark hair. "You're dead clever to make such gorgeous things."

"You make gorgeous things as well! You make gorgeous poetry," she said, not a hundred percent sincerely. (She's read some of my poems. She always says nice things, but I know she doesn't rate them very highly.) "And now you've got harp playing too!" She lit a cigarette. Meow spends a lot of time passive smoking. I gave the back of her head a sympathetic fondle.

"But this is *music*," I told Christina, uttering the word in a reverential whisper. "That's something talented people do, not me!"

She tutted. "As far as I can see you've got

all the necessary attributes: Fingers, thumbs. Sensitivity. A harp."

"Yes, fingers and thumbs I have; sensitivity — possibly! A harp, yes, now! But there's an important something I'm lacking."

"Don't tell me," she said. "I know. Confidence."

"Well, yes, but that wasn't what I was thinking. There's another thing I'm lacking too."

She puffed out a cloud of smoke. "Go on."

I frowned. "My husband's approval."

She flipped her hand back in a dismissive gesture. "Minor detail. Unimportant. One to be sorted out later. In the fullness of time."

The fullness of time. When, I ask myself, will that arrive? It's a delicate matter and I'll have to pick the right moment. I'm a wimp and I know it. Clive is great, but occasionally, when I'm stupid, there are repercussions.

Like that time when Clive and I went to badminton club and ended up playing doubles with Sarah (local sweetie pie) and Terry (local outrageous flirt). Terry was plying me with rather personal compliments and I was flirting back — only a little — because I know he's harmless. Suddenly I felt a great thwack on the back of my shoulder that sent me reeling. Clive had hit me with his racket. There was a small moment of stunned silence between us all before he leaped in with an apology. "Oh God, El, my poor honeybun! Are you all right? I'm so sorry! I don't know what happened. I thought the shuttlecock was heading this way . . . I'm sure it was! I thought you'd get out of the way." The shuttlecock had been stationary in Sarah's hands.

We'd trooped off to the pub after the game. I wasn't really hurt, but I think we were all in need of a little something to steady our nerves. There was no more flirting and nobody mentioned the accident again.

In wobbly moments I still wonder, *was* it actually an accident?

Too many strings! How will I ever find my way around them all? Red strings are Cs, black strings are Fs — and all the others are sheer guesswork. Lovely guesswork, though. I concentrate hard and try to pick out the first line of "Danny Boy." It almost works.

Dan peers round the door. He's wearing an earnest expression and clearly has something important to say. I wait, wondering what's coming. Am I trespassing too much on his generosity? Am I coming too often? Am I disturbing him with my slow, plodding attempts at harp practice?

He scrutinizes my feet, then slowly raises his eyes to my face. "Ellie, I have a question for you."

"Ask away!" I say, breezily.

He clears his throat. "My question is this. Do you like plums?"

Do I like plums?

"Yes, very much. Why . . . ?"

"Plums," he repeats, as if the future of the universe rested on that word. "There are lots. Of plums. Several hundred. On my plum tree. In the back. Several hundred is more than I can eat. And waste is a thing I don't like. So I was thinking you should take some plums home. For yourself and your husband."

Dan doesn't know that Clive doesn't know. Too much explaining . . .

Dan leads me outside to a little enclosure behind the barn, a bumpy field with three trees. A tiny woodshed stands at one end, stacked high with logs. Robins and coal tits flutter and chirrup in the hedge along the back. September sunshine streams across the grass, threading gold through the green.

"My orchard!" Dan announces.

"Glorious!" I exclaim.

One of the trees is a tall cherry, one an apple that looks as though the fruits have already been picked. The third is bowed low with the weight of plums, amber colored with a rosy blush. The air is thick with their scent.

"We need a trug," Dan says. "Luckily a trug is a thing that I have."

He disappears into the woodshed for a minute, then reappears with the traditional oval basket for gathering fruit and vegetables.

We set to work. The plums are oozing stickiness and surrounded by bees. Dan, I assume, doesn't have much in the way of family and friends he can share them with. So far I've never seen another person on my visits. But he's mentioned his sister, Jo, a couple of times. I wonder if she has much of a say in his life. He implies that she does, yet I know that Dan has a mind of his own — nobody more so.

"Are you getting on well with your harp?" he asks, as he does every day.

"Yes," I reply. "It's a delight. But my fingers keep getting muddled up. I'm hopelessly uncoordinated. The books help, but I was wondering if . . . if you could show me a little basic technique?"

He shakes his head. "I don't play the harp. I only make them." He brightens. "I can teach you how to tune up if you like."

"Do I need to learn that? It never sounds out of tune to me."

"That's because I tune it every morning before you arrive."

I am touched, and not for the first time.

"Oh, Dan! I'd no idea! Thank you! And yes, please, I'd love it if you could teach me to tune up."

We munch a couple of plums, spitting out the stones. Dan seems to be spitting with care and precision. "I'm hoping they'll grow and make more plum trees," he explains.

"You need *more* plums?"

"No, but the world could always do with more trees." He glances at the trug. "So far we have forty-three plums. How many would you like?"

I'm amazed. I wasn't aware he'd been counting.

"Another forty-three!" I answer boldly, hatching a plan.

He smiles approval. The sunlight is touching the curve of his cheek and, as he stretches high to reach the fruit on the upper branches, I register again his extraordinarily handsome features. If the universe had planned things differently . . . If I had been single . . . If he had been the sort of person who looked at me the way I was now looking at him . . .

"I've just had a thought!" he cries, his hand circling a plum. "It is a thought I had before, but then I forgot it. Now I've had it again! Shall I tell you my thought?" He has an air of eureka about him.

"Yes!"

"You could take harp lessons with my girlfriend!"

"Your girlfriend . . . ?"

"Of course!" His hands start twitching oddly. "You must have lessons with Roe Deer!"

"With *Roe Deer*?"

"Yes," he says. "My girlfriend Roe Deer. She lives in Taunton. It is twenty-three point one miles from here. I think she'll be happy to teach you." Then a shadow crosses his face. "But you may have to pay her. She's a bit funny about money."

"Of course she'd need paying." It isn't the money aspect that's bothering me. "Could I phone her?" I ask.

"Yes, of course. Her number is . . ." And he reels off a number he obviously expects me to remember.

"Could you write it down for me?"

When we've gathered eighty-six plums,

two large trugfuls, we return to the barn. He takes me to the notice board with all the photos of women playing harps.

"That's her!" he says, pointing.

It's the sizzling sexpot of a blonde whose image has haunted me right from the beginning.

7
DAN

My sister Jo arranged it all because she wants me to sell more harps. It was the first time I'd had a radio reporter in my barn.

He was ginger haired and blinked a lot. He had a wart on his left cheek with tiny hairs sprouting out of it. He had ginger nose hairs too. He was wearing jeans, black, and a jacket, leather. He said we would be on air after he'd counted three two one. He held up three fingers in front of my face. "Three, two, one," he mouthed. Then in a completely different voice he said: "Delighted to meet you, Mr. Hollis! So this is your workshop?"

Yes, I said, it was.

"I must say, it's quite a place. An old barn, up a steep lane, miles from anywhere — the last place you would expect to find a business. There is quite a rustic atmosphere in here, with the low beams and a trestle bench or two. But everywhere I look there are harps; harps of all different shapes and sizes. Very intricate and beautiful they are too! You seem to be pretty well set up, Mr. Hollis. How long have you been established here as the Exmoor Harpmaker?"

I told him twenty-three years.

"Twenty-three years! Quite some time! But I must say, that seems impossible, looking at you. You don't seem that old."

I told him I was thirty-three.

"Right. So that means, according to my calculations, you started your own business when you were a mere ten years old. Is that true?"

I told him yes.

"Were you actually able to construct a harp at that tender age?"

I told him yes.

"That must have been quite a difficult skill to learn."

I told him yes.

"Did you have anyone to help you?"

I told him yes.

"Let me guess. Was it perhaps a kind uncle who was skilled in carpentry? A neighbor? But no, there wouldn't be any neighbors out here, would there? Was it your father?"

I told him yes. It was my father.

"Ah! So he was a harpmaker before you?"

I told him yes.

"And you always knew, did you, right from square one, that you would follow in his footsteps and make harps?"

I had to think about this. I would know the answer for sure if the question hadn't been so cryptic. It all depended on the timing of Square One. If Square One occurred at my birth, then the answer was no. I don't remember being born very clearly, but I am pretty sure making harps was not uppermost in my mind when it happened. Perhaps Square One was on my first birthday, when I turned one. In this case, again, I don't think I had great harpmaking aspirations. If, on the other hand, Square One was later on, when I was starting to want more than baby food and nappy changes, then the answer might well be yes. I was about to tell the radio reporter this when he started asking more questions.

"Could you tell us a little bit about your harpmaking journey? How you fell in love with the profession? How your father helped you along the way? How you fitted it in around school?"

I asked him which question he wanted me to answer first.

"Well, maybe if you tell us about the first time you realized you wanted to be a harp-maker . . . ?" And he raised his eyebrows at me. They were very bushy and ginger.

"Certainly," I said. "The first time I realized I wanted to be a harpmaker was when I was seven and a half years old. It was Saturday, the twelfth of June, and there were green dragonflies in the garden. I was wearing new shoes my mother had got for me, but they dug into my heels too much. There were four different types of moss growing on the stone by the gate. We had scrambled eggs for breakfast. The weather was fair to middling."

"Right," he said. "Great to have all those details. So what happened exactly to put harpmaking into your head? Were you inspired by a harp your father had made?"

I told him no. My father did not make harps then. He did not make many musical instruments, but he worked with wood generally. He carved things like bowls and candlesticks and statues most of the time and sold them to tourists. He did some furniture too. My mother was not very interested in wood, but the thing she was interested in was getting free babysitting for me. I was a problem because I did not always do the things I was supposed to do. When I got excited I flapped my hands around and made strange noises and she did not like that. She said if I would promise not to make strange noises and flap my hands around I could go to Storyland in Dulverton. Storyland was on Saturday mornings. Me and five other children got to sit on beanbags in the village hall and listen to a large, gray-haired lady who read stories. I had the beanbag with blue and yellow penguins all over it. It was very difficult for me not to make strange noises and flap my hands around when the storytelling lady came in, but I didn't because I wanted to be allowed to come again next week and the week after that and in fact the thing I wanted was to live in Storyland and listen to stories forever.

"This is very interesting," cut in the radio man, "but I'm sure the listeners out there are wanting to hear about the actual harp-making."

"Yes," I said. "That's exactly the thing I am going to tell you." I went on to explain that it was in Storyland that I met my first harp. One day — the day of the green dragonflies and uncomfortable shoes and the four types of moss and the scrambled eggs — my mother had dropped me off as usual and I went in and sat on my yellow and blue penguin beanbag. And there in front of me, placed in the middle of all the beanbags, was the most beautiful object I'd ever seen. But I kept on at harpmaking

It was like a swan and a heart and a loom and a sailing ship and a hazel tree and a wing and the swell of a wave and a woman dancing and ripples of light on water — all at the same time. And it was made of wood! All of us kids were gawping.

Then a lady who wasn't our normal story-telling lady stepped up. She had white skin and tremendously long hair. She said she was filling in today and she was going to tell us a story with some musical interludes on her harp. I have to admit, I couldn't stop my hands from flapping then and a bit of a gurgle came out of my mouth, but nobody seemed to mind. When the lady started, it took my breath away. The harp not only had the most beautiful body, but it had a soul too. And a voice — the most softly powerful voice I had ever heard.

"I still remember the story the lady told us that day," I said to the radio man. "Would you like me to tell it to you?"

"Perhaps not now," he said, glancing at the microphone. "Back to the harpmaking?"

So I related what happened next when I got home from Storyland. What happened next was this: I ran straight to my father and told him he must make a harp. He told me steady on, son, that's easier said than

69

done. But I kept on at him every day over the next year and eventually he did do it. His first harp wasn't very good, of course. But he became intrigued and that led him to make another the next year, and I helped him. By the time he made his third harp he had bought the barn and I was making my own one simultaneously. I was then ten years old.

"Quite a boy!" said the radio man. "Your parents must have been very proud of you."

"Must they?" I said.

"I would have thought so. If *my* son made a harp at age ten I'd be proud. Can't imagine that, though. Could never drag him away from the computer games for long enough, the little blighter! Still, your father must have been a great inspiration to you. Do you mind my asking, is he still around?"

"No," I said. "He died in a car accident when I was sixteen."

"Oh, I'm sorry to hear that. And your mother? Is she alive?"

"She died a few months after my father. She died because of a hospital operation that went wrong. I was sad that year."

"Phew! I'm not surprised! That's hard on a teenager. Do you have any other family?"

I informed him that I had an older sister Jo. I told him how, after our parents died, Jo lived with me here in the Harp Barn for a while and helped sort things out. I mentioned that Jo still does the business side of harpmaking for me. And that she is much cleverer than me. I can only do harps. She can do money.

"I see. And how many harps do you make in a year?"

I answered that it depended on the year, but normally it was only about thirty-six.

"Only! And I believe all your wood is locally sourced, from the woods of Exmoor and the surrounding region?"

I answered in the affirmative.

"And you use an Exmoor pebble in the woodwork of each harp?"

I told him this was indeed the case.

"I notice that all the harps here, beautiful though they are, are on a fairly small scale. Have you ever considered upsizing and making proper harps?"

"Proper harps?"

"Sorry, perhaps I'm using the wrong terminology here. I mean the large harps, the classical harps, the harps you see in orchestras."

"Not proper harps!" I told him.

"I don't quite follow you."

There was a gap here as I thought about him following me and wondered if that was a thing I wanted. I was pretty sure it wasn't.

He scratched his head. "Er, although you have been building Celtic harps all these years, you don't have any desire to try and construct a classical harp, a concert harp?"

I told him no.

"Don't you think it would be grand to see a harp that you had made, one of your own harps, playing Mozart in Carnegie Hall?"

I told him no.

"So you have no interest in classical harps?"

I told him no.

He rubbed his wart. "I confess, I am surprised. Why is that, Mr. Hollis?"

I decided to explain by using analogies and rhetorical questions. My answer to the radio man was this: "Why take a saccharin tablet when instead you can suck an organic honeycomb? Why settle for a racehorse when you can have a unicorn?"

He gave a low, gravelly laugh. "Ah, I think I get your drift. Well, it has been a pleasure talking to you, Mr. Hollis. I wish you all possible success in your future harpmaking. And if anyone out there is interested in buying an Exmoor harp, please do not try and contact Mr. Hollis directly, as you won't be able to. Instead you can contact Mr. Hollis's sister, Jo, whose email link can be obtained from our website. She will be happy to talk business with you. That's right, isn't it, Mr. Hollis?"

I told him yes, that was right.

8
ELLIE

And yet again the vision comes
That golden day when you and I
Were gathering the glowing plums . . .

I crumple the poem and shoot it into the bin. I pick up the phone.

"He's got a girlfriend!"

"Who? Clive?"

"No, you dumbo! Dan!"

"Ah, your Exmoor Harpmaker." Christina always sounds amused when I talk about him, which is slightly annoying. I try not to mention him, but sometimes I can't help it. It isn't as if I can talk about him to anyone else.

"Does it matter?" she asks.

"I'm not sure." I stare out the window up at the hill. "It depends."

"Tell me more." I can hear the flick of her lighter down the phone. She'll be settling down on her settee with a cigarette. Meow has probably just jumped into her lap. I should ask about Christina's day at the shop, ask if Alex has rung and if he is still enjoying university life, but that will all have to wait.

"She's a professional harpist. She's stunning. Blond. Enormous cleavage."

"So it matters that much?"

I have to laugh. "Stop jumping to conclusions. I'm just surprised, that's all."

When Dan first mentioned his girlfriend I'd envisaged someone small, sweetly shy, perhaps even a little gauche. I scold myself for my own crassness. The photo certainly put me to rights.

"Didn't you say Dan was totally gorgeous too?"

"Those weren't my exact words, Christina, no. He's dashing in his own way, I'll admit. Still, he's . . ." I try to explain what I mean but don't seem to be able to express myself very well. I tell her about Dan's unique take on things, his simple lifestyle and his self-sufficiency. The more I talk, the harder it becomes to understand how somebody who looks like Roe Deer can fit into the picture.

"Are you saying he's not really boyfriend material?"

"No, no. It's more that I don't see him as

a man who would particularly want or need a girlfriend." There. Maybe that's what was troubling me. I made a wrong judgment.

"Have you mentioned anything to Clive yet?"

"No. I can't seem to coax myself to come clean. Honesty doesn't seem a good policy . . . but neither does dishonesty."

"I bet you're guilt-tripping."

"Yup." For me, guilt is not so much a habit as an addiction. I blame my parents. My mother, anyway. She was relentless. Stalwart moral values are all very well, but when the merest whiff of fun brings on a scolding . . .

"Hey, Ellie! Your harp playing is a *good* thing," Christina insists.

"But my secrecy is a bad thing."

"Sometimes it's good to be bad." One of the reasons I like Christina so much.

When I replace the receiver I realize I haven't asked about Christina's day at the shop, or about Alex. I tell myself it's OK; she's used me as a sounding board enough times so it's fine to do the same to her every once in a while. But I'm not impressed with myself.

The longer I leave it, the more difficult it's going to be. If I say something now he'll already be hurt — and when Clive is hurt he lashes out. If only I could find a way of telling him without mentioning Dan. I'm on slippery ground. I don't have many male friends, but if I so much as mention them Clive gets tetchy. I suppose it's not surprising in view of his history.

When I first met him, Clive was dating my colleague Jayne. It was the Christmas meal of the library staff and Clive was Jayne's plus one. I didn't have a plus one of my own at the time and felt rather a misfit. The struggle of staff party small talk was less bad than usual, however, because I was sitting opposite Jayne — fun, chatty Jayne. Hair jumping out of her pigtail, lipstick clashing with her sweater, she was all bubbles and chaos. I was impressed that she was with this crisply dressed Clive guy, who seemed to me a very cool, smart sort of a person. He kept everyone's glasses topped up. He and Jayne aired their views on the films made from classic books. The newer version of *The Thirty-Nine Steps* wasn't bad, they said. Nobody had produced a *Great Expectations* as good as the book. As for *Charlie and the Chocolate Factory*, Jayne (who had written a thesis on children's literature) approved of the film and was prepared to put forward its merits until her jaw ached. Clive affectionately disagreed. They were both keen to hear my opinion, but I hadn't seen it. I tried not to look at Clive too much. What was it about him that fascinated me? The intensity of his eyes? The faint stubble on his chin? The pronounced line of his jaw? I came to the conclusion it wasn't so much his physical attributes as his combination of sensitivity and firmness.

"Clive seems nice," I commented to Jayne at work the following week as we were cataloging books together.

"You think so, do you?" she said with bitterness.

"What's wrong, Jayne? Has something happened between you?"

She curled her hand into a fist. "That man! I hate his guts."

"Why?" I asked, bemused.

"He only went and smashed my Beatrix Potters! Every last one."

I looked at her quizzically.

She told me how she'd been collecting Beatrix Potter china for years. She adored the stuff. Peter Rabbit plates, Squirrel Nutkin mugs and Jeremy Fisher eggcups were all on show in her flat. But apparently, after a flaming row, Clive had laid into her collection with a hammer.

I was horrified. How could such a pleasant, well-mannered guy behave so violently? I started to hate him too. I didn't know Jayne that well, but I did my best to comfort her. She was pretty upset — though more, it seemed, over her broken Mrs. Tiggy-Winkle teapot than her broken relationship.

Not long after our conversation I spotted Clive in the street. There was a grayness to the skin around his eyes and a heaviness in his walk. I would have hurried on in view of his appalling treatment of Jayne, but he hailed me at once.

"Hello, there! Ellie, isn't it?"

"Hello, Clive." Frostily.

He sensed that I was fending off any further dialogue. "Did Jayne tell you?"

I nodded.

"She was . . ." His face darkened. "She . . ." He couldn't get any more words out. I watched him suffer for what felt like minutes. Then at last he managed to shape the words. "She was sleeping with another man behind my back."

"Oh! She didn't tell me that!"

"He was a friend of mine. A close friend. That's what I thought, anyway."

I saw the pain. I couldn't condone his way of dealing with it, but a shard of sympathy slipped into my heart. I suggested coffee.

"I won't be very good company," he mumbled.

"Doesn't matter!" I told him.

We ended up opposite each other in the Apple Tree Café, sipping cappuccinos and carefully skirting around any topics that verged on the personal. The background music hummed a non-descript tune. I sat rearranging the brown paper cylinders of sugar in their bowl, reviewing my opinion of Jayne. At the same time I was keenly aware that this man was now single. Available. Not that I was interested, not when I knew what he was capable of. And yet . . .

As we talked, his manner was brightening. He seemed to be gathering strength, building himself up again.

I decided I should ask something about his job. I'd spouted on for ages about how much I loved being a librarian and he'd honored me with flattering levels of attention.

"So what, um . . . what *is* an actuary?" (I'd asked the very same question to Jayne when she started going out with him and her answer was, "Dull.")

Clive's eyes narrowed. A look spread over his face that started off defensive, passed through apologetic and then settled for resigned.

"Do you really want to know? Jayne was never very interested."

"*I* am," I told him, seizing the opportunity to demonstrate exactly how much nicer I was than Jayne.

He took a gulp of coffee. "OK, then, I'll tell you. It's number crunching and statistics. It's masses and masses of spreadsheets. It's trying to explain complicated concepts with the aid of overly simplistic diagrams to clients who haven't a hope in hell of understanding. It's working for a company that rips people off big-time. In my case it also involves having a boss who's an obnoxious git. But the salary's good."

I was silenced, but I appreciated the fact that he didn't overwhelm me with technical details.

He paid for the coffees. I didn't protest in view of his large salary.

"Well, this has been nice, Ellie," he said. "We must do it again sometime."

I wondered if we would.

At home I googled "actuary." Wikipedia informed me that there are two components of risk assessment: the magnitude of potential loss and the probability that loss will occur. The price of your insurance is worked out on these. Clive must be very good at calculating probabilities, I thought. What

81

are things worth and how likely are you to lose them? Life's relevant questions.

I'm no good at making calculations myself when it comes to risk. I might agonize, but in the end it's always my guts that dictate whether I dive in or hold back. Clive, I decided, must be way more logical in his approach.

When he rang the next day to ask me out I said yes. Then fretted. I still hadn't processed my feelings toward him. But I was flattered. Worried. Excited. Would I tell Jayne? I thought not.

Clive was on the rebound and I questioned if he would have liked me otherwise. It mattered what he thought of me. I was bound to be a disappointment, wasn't I? He'd think I was dippy. I'd never find enough intelligent things to say. I chose a few topics and rehearsed conversations in my head.

During the date I forgot everything I'd rehearsed, but it didn't matter because Clive did the work. He was entertaining in a way I hadn't expected. His mother, I learned, had a habit of adopting sickly dogs and her house was permanently filled with limping terriers. Smelly ones. Clive said they'd replaced his father, who also stank. (Metaphorically. The father had run off with his secretary years earlier.) I told him about my own parents. My mother, who at that stage was still criticizing my every move, who often said: "When Ellie walks into a room things go wrong." My father, who winked at me but would never contradict her.

"Well, *I'm* contradicting her!" Clive said. "Nothing's gone wrong *here* since you walked in, has it? Quite the reverse!" With a look that melted me.

We also talked about Jayne and . . . was it that date or the next that he told me I was worth twenty Jaynes?

It felt so good to be appreciated, as if a warm, furry animal was nestling inside me.

Six months later Clive supported me through a big crisis. Thanks to a new automated system my job at the library became redundant. I was devastated. Jayne had already moved on to work in a university library and was no longer in touch, though I heard she was doing well. I had never told her I was dating Clive.

I wished I had Jayne's self-assurance. I applied for lots of jobs I didn't really want, with very little success. My father tided me over with small sums of money. My mother sighed. But every time I got another rejection a bouquet of flowers arrived from Clive. His devotion touched me and boosted my drooping confidence. Then, during a windy wander along the beach, Clive proposed. I was taken aback, especially when he stuck his hand in his pocket and took out a ring. I gawped at it. Diamonds and emeralds. Expensive.

"Clive, you're serious!"

"Of course I'm bloody serious!"

That a man should want to spend the rest of his life with me seemed a marvel beyond all marvels. Especially a successful and attractive man. Everything about him was attractive then, even his mood swings. My heart launched into a spinning dance of gratitude.

"Yes!" I whispered, but my voice was drowned in the crash of waves.

"Did you say yes?" he shouted.

"Yes. Yes, yes, *yes*!"

It felt like such a big adventure.

"I'll be earning enough money to support both of us," he pointed out when we'd got a little farther down the beach. "You won't need to lift a finger."

I pretended to gasp. "Does that mean I have to do all the cooking and cleaning?"

"No, of course not! Not unless you want to!"

Without a second thought I assured him that I did want to. "It's only fair!" I said. "We'll be an old-fashioned couple! You

84

Breadwinner. Me Housewife!" It was all a bit of a joke at the time. But I never did get another job and the housewife role seems to have stuck.

"So, what shall we do for your birthday?" he said, putting a hand on my shoulder, making me jump. I put down the book I hadn't really been reading.

"I don't know. I hadn't thought."

"A nice meal out? Cinema? A trip somewhere? C'mon, El! What would you *really* like to do?"

Really I'd like to make a trip up to the Harp Barn, but as my birthday fell on a Saturday that would be impossible.

"Um . . . we could invite some friends out for a meal?"

"Friends?" he said, as if the word was foreign. "Who do you have in mind?"

"Well, there's Christina, of course . . ." His forehead creased slightly. "It wouldn't have to be just Christina," I went on quickly. "We could invite Phil and Rachel — or do you have any friends from work you'd like to invite? Andy, perhaps?"

Andy was the only colleague Clive ever mentioned with any degree of enthusiasm.

"Oh, not Andy," he said.

"Why not? He seems nice." I tried to

remember the couple of occasions I'd met Andy, but all I could recall was that he was a big man with a big beard and a big laugh. "He's single, isn't he?" I added. "Perhaps he might get on well with Christina."

"I doubt it. He's only good for crude jokes. I'm sure Christina would find him very dull."

He opened the cupboard and got out a packet of pork rinds. He pulled it open and offered me one, even though he knows I'm not keen. I wrinkled my nose and waved them away. The smell was disgusting. He threw a couple into his mouth and crunched them loudly.

"Why don't we have a snug pub lunch somewhere, just the two of us?"

"Sounds nice," I said. It did in a way, but, if Dan and my harp were not an option (and they weren't), I'd quite fancied something a bit more like a party, with other people involved. I don't really get to see other people as much as I'd like. Clive works on the principle that we only need each other.

"Just the two of us, then! Where shall we go?" Clive asked, screwing up the top of the pork rinds packet and putting it to the side. "I know! How about the Crow's Nest? That little place up near Doone Valley."

I considered. "Well, it's great to have food

with a view. But I got very cold last time we were there. I'm sure the climate's a degree or two colder than it is here. I suppose the air gets a bit thin up there on the top."

"Nothing wrong with being thin on the top," he said, running his hands over his head.

" 'Course not, hon!" Then I remembered that the Crow's Nest serves a local brew that Clive particularly likes.

"The Crow's Nest *is* lovely," I said.

"Sorted, then!" he said.

It's just as well one of us is capable of making decisions.

9
DAN

My girlfriend Roe Deer says it's disgraceful how people are so seldom prepared to pay for music. Have people no idea, she asks, how many years of hard work it takes to learn an instrument? How many hours of practice every day? Not to mention the challenges of lugging a harp about to gigs, getting it insured, replacing broken strings? Not to mention the stress of live performance. Then there's the hassle and expense of setting up and maintaining a website, doing your own publicity, recordings, photo shoots, etc., etc., etc. My girlfriend Roe Deer is very aggrieved about these things because, she says, you wouldn't expect a plumber to come out and fix your taps for free. You wouldn't make comments about how lucky he is to have that talent and what a pleasure it must be for him. You wouldn't assume that plumbing is its own reward. You would pay him handsomely. Handsomely is what you should also pay some-body (i.e., her) for playing the harp.

I agree with my girlfriend Roe Deer. Not so much about the money (I am not a money person) but about the value. Doctors and dentists minister to our physical needs. Prime ministers minister to our political needs. Plumbers minister unto taps. But harp players (and indeed all musicians) minister unto something else. The something else is much deeper than the bits we can see, but far more important. In my opinion music ministers to the real person that hides inside the person-shell. In my opinion the real person inside the person-shell craves and needs music every day; otherwise, the real person shrivels up into a nothingness.

This morning I woke up and the windows were dripping with condensation, but the sun was powering through it. I pulled on my boots and jacket as quickly as I could and rushed outside. The air was glittery and scented with damp pine. The ground shimmered with dewdrops. Every grass blade gleamed silky silver and every stone along the lane shone like a diamond. I felt very rich to live on Exmoor. The birds were enjoying it as much as I was. So many tweetlings and twitterings! A buzzard too, cruising above the clouds, casual as you like. The clouds today were white, glossy, freshly scrubbed and combed.

Hills stretched out all around me, some decorated with skewed checkers of fields, some spotted with sheep, some wooded; pine patterns, oak patterns, beech patterns. Others rose up proudly ragged with gorse, heather and bracken, the colors of the moor.

When I arrived back at the barn my eyes and lungs and soul were full of Exmoor. Ellie was just arriving at the same time. She clambered out of her car wielding her big canvas shoulder bag and also a large-sized cake.

We went in together. Ellie put the cake on the table.

It was a brown cake, round, with thick squishy icing. She'd stuck three fir cones on the top. I thought this was a good decoration — much nicer than plastic penguins, which are what my sister Jo always sticks on a cake. If ever my sister Jo makes a cake, that is. Which is not often.

I said to Ellie that this was a first for me. I had never tried fir-cone cake before. She laughed a big laugh in her slightly snorty way. "It's not actually fir cone flavored, it's a chocolate cake," she told me. "I've just got it. It's from the bakery in Porlock. I would have made one myself, but I . . . well, I ran out of time. I did add the fir cones myself, though. They're from the woods down in the valley."

I examined the fir cones admiringly.

"I was careful to wash them in case of bugs," she said.

I commended her for her wisdom. Bugs would do nothing to enhance either the flavor or the texture, I believed. I had eaten a bug only once in my life, as it had alighted on an egg-and-cress sandwich at precisely the wrong moment, i.e., a split second before the sandwich entered my mouth. The experience was not pleasant, either for the bug or for me.

"Cake!" Ellie affirmed, rubbing her hands together. "I thought it would make a change from sandwiches."

"What's wrong with sandwiches?" I asked.

"Nothing," she said. "But I like cake so much! And" — she blew some sawdust off a chair, sat on it and looked up at me from under her eyelashes — "it's a little celebration."

I asked what we were celebrating.

"Can you guess?" she said.

I am not good at guessing, but I thought I'd give it a go. I asked if we were celebrating the fact that she potentially had a new harp teacher. One end of her mouth turned down a bit and she said, "No, not that."

I asked if we were celebrating a new poem she'd written.

"No, I haven't finished any in a while," was her answer.

What else could we be celebrating? I looked out the window for inspiration. My eyes focused on the leaves of the beeches. Each tree seemed to have ideas of its own. Some were determined to stay green. Others were fully committed to being yellow. While others clearly thought bronze was the way to go. But they were all dancing together in beautiful formations in the sunlight.

I asked if we were celebrating the Glories of Autumn.

Both corners of her mouth lifted this time. "A lovely idea, but no. It's something that happens every year in the autumn, though, on a certain date. It's not actually today, it's tomorrow, but I won't be seeing you tomorrow so I thought we could celebrate today."

She looked at me with a look of expectation. I told her that if there's one thing I'm bad at, that thing is guessing, and I'd be really, really grateful if she could enlighten me now about what we were celebrating because I was starting to feel stressed about it.

She pointed to the cake. "That's a clue. If it had candles on it, it would be even more of a clue."

"Ah!" I said. "It's someone's birthday!"

"Dan," she said, "it's *my* birthday! Not today, tomorrow." This was evidently an important point and worth saying twice.

"Ellie," I said, "happy birthday *tomorrow*!"

"Thank you!" is what she replied.

I then started wondering if she was expecting me to give her a present and, this being the case, what sort of a present I could produce at short notice. Presents are difficult, just as guessing is difficult. It is no simple task working out what people want and what will make them happy. When my girlfriend Roe Deer has a birthday I spend a lot of time thinking very hard indeed. She already has three harps now, so it has to be something else. I've tried giving her CDs, soap, harp strings, potted plants, carved wooden animals, but they never seem to be right. As for my sister Jo, she has a birthday every February and every time it happens she says: "Dan, please don't get me anything. You'll only agonize and I'll only end up with something I don't want. Just give me a fiver and I'll buy myself something nice." So that is what I do, and that is what she does. It's much easier that way.

Luckily on my own birthday (the twenty-first of May) I am allowed to choose exactly what I want to do. And what I choose to do is nothing. Other people seldom take this option, so their birthdays are fraught with difficulty.

Another thing about birthdays: There is always the worry that I might get invited to a party. That would be spectacularly bad news. I have been to several parties in my life and it's always a disaster.

Thomas's party three years ago, for example. I only managed to stay for twelve minutes because of the noise. Thomas's wife Linda has never forgiven me for that.

Roe Deer's party six years ago, for example. I only managed to stay for nine minutes because I was being jostled by so many people. I had to get out quickly so did not say good-bye. Roe Deer has never forgiven me for that.

"Dan, what's troubling you?" asked Ellie the Exmoor Housewife.

I told her I was worried about giving her the wrong present and also worried that she was going to invite me to a party.

She laid a hand on my arm.

"You can put your mind at rest. I'm not

going to invite you to a party. I haven't had a party in years. I'm going out for a meal with Clive tomorrow, that's all. As for a present! You mustn't even think of it! For heaven's sake, you've given me a harp!" Her eyes sparkled. "That's enough of a present to last a lifetime! You mustn't even think of giving me anything else."

I was glad she'd said this. And glad I'd given her the harp. Giving her a harp *was* a good idea. I knew that at the time. At the time that was something I'd realized more than she had.

Ellie took her enormous canvas shoulder bag from the floor and delved around in it. "As a matter of fact, I've got a little present for *you*!"

I didn't know what to think. "For me?"

"Yes."

She pulled out a jar of jam, then another, then another. Lots of jars of jam. They had little frilly hats over their lids, checked blue and white, fastened with rubber bands. They also had labels stuck on the side with the word *Plum* written in purple ink. She gave me the jars, one by one. I put them in a line along the edge of the table and counted them. There were seven.

I thanked her profusely. I was very enthusiastic because nobody has ever, ever given me seven jars of jam before. Let alone ones with checked blue-and-white hats.

"I hope it's OK," she said, turning a little red. "It's my first attempt at jam making. It was quite an adventure. Your plums were so juicy! I made a sticky mess all over the kitchen. Then I was worried it wasn't going to set, but it did. There were eight jars altogether, but I gave one to Christina because she gave me the recipe. I hope you like jam. You do? Phew! I had a bit of a panic in case you didn't. Sorry — I'm babbling. Let's eat that cake."

We had cake together and Ellie had a fit of giggles because we got so chocolaty. While we were licking our fingers I asked her if she had rung my girlfriend Roe Deer about harp lessons yet. She stopped giggling abruptly and said no, she hadn't got round to it yet, what with jam making and birthday arrangements, but she would get round to it very soon. Then she asked if Roe Deer came up to the barn to visit me much and added that she was surprised she hadn't bumped into her before now. I said not very much these days, no, and oh.

After we had eaten two slices of cake each and both of us had taken a trip to the bathroom to wash the residual chocolatiness off our hands, I had an idea. Whether or not it was a good idea I didn't know, but I thought I'd suggest it anyway because to me it is a proper way of celebrating a birthday if celebrating is what you want to do. So I told Ellie it was very lovely to eat cake together but we should also do something outside because outside was special and today there was sunshine, which made it even more special.

"What did you have in mind?" she said. "A walk?"

I told her that the thing I had in mind did involve a short walk, yes.

We put on our jackets and went outside. I took her down the first bit of lane, then over the stile and into the field with lots of molehills. At the far end of this field is an old stone wall covered in layers of shaggy moss. Behind the stone wall are sixteen tall birch trees.

The birch trees were looking very happy today, with their white trunks arching gracefully upward, their branches swaying in the breeze and their leaves fluttering every shade of yellow.

Ellie gazed up at them. "Ah, you remembered they're my favorite!"

I reached up and pulled a bough toward us to inspect the brown catkins. They were made up of dry clusters of tiny winged

97

seeds. Some were beginning to disintegrate, which is what they do when they are ready to fly. On the next gusty day they'll suddenly get adventurous. They'll unhitch themselves, launch out into the air and soar away on the wind. They'll travel huge distances. But some of them won't because the next thing I did was to proffer a twigful to Ellie.

Ellie looked at me with questions in her eyes.

"Take some," I told her. "We're going to plant them. I have compost and I have seed trays. First we'll plant them in the seed trays, where I can look after them, but when they are saplings big enough to look after themselves we can plant them out in the countryside. We're going to create a new coppice of birch trees. For your birthday. An Ellie coppice."

"Oh, Dan," is what she said as she helped herself to birch seeds. "What could be more wonderful!"

10
ELLIE

He's leaning against the car, waiting. I feel bad. But it's my birthday so I'm allowing myself a few more minutes. The autumn light is beautiful this afternoon, the way it clings to the magentas and browns of the heather and beams out honey colors from the gorse. I crouch among the prickles and play with the focus of my camera. I zoom in on a single gorse flower, ensure the edge is sharp as crystal and press the shutter. Not quite satisfied, I adjust the focus again, converting it to a blurry kaleidoscope of color, then take another shot. I'm not sure which one I like better.

"Got something good?" Clive asks as I join him.

"Yes, I think so."

"And we're going for a walk now, are we?" He's using his *you're-the-boss* voice.

"Well, just a little stroll to the viewpoint perhaps?"

"Right you are." He zips up his jacket.

We've had a pleasant meal at the Crow's Nest; the risotto wasn't exceptional, but the lemon meringue pie made up for it. Clive told me all about the new rowing machines at the gym and I enthused about the book I was reading. We noticed that the family having a meal at the next table weren't talking to each other due to an urgent need to use their smartphones. Clive indulged in a rant about selfie culture in a voice that was a little too loud. I stole an anxious glance at the teenagers to see if they'd taken offense, but they were far too preoccupied to be aware of our existence, let alone our topic of conversation.

Now, as we tramp side by side across the moor, I'm thinking about Dan and the birch seeds we planted yesterday. And, with a sudden surge of realization, I'm aware I've been thinking about Dan *all day.* Mentally conjuring up his features, his voice, his smile . . . wondering if he's thinking of me at all. That's stupid, of course. He'll be thinking instead of his beautiful, talented, sexy girlfriend.

I turn to view the horizon. The line of the land swells and puckers; the line of the sea seems to curve slightly downward. The islands of Flat Holm and Steep Holm rise like sea monsters out of the blue. I'm grateful for the blast of cool wind against my hot face.

"All right, El?"

"Yes, just admiring the wonderful colors."

Dear God! Thirty-six now — that's how old I am. I wish I wasn't. Thirty-six is way too old to be feeling such crazy, overwhelming teenage-crush feelings. If it wasn't so pathetic it would be funny.

Anyway, I'm happily married, aren't I?

Of course I am.

I clutch my husband's arm. "Thank you for today, Clive! And thank you for — you know — *everything*! You're my rock."

During tides of emotion little limpets have to cling to rocks.

"So I'm rugged, am I?" he asks.

"Oh yes!"

"And strong?"

I feel the muscles of his arm, feel them flex under my touch.

"Extremely strong!"

He looks pleased.

This is the perfect opportunity to tell him about my harp playing. He's obliged to be extra nice on my birthday, the sun is shining and he's had a couple of beers. If I can make him understand how much I love the harp, he'll surely be happy for me.

I'll do it. I'll do it now.

"Clive, when I was sorting out the spare room the other day I found your old guitar . . ."

"Oh, did you? Covered in cobwebs, was it?"

"Well, I gave it a bit of a dust, yes, but it was nice to see it again. It reminded me how you used to love strumming away."

"I only knew four chords."

"Well, it sounded good to me, anyway. You put a lot of expression into it, especially when you sang. You seemed so happy."

"Ellie, it was *painful.*"

Perhaps I should try a different tack.

Five or six Exmoor ponies wander out from behind a hillock, manes wild, tails ragged, noses velvety. They look at us with gentle, uncertain eyes, then move slowly away.

Our shadows are getting longer. I sift through my brain, hunting for inspiration.

"Sometimes I think I should branch out a bit," I comment. "I mean, I don't really have any hobbies, do I, apart from poetry. Do you think I'm getting a bit dull?"

"Of course not, El! You could never be dull. What are you getting at? Are you bored?"

"No, no, not at all. I just wonder if I could

do something more with my life."

"Like?"

Play the harp, play the harp, play the harp!

But I can't say it. My mouth has gone dry.

I look sideways at Clive. He seems extra large as he strides beside me, his strips of sandy hair lifted slightly by the breeze. I know he can be incredibly supportive in certain situations, but I'm just not convinced this is one of those situations.

Anyway, how can I talk about Dan now without my voice and face giving away too much? No, I simply can't do it today. I'm too obsessed, too jittery. If Clive presses me to give up the harp I actually feel I might cry.

It's best if I leave my disclosure until I've met Dan's girlfriend. Once I've got to know her I'll surely succeed in getting more of a grip on myself.

I sit on the windowsill next to the phone and look out. Beyond the boundaries of our garden the slope of the hill leans heavily against a darkening sky. Drizzle spins through the air and spits onto the windowpane.

The number I need is on a scrap of paper, folded up in the front pocket of my bag. I pull it out and gaze at it. Dan's handwriting is very neat and slants slightly to the left. I toy with the receiver for a minute, then dial a different number.

"Hi, Mum, it's me, Ellie."

"Who?"

"Ellie. Me!"

"Oh, Ellie, is it? Hello, Ellie."

"Mum, just ringing to see how you are. Everything OK?"

There is a silence. I count the seconds. I can hear her breathing, slow and slightly wheezy. "There's a black dog outside on the grass."

This may or may not be true. "Ah, is there?" I say brightly. "Well, that's nice. You're all right, are you?"

"He is sniffing at the dahlias. It shouldn't be allowed."

"Mum, it's fine. Tell me, how are you? Are the carers being good? Have you seen Vic today?"

"Vic?"

"Vic. Your other daughter."

"No, I don't think so. Haven't seen her in years."

I know for a fact that Vic goes to the home twice a week. She's the dutiful daughter now, living close enough to do that. I am three hundred miles away so it isn't quite so easy. And the distance is more than just a geographical one.

"Mum, can I ask you a question? Did you ever think I was musical as a child?"

"You might be one of several." She hasn't understood. The conversation, as usual, is going nowhere. Part of me wants to tell her about my harp playing. The secret would be safe, as she'd probably forget it anyway. But it's all a bit pointless. How I miss my dad!

I ramble on for a while, then say my good-byes and put the phone down. The sky has grown a heavier shade of gray. I consult my watch. Clive will be back home if I leave it much longer. I pick up the paper Dan gave me.

I brace myself and ring the number written on it.

"Excuse me. I'm ringing to speak to Roe Deer."

A peal of laughter.

"Sorry, but I was given this number."

"Yes," she says. "And I can guess who gave it to you. Was it by any chance Dan Hollis?"

His name reassures me a little. "Yes, it was, actually. Are you Roe Deer?"

"Not exactly. I'm Rhoda Rothbury, but Dan likes to call me Roe Deer. One of his little eccentricities. And you are . . . ?"

"My name's Ellie Jacobs," I stammer. "Dan suggested I should contact you. I'm ringing to ask about harp lessons. I'm trying to learn on one of his harps, but I badly need a teacher."

"I see." Her voice is clear and intelligent; sharp, even. "So you're a complete beginner, are you?"

We sort out a few logistics. She apparently prefers to give lessons from her house in Taunton, but she might be able to teach me at Dan's barn once in a while. Her normal rate is thirty-eight pounds an hour. She asks if I'd like to meet up first and take it from there.

"Oh yes, I think that would be best," I bluster. I'm not sure how many lots of thirty-eight pounds I can manage without Clive noticing. He goes through our joint account statement with a fine-tooth comb every month. I'll have to be devious and pay her cash. Besides, I want to meet her first. And find out how well she really can play the harp. And find out if she can teach, which is a different matter. And find out other things.

11
DAN

Today I'm working on a twenty-two-string Celtic harp. I'm fashioning it from recycled wood from a pew. The reason I'm using a pew is that the committee of one of the local churches decided they needed to set up a coffee-serving station inside the church and the pew happened to be where they wanted to put the station and nobody ever sat on that particular pew anymore because the congregation had shrunk considerably since Reverend Harrison arrived with his long sermons, but the thing the congregation needed more than ever was coffee. Therefore the pew had to go, therefore they ripped it out. My sister Jo (who is always seeking out wood on my behalf) asked if I could have the pew. The church committee met up and discussed it and discussed it. It took them a while, but in the end they agreed on the answer: yes.

I like this wood and respect it, very much.

For generations it was a yew tree, growing through the wind, rain and sunshine of life, expanding steadily in its gnarled, knobbly way. Birds perched in it and little creatures curled up in its roots. Then it became a pew and generations of people sat on it, praying. They must have felt all sorts of things going in and out of their hearts as they sat through baptisms, weddings, festivals and funerals. Now the wood will transform again, and one day some skilled harpist will draw music from it, music that will make hundreds more people feel things. Another miracle.

The harp is coming on nicely. I've made the base, backbone and sound box complete with ribs, liners and spacing bars. The soundboard is ready to be drilled with twenty-two tiny holes. I've also shaped the neck and ensured the harmonic curve is curved exactly the right amount. It is all filed and planed to perfection.

The pillar will bow outward then inward a little before sweeping out at the top, elegant, swanlike. I begin sheering off thin layers with my plane. The yew wood is mellow, yielding, full of interesting swirls, light and dark.

Today is Ellie's birthday. Yesterday we ate cake and planted birch seeds to celebrate. Ellie will be out today, she told me, eating at a pub with her husband and then going for a nice walk, also with her husband. Her husband's name is Clive.

I do not like the name Clive.

I look at the pillar of the harp and I realize I have planed off too much. The pillar is now too narrow at the top. I don't usually make mistakes like this. Now I'll have to cut a fresh piece of pew wood and start it again. I'm not happy about what I've done. I don't like to waste the precious wood, because I love yew.

Thomas and I have been friends for twelve years and he always knows what's in my letters.

"A letter from your sister and a fuel bill and an order of harp strings," he says to me as he hands them over four days after Ellie's birthday and the planting of the birch coppice. We are just outside the barn, standing in the lane. Thomas is wearing his green fluorescent sweatshirt with his shorts. He also has on very large-sized sneakers, green and white with orange laces. The weather is misty and you can't see much beyond the first hill. It is very quiet. Even the birds can't be bothered to sing much today, apart from one solitary crow — and I'm not convinced he knows much about singing.

"Thank you," I tell Thomas, taking the letters. "I don't need to open them now."

I do, though, because that's what you are supposed to do with letters. Thomas leans over my shoulder and reads them too.

"Your sister is still working at the school, then," he comments as I peruse the first letter.

I nod. Together we read that the teachers are snotty to her, that there is one who she particularly dislikes, that this one never says hello because she is only a cleaner, which in his head means a lesser mortal.

"Shameful," mutters Thomas. "Poor Jo!" He has never met my sister Jo but has read a lot of her letters and so feels he knows her quite well. He shakes his head sorrowfully. "She deserves better. Next!"

We look at the fuel bill.

"Ouch," he says. "Oil isn't getting any cheaper."

He is right about this. It is not getting cheaper at all. It is doing the exact opposite.

Thomas sighs and points a long finger at the package. "How many harp strings have you got in there, boyo?" he asks.

I open it to check. "Four sets. Three sets of thirty-six and one of twenty-seven. A hundred and thirty-five in total."

He whistles. "I bet they're not cheap and all!"

I agree that they are not cheap.

"Stag's Head tonight?" he suggests.

"Good idea!" I say.

"I'll pick you up at eight."

He came to collect me at eight thirty-seven in his red van. I got in next to him. The three Alsatians were leaping about in the back sounding as if all hell was let loose. When all hell is let loose it is a very noisy experience and hurts your eardrums. Eventually one of them stopped barking and started licking the back of my neck instead. It felt quite nice. Wetly warm and warmly wet.

Thomas was grumbling, as he likes a good grumble. His grumble today was all about how lemonade just didn't do it for him and tonic without the addition of gin was a whole load of no fun. As we parked, he started saying that alcohol did not actually affect his ability to drive at all. If anything, it sharpened his perceptions. As we got out of the car and approached the pub door he was concluding that drunk-driving rules did not apply in the countryside in any case because there was nobody to run over. He also mentioned that he was particularly parched today and a little tipple would be welcome to calm his nerves due to the fact that he had had an argument with his missus. In fact, a pint of cider would be of great medicinal value.

"Are you saying you'd like me to buy you a pint of cider?" I asked, as he was being a bit obscure about it.

"Oh well, if you're offering, mate . . ." is what he said.

The people working behind the bar were two in number. One was the woman who blinks many times a second and who wears S-shaped dangly earrings and who has plucked out all of her eyebrows and painted them on again a bit higher up. The other was the shiny-faced man who says "No worries" a lot. I asked him for two pints of cider. "No worries," he said.

I took the ciders back to the corner table where Thomas had settled himself. Thomas tipped half a pint of cider down his throat, then wiped his mouth on his sleeve.

Our conversation went like this.

"So I see you have a new girlfriend?"

"What?" I said.

"You have a new girlfriend. Brown haired, slim, cute. Don't try and pull the wool over my eyes, mate. I've seen her. I've coincided with her leaving the Harp Barn a couple of

112

times now, you dog. Come on, what's the story?"

I told him I had no intention of pulling wool over his eyes. Moreover, I was no dog. And as for having a new girlfriend, I didn't. Not at all. I was quite happy with the old one, Roe Deer. Not that Roe Deer was old, I hastened to add — just that she had been my girlfriend for six years now, which just went to prove how serious our relationship was. The woman that Thomas had seen emerging from the Harp Barn was none other than the Housewife of Exmoor and the story was that she had a list of things to do before she was forty but it was looking as though she was not getting through them very fast; in fact, it was looking distinctly unpromising, as she had reached the age of thirty-six years and four days (I now knew this exactly) but when I first met her she was thirty-five years and three hundred and thirty-three days and at that time not even one of the items on the list had been achieved. So I had given her a harp.

Thomas sucked his cheeks in and then blew them out again.

"You gave her a harp? As in — *gave*? As in — no cash?"

I confirmed that no cash was involved.

"You must like her a hell of a lot, boyo."

I told him that indeed I did.

"Well, now, that sounds like a beautiful relationship, if you know what I'm saying — nudge, nudge, wink, wink. I'm sure she must find you difficult to resist after that one, you dirty dog!"

I assured him for a second time that I was not a dog, and certainly not a dirty one, and I told him that she was a married lady who ate triangular sandwiches and she was quite able to resist me. And as I had mentioned before, I had a girlfriend already, Roe Deer.

"Oh yes, of course, Mr. High-and-Mighty, so you do! OK then, let's switch to her. Another tasty morsel. How are things with the gorgeous Roe Deer?"

I said that things were just fine. Also that I hoped Roe Deer would shortly be teaching harp to Ellie at the barn on a regular basis so that Ellie would become a more confident harp player. I added that Ellie was the thirty-six-years-and-four-days-old Housewife to whom I'd given a harp.

Thomas's eyes had a bit of a glazed look. "So the Roe Deer might be coming to the Harp Barn more often?" he asked.

I asserted that I believed this to be the fact.

"How do you do it, mate?" he said. "I'm

stuck with a thirteen-stone hormonal harridan who does nothing but moan at me, and you have two gorgeous goddesses at your beck and call."

I pointed out that they were not goddesses, they were harp players.

"Same difference," he said. "Harpists, angels, goddesses, whatever. But I'm guessing they're not that holy. Especially Roe Deer. Nobody can be holy who dresses like she does. Nobody can be holy with breasts like hers. Her breasts are — well, not to put too fine a point on it, they are *bloody marvelous*!"

I agreed that Roe Deer did indeed have very marvelous breasts.

"Ah, so you admit it! You are like me. You have a . . ." He paused. ". . . a high regard for large coconuts."

I said that yes, I did. I liked coconuts whatever size they were. And also, I did like women's breasts.

"Especially Roe Deer's?" His eyes were a bit fuzzy. He took a slosh of cider.

Yes, I told him, I did especially like Roe Deer's breasts. I had spent many a happy moment studying them and wondering what wood I would use to carve them out of if ever I carved them in wood. I had come to the conclusion that maple might be best.

He laughed and slapped me on the back and called me a good man.

I commented that Roe Deer's breasts were also satisfactory in that they were very nice to stroke when she was lying naked in bed.

He choked and a spray of cider spurted out of his mouth and across the table.

"The next round's on me, boyo," is what he said after that.

On the way home there were three deer on the road, their eyes shining in the headlamps. They did not linger for an instant but pranced away into the woods, their white bottoms bobbing up and down. It made me think of Roe Deer again.

I hope Roe Deer will come and teach Ellie the harp. It would be nice for them to play harps together in my upstairs room. I could bring sandwiches for them both, cut into triangles. Jam sandwiches, made with the frilly-hatted jam that Ellie made from my plums. When Ellie gets good enough at the harp, perhaps her husband will want to come and listen, and I can make sandwiches for him too. And Thomas can come as well, although he will probably not listen to the harp much, he will just look at Roe Deer's breasts. I don't think she will mind. She is very tolerant that way. She is not like my sister Jo. If any man looks at *her* breasts (which are also of a notable size) she slaps him in the face. I must never introduce her to Thomas.

I have not told my sister Jo that I have given Ellie a harp. I considered telling her about it after the radio interview because she was pleased with me about that — she said it would generate business. But I didn't get around to it. In fact, I don't want to think about Jo's reaction if ever I do get around to it. It is easier to just make another harp.

12
ELLIE

That scent of earth and vegetation, that crispness in the air; the unmistakable sense of autumn stirring. The beeches at the end of the garden are smattered with coppery red, but the sunlight only manages to reach their top branches. Much as I love my home, I sometimes need to escape out of our shady valley and up onto high ground.

My heart accelerates as I change gear and climb the steep hill out of the village, the sky widening out beyond the pines. On the brow of the hill I honk my horn several times to disperse the usual crowd of pheasants who are wandering aimlessly around in the road.

I'm twenty minutes early. It's nosiness. I want to see if Rhoda — Roe Deer — is there already. Not that it would mean anything. She can see Dan for as long as she wants after I've gone anyway. Maybe evenings are their times together. Or nights.

When I arrive there is no other car parked.

Dan is in the back of the barn scrubbing pebbles.

"Look, Ellie!" His sleeves are rolled up, his hair a shambles. His glee is infectious.

I drag my eyes away from him and focus on the pebbles. "From this morning's walk," he tells me. "The orange one is almost a perfect oval. And this one has a silver streak across it if you hold it in the right light. And this one's rough, but look at the colors of all the speckles!"

I've never been that interested in pebbles before, but in Dan's presence I begin to see them with new eyes. They are artworks of infinite variety and beauty. Later perhaps I'll write a poem about them. Now I have other things on my mind.

"Will you help me to tune up before Rho— er — Roe Deer arrives?"

"Yes, all right. Good idea!" He dries his hands. He's shown me the tuning-up process a few times, but I'm far from confident.

I follow him upstairs. He takes a tuning key from his pocket and tries a few strings, adjusting them by placing the key over the pegs and turning it an infinitesimal amount.

"Now, why don't you try this one?"

I lean in to pluck the string.

"Sharp or flat?" he asks.

119

A week ago I didn't even know the meaning of the words. Now my ears are beginning to distinguish tiny differences.

"Sharp."

His smile is dazzling. He presents me with the key. I loosen the string slightly.

"There!" He plays a long arpeggio with his left hand. His hands are large and tanned, with roughish skin, but his touch is sensitive.

I'm captivated. "Are you sure you don't play the harp? That sounded amazing!"

"I only tune up and play chords and arpeggios."

"Aren't you tempted to learn some tunes?"

He shakes his head. "Tuning up, chords and arpeggios."

As I straighten up, my arm brushes against his. Inevitable, unstoppable, a tide of warmth floods through me. His face turns quickly toward me as if he felt something too.

"Dan!" calls a voice from downstairs. "Are you there?"

I follow him down. He darts across the barn to kiss the woman of the photo. As he draws back, I get my first glimpse of her face. Even from this distance it looks airbrushed. Her skin is flawless, her golden hair swept back and pouring over one shoulder. She's dressed in a figure-hugging wraparound dress and a long, loose coat of deep turquoise reminiscent of a summer sky. Her hair shines against it like a wheat field. Every detail has been carefully put together. I come closer and introduce myself. I watch her lips curve into a gracious smile and her sapphire eyes fasten on me with interest.

"Sandwiches?" Dan offers.

"Yes, please," I reply eagerly, then start apologizing as I realize it wasn't me he was talking to.

A firm "No, thank you" comes from Rhoda, though. I guess that to retain a slim figure like hers she has to exercise strict self-discipline. Or maybe she's just lucky. She is perfectly designed and sleekly finished. Her cleavage gapes so much I can't stop looking at it, even though I'm not that way inclined. I notice Dan looking at it too. Alas, I can't boast much in that department. And with my tatty jeans, bird's-nest hair and poor posture, standing next to Rhoda is, I realize too late, a spectacularly bad idea.

"So, Ellie, tell me about your musical experience," she purrs, sliding manicured fingers through her silky waves of hair.

"There isn't any," I answer glumly.

"What, not at all?"

I wilt. "Well, I sing about the house a bit and I've got quite a lot of CDs. I like listening to music." It sounds so lame.

Dan's loitering at the bottom of the stairs. "Ellie is naturally musical," he puts in. "Very. I know that because, even though she's a beginner, I love listening when she plays."

When Dan gives a compliment I feel it much more than I do with other people. Perhaps because I know he never lies. I flush.

"Well, I try! I do try hard, and I do love the harp."

Rhoda nods. "That's a good start, then."

I'm aware of the sparkles in Dan's eyes, but I daren't look at him right now.

"I'll make you four sandwiches, Ellie. Brown wholemeal bread; triangular; cucumber and tuna mayonnaise. Will that be all right?"

"Lovely!"

He propels himself upstairs to the kitchen.

Rhoda and I stand amid the throng of harps. I still feel it's a massive privilege to be here, in this quiet, artistic, sweet-scented place, in their elegant company.

Rhoda crosses her arms. "Which is yours?"

"Oh, mine's upstairs in Dan's little room.

I play it there. It's one of the cherrywood ones."

"Cherrywood. Nice," she comments, her voice conveying the strength of a superior knowledge. "They always have a lovely tone."

"Yes, it's very special."

"Why don't you take it home?"

I'll have to tell her. But how much? She seems to be assuming I've bought the harp. Dan can't have told her it was actually a gift. I imagine it might cause friction between them if she knew. Would she kick up a fuss? Is she the jealous type? Now that she's seen me, it's hardly possible she can view me as a rival. Still, I wonder if she minds that I come to the Harp Barn so often and see so much of her boyfriend.

"I'd love to take it home, of course, but I haven't actually told my husband that I'm learning. The plan is to surprise him one day, when I'm really good." This sounds reasonable. It at least bears some resemblance to the truth. Rhoda seems to accept it, anyway.

"Well, it's nice for Dan to have someone to share his sandwiches with," she acknowledges.

On cue, Dan comes down and presents me with four triangular sandwiches laid out in a star shape on a plate.

Rhoda strolls about the barn examining the harps. I traipse after her, nibbling at the sandwiches, not sure what to say next.

She turns to Dan. "Ah, you've finished the *Elfin* now."

"Yes! Last time you saw it there were no strings and no pebble. Now it has twenty-six strings and one pebble. It's a good pebble, isn't it, Roe Deer?"

Or was it Roe, *dear*? Either way, it was uttered with affection. I pluck at my eyebrows nervously.

She strokes the flat bluish pebble that is shining against the pale wood. "Yes, it goes well."

"The sound is good too, I think," he replies. "Not loud, but quite resonant. Give it a go, Roe, and tell me what you think."

She leans over and plays it from above, without even bothering to get into the right position. The strings ring out under her fingers. The melody flows once through, clean and simple, then again with exquisite harmonies added. I catch my breath. This is real music.

Seldom have I felt so envious. I need to keep reminding myself she's been playing since she was a child. I can never expect to catch up.

Dan is beaming. He must be horribly proud of her.

Rhoda looks at me from under her luscious lashes. "So, Ellie, I have to rush off now, but we can arrange a lesson if you like. Don't worry, I shan't be offended if you don't like," she adds with a charming smile.

I do my utmost to reflect some charm back at her. "I'd like it very much."

The jam is delicious, though I say so myself. Dan and I are both wolfing the sandwiches. I silently offer up thanks for Christina's recipe.

"Are your lessons with Roe Deer going well?" he asks.

Well . . .

Rhoda is a good teacher. We now have lessons in her house in Taunton. She has three harps of her own, so I play one of hers when I'm there. She's shown me where I've been going wrong. I need to sit up straighter, relax my wrists more and bring my hands in closer to the harp. My elbows keep sinking; I must check that they don't. I must pluck a little higher up on the strings. My fingers should be pinging back into my palms with every pluck. My nails should be a bit shorter. I need to practice triads, scales, rhythms and placing my fingers in

125

advance.

I ache to make music as Rhoda does, her fingers rippling over the strings so fast you can hardly see them. I have a long, long way to go.

Do I like Rhoda? I'm not sure. She's been kind and helpful, but I can't quite warm to her, somehow.

"I'm learning a lot," I tell Dan.

Rhoda doesn't seem to visit Dan very often. He must be the one who visits her. He does have a battered old Land Rover out back, but I've always had the impression he doesn't drive it very often.

"Roe Deer is the best harpist I know," he informs me.

"Yes, but you *would* say that," I point out grumpily. "She's your girlfriend."

"Yes, I would say that. Because it's true. She *is* the best harpist I know. And yes, you're right; she *is* my girlfriend."

I'm not keen on the pride in his voice and not keen to talk about their relationship. I'd rather fish for compliments. "She says I have a good ear," I boast.

My ears are mostly covered by bushy hair, but I get the impression Dan is trying to examine them — without looking as though he's examining them.

"You have *two,* both of them good!" he

replies at last.

"Gee, thanks. I'll take that as a compliment."

He pauses. "The thing about ears is they're for listening. Yours are no exception. It would help your harp playing if you sometimes used them for that."

I am stung. "I do listen! I listen all the time!"

Again, a small patch of silence. I feel my words hemmed in by doubt.

With all her clever tips on technique, that's one thing Rhoda has never told me — to listen. I used to listen when I first started, when I was messing about with the harp on my own, but perhaps not so much now. What with the hand positions and posture and trying to read the music correctly there are an awful lot of other things to use up my slim powers of concentration.

I snatch up the last sandwich, cross with Dan for his astuteness.

He stands up. "I'll go and make coffee."

"You're so mean! You always make coffee, but you never offer me any!" I moan with my mouth full.

He laughs as if I've said something hilarious. "Oh, so you want to drink it?"

Sometimes my patience wears thin. "Absolutely! That's what it's for, you know, coffee. For drinking."

"No, it isn't. Not at all," he answers. And I see that in his world this is an incontrovertible truth.

"What on earth do you use it for, then?"

"Sniffing."

My annoyance gives way to incredulity. "So you don't ever drink it?"

"Nope. I make it, which is a thing I enjoy. I waft it around the room a bit, which is another thing I enjoy. I sniff it, which is a third thing I enjoy. Then I pour it down the sink."

"Dan! I'd assumed you were guzzling it all by yourself in the kitchen. But you're throwing it away! That's a crime! That's such a waste!"

"Why a crime? Why a waste? I don't like the way it tastes. It tastes like woodworm. I like the way it smells. It smells like sunshine and harvest fields and hope. I've been making coffee for years and wafting it around and then pouring it down the sink. It's a thing I do a lot."

I can't help but laugh. "Well, when I'm here, please don't pour it down the sink anymore. Give it to me to pour down my throat!"

"Oh. Oh. I wish you'd told me that's what you wanted! I didn't realize. Not at all. I'm

128

supposed to realize that sort of thing, I know, but sometimes I don't . . . see things that other people see . . ."

"Dan, Dan, it's fine! It doesn't matter!" I put my hand out to him. He takes it briefly. Our eyes meet. In an instant my insides turn to mush.

While he is making coffee I repeat the mantra over and over to myself. *Clive is my rock. Clive is my rock. Clive is my rock.*

13
DAN

One of the not-so-good things about being the Exmoor Harpmaker is that Exmoor is a place with quite a few murderers wandering about. I pointed this out to Thomas when he brought my letters this morning.

"What?" he said.

I repeated my observation.

Thomas replied that as far as he knew he did not know of any murderers in the locality and if I did then I should certainly inform the police about it pronto. I said in reply that Exmoor was certainly rife with murderers and at this time of year I saw them out and about everywhere. He said unless I explained myself quickly he would refuse to give me my letters and there was one from my sister Jo today that looked very interesting indeed. What murderers was I talking about, he wanted to know. I said the letter from my sister Jo was probably not in the least bit interesting, but, just to clarify, it was not people who were being murdered, it was birds.

Oh, he said. I'd had him worried for a minute there. He supposed I was referring to the shooting season.

I confirmed that indeed I was.

He handed over my letters (junk mail and the letter from Jo, which, as I'd suspected, turned out to be a cheerful rant about this and that and an inquiry after my health) and said he respected my views, mate, but shooting pheasants hardly counted as murder. He didn't reckon pheasants were so important in the great scheme of things. I asked him why not. He shrugged and said they were stupid creatures who made a big flap about nothing, always got in the way of his van and populated the roads whenever he was in a hurry, not quite moving to the shoulder in time but not quite consenting to get run over either. And although he didn't really understand this shooting lark and it was all hooray henrys who did it anyway, nevertheless he did quite enjoy a pheasant when it was steeped in gravy and with a nice well-roasted spud on the side. He added that he might sometimes moan about his missus, but in all honesty, one thing in her favor was that she cooked a mean roast.

("Mean" means lots of things. It is a verb that tells you people are not being accurate in what they say; they are hiding all sorts of extra things under the words. For example, when Roe Deer calls me a lemon, what does she *mean*? She does not mean I am a yellow citrus fruit. Not at all. At least, I hope not. "Mean" is also a noun that describes a sort of average, which is a number divided by another number. For example, the mean number of sandwiches I eat in a day is the total number I eat in a month divided by the number of days in the month. "Mean" is also an adjective that indicates a lack of generosity. For example, Ellie said I was being mean when I didn't give her any coffee and I poured it down the sink instead. This was not a compliment. But when Thomas uses it, especially before a food or drink word, "mean" is a huge compliment. "This is a mean cider," is something he says at the Stag's Head very often indeed.)

Anyway, I observed, I did not like the bang of guns. Not at all. I also did not like finding bits of lead shot lying about the countryside. Lead is a poisonous substance that does not do the countryside any good whatsoever. Neither, I told him, did I like the fact that these poor birds are bred and fattened up and then let loose in the wild purely for the purpose of providing sport for the —

"— the hooray henrys," Thomas supplied.

If the hooray henrys were very hungry indeed, I said, and were prepared to do all the other bits involved — the rearing, feeding and tending, then later the plucking, stuffing, cooking, steeping in gravy and putting of spuds on the side — then that would be more excusable. But it didn't work like that. Also I did not like the way the hooray henrys paid local lads a pittance to beat the birds out of the bushes and into the path of the gunfire to make it easy for themselves. To me that seemed mean (not like Thomas's cider; like Ellie's coffee) and unsportsmanlike. In fact, it was by far the most unsporting sport I could think of.

Thomas said that I had a point, but he still thought they were silly birds and he still liked them on a plate with gravy and spuds.

Roe Deer arrived at nine forty-five this morning, fifteen minutes before Ellie's lesson. She was wearing a purple skirt, very short, and black boots, very long. Her hair was loose but had a single plait plaited into it over her right ear. In and out of the plait was wound a slender purple ribbon, same color as her skirt. When she came in she placed a kiss on my cheek and put her head a little to one side. This is what she said: "Dan, I think I've got a commission for you."

I asked her why she thought that.

"Well, the husband of one of my harp students rang me out of the blue. The lady is very keen on learning, but she doesn't have a harp of her own. Anyway, this guy wants to give her a harp for Christmas."

I said that sounded like a nice Christmas present to me.

"Yes, Dan, but the point is, he wants a handmade one."

She seemed to be waiting for a response, so I said, "Oh."

She tossed her hair (including the plait) over her shoulder. "I recommended you, of course. I told him to look at your website, and he's done that. But he says he wants you to make a particular one, one specially for her, out of some wood he's got."

I asked what kind of wood.

"Apple," she said. "It has some special significance for them. I think he said it's from a tree that was in her grandmother's orchard. Something like that, anyway. And he wants you to carve her name in it as well. I warned him you have your own ideas and might not like that, but he was quite insistent. Seems a stubborn type. Maybe even more stubborn than you!" She laughed. Her laugh came out in a quick puff of air into my face. Her breath was minty.

I asked if the apple wood had been seasoned, as apple wood has a high shrinkage rate. It doesn't do to be in too much of a hurry when you make an apple wood harp. She shrugged. "You'd better get in touch with him yourself," is what she said. Roe Deer does not like answering questions. In any case there was not time for me to ask any more of them because that was the moment Ellie knocked at the door. I went and opened it.

It is nice to hear music as I work. Scales, arpeggios, snatches of tunes played first fast (Roe Deer) and then very slowly and repeated lots of times (Ellie). I like both types of sound. I hum along a bit.

I am doing my quiet jobs today. Washing pebbles, sweeping up sawdust, sorting strings, a little gentle sandpapering, gluing and clamping.

Roe Deer did not bring any of her three harps so I have lent her the thirty-six-string sycamore *Harbinger* for teaching purposes. Good for them to have a harp each. Teacher's harp, student's harp. Sycamore harp, cherry harp. Girlfriend harp, Housewife harp. It is all most satisfying.

It was the third Saturday in October that it happened. I had been watching the ants. The weather was coolish and grayish, and they were not scurrying around with their usual frantic dedication. They were slow, extra slow; positively plodding. I had on my anorak, padded, so I was not too cold. I sat on a cushion of moss nearly at the top of the oak woods and I watched them for sixteen minutes. I counted two hundred and twenty-three ants in that time, but it's possible I counted some twice. We should allow a margin of twelve ants either way.

After ant-counting activities I headed on toward the open land. The sky was purply and seemed to be doing its best to hang on to the water droplets that made up the great gray clouds. The wind was gusting once I'd come out of the shelter of the trees. I headed northward until I reached the crest of the hill and could see the sea. It had a raked look about it and was an odd greenish brown. I carefully selected today's stone and placed it on top of the cairn. Not many sounds. The wind in the trees. The distant whinnying of a pony.

Then suddenly there was a crashing in the bushes to my right. I knew what it was straightaway. It was the sound of the beaters. Almost simultaneously the air was rent with a cacophony of gunshots. I crouched down and put my hands over my ears to try and block out the noise, but it burst through my hands and into my eardrums and into the center of my head. It felt as if it had split open my skull. It cudgeled my brain. I just wanted it to stop.

I closed my eyes. I opened them again. There, in front of me, was a streak of color: brown, red, green and white. It was flapping madly across the moor. Wings arched, eyes wide in terror, desperately seeking cover. It was right out in the open, with nowhere safe to go. For a moment I was rooted to the spot, then I catapulted myself toward it.

I ran. I caught it in my arms. Everything spun in slow motion. Me and pheasant, pheasant and me. Feathers, beak, tail, wings, legs, claws, anorak, arms, head, boots, prickling grass, panting breaths — all of them mixed up together. Then the air split again, like a roar, like an earthquake. I felt a sharp pain ripping through me. Something shrieked — it may have been me. The world turned upside down.

Gray figures were shouting and running

toward me. I was sprawled on the ground, trying to keep hold of whatever it was I was trying to keep hold of. A warm patch of red was seeping through my clothes.

14
ELLIE

"Shall you get it or shall I?" asks Clive.

I'm busy washing up last night's dirty dishes and he's crouching at my feet repairing the door of the cupboard under the sink. I've been on at him to do it for ages. Annoying that he's chosen to do it just now, when I'm trying to use the sink, but it's good of him to do it at all. He's had a stressful week at work. He hasn't told me in so many words, but Supertramp is on extra loud and I know that's one of his methods of winding down.

"I'll get it," I tell him, drying my hands. "I'm expecting a call from Vic. She was going to take Mum to the dentist's this morning. That's probably her, reporting back."

I cross the kitchen and pick up the receiver. "Hello?"

I can hear it's a man talking down the line, but I can't hear one word of what he's saying. "Just a minute," I yell and reach across

139

to the volume switch. Supertramp pipes down, continuing to scold "Dreamer" in more hushed tones.

"Sorry about that," I say down the phone. "I couldn't hear you. Hello."

"Good afternoon," replies a cultured voice. "Is that by any chance an Ellie Jacobs, a . . . er . . . housewife of Exmoor?"

My heart stands still for a moment. Only Dan would call me that, yet clearly this is not Dan.

"I'm Ellie Jacobs, yes."

"Ah, good. My name's Lawrence Burbage. Hope you don't mind my ringing you like this. It's just that there's been a spot of trouble."

"Trouble?" I echo faintly.

"Yes. I've a young chap with me who says he knows you and you might be able to help. I found your number through directory assistance."

"Oh . . . ?"

"Dan Hollis. You know him, I take it?"

"Yes. Yes, I — I do." Clive is still crouching at the cupboard but has turned to view me across the room, curiosity spread all over his face.

I can hear a strange, strangulated sound coming over the phone, then the voice continues. "I'm just dropping him off at the hospital now, but I do have to get back to the shoot. All rather awkward, actually. I think he should have somebody with him, which is why I'm calling. He seems rather . . . well, shall we say . . . lost."

"What's happened?" My chest feels tight.

"Well," he answers, "nothing to panic over, let me assure you, but to be honest the man's been rather a damned fool. Ran out in front of a gun and got himself shot. Pretty nasty, actually. Bleeding all over the place . . ."

"Bleeding?"

"Yes. Great trails of blood everywhere. Thought I'd better get him to the emergency room quickly. Got him to the hospital in Taunton all right, but I think the whole episode must have turned his head. Right state he was in, rocking and blubbing and not making any sense. I'd not mind so much taking him in the car, even though blood is a darned nuisance to get out of leather seats. You do your duty toward your fellow men, even if they do display extraordinarily stupid behavior. But having to transport the damned bird too . . ."

"The . . . the *what*?"

"The pheasant. Your young chap insisted on taking the bird with him. Simply wouldn't let go of it. Brought it all the way

141

tucked under his arm. In my Range Rover, I'll have you know. Anyway, I thought I'd better let a responsible person know what had happened. He came up with your name. I presume you are responsible for him?"

I glance rapidly at Clive. He is opening and shutting the cupboard door with one hand, a screwdriver in the other, but he still looks interested.

"Yes, I am," I say.

"Oh, good." Lawrence Burbage sounds relieved. "I do feel I've gone beyond the call of duty on this one. I'm just dropping him off at the waiting room in the ER now. I can't hang about all day, though. I'll get back to my chaps now if you don't mind, and leave it to you."

Anger flares up inside me, along with a desperation for more details, but without telling Clive the whole story there isn't much I can do. "Oh yes, that's fine," I bluster. "Thank you. I'll see to it that everything's all right."

I put down the receiver, my mind flipping feverishly around.

Clive stands up and stretches. "What was all that about?"

"It's somebody from the hospital in Taunton," I answer quickly. "It's about Christina. She's had a little accident. She's all right, but she needs a friend. I must go and see her."

"An accident? What sort of accident?"

"An accident with a can opener," I improvise. "It sliced into her hand. Really quite nasty, and she can't drive. I'd better take off straightaway, hon. I'll be back as soon as I can. Get yourself lunch. There's a quiche in the fridge. If it's going to be a really long time I'll ring you."

He starts moaning about how Christina's timing is impeccable (not) and doesn't she realize that most people have things to do on a Saturday morning, but I'm not listening.

I rush from the house, giving thanks to all the gods that it wasn't Clive who'd answered the phone. I feel so stupid. I should have told him long ago all about my harp playing and my visits to the Harp Barn. But now isn't the time. I just need to make sure Dan is all right.

My head's a mess on the drive to Taunton. A blur of horrible possibilities, images full of blood and gore. I curse when I get stuck behind a slow tractor and recklessly overtake it on a bend.

The hospital car park has me driving round in circles for ages before I find a space. I launch myself into the nearest building and rush up and down passageways searching wildly for the ER. There are a multitude of signs and arrows around, but not the one I'm looking for. Everyone I meet looks too ill to ask.

At last the department appears, right there in front of me. The receptionist is a plump, middle-aged woman with platinum blond hair and a supersized smirk. The smirk grows even bigger when I say I am here to see Dan Hollis.

"Ah, the pheasant man." She grins. "Down to the end of the corridor and the last door on your right. Just follow the trail of disaster."

I speed down the corridor, noticing no particular signs of disaster as I go, just a rather strong smell of bleach. I knock and put my head round the door of the room. The first thing I see is Dan, sitting with his leg in bandages and his arms wrapped around a fat pheasant. His head is bent low over the bird. The pheasant also appears to be bandaged and is looking droopy and fed up. A young nurse with a clip file is seated beside Dan, gently remonstrating. Her small, round face betrays signs of frustration and helplessness.

"Dan! What on earth happened?" I cry. He looks up. He is deathly white.

"Ah, ah, ah," he murmurs.

"Dan, it's all right. It's me, Ellie. Are you OK?"

"Not OK, not OK," he tells me. "I've been shot."

"So I gathered." I step toward him. "Is it very painful?"

He doesn't answer so I turn to the nurse. "How bad is it?"

"Not so very bad," she reassures me. But behind the veneer of professional confidence I detect a note of panic in her voice. "He's lucky the femoral artery wasn't damaged. Although to be honest the shot sank in deeper than we would have liked. We've removed it, of course. The main thing is to keep the wound clean to avoid infection. That means changing the dressings regularly, which will be difficult for him as the wound is at the back of the thigh. Perhaps you could help with that?"

"Of course."

"We've given him some pretty strong pain relief, which should have kicked in by now. I think it's the shock more than anything that's the problem. And . . . um, he won't let go of the pheasant. He just won't let go, no matter what we say. Which is why we've had to put him in this room on his own. We're not allowed to have birds in here."

"No, of course not," I say sympathetically. "We'll have to persuade him to let go somehow, or else use force, I'm afraid. Are you his . . ."

"Friend," I put in firmly. I turn to Dan. "Dan, you must let go of the pheasant."

He strokes the bird protectively. "No."

"Dan, you have to!"

"No."

"Dan, please!"

He wraps both arms around it.

"Dan, you can't hold it forever. Just let go."

"No. I *will* hold him forever if need be."

"But why?" pleads the nurse.

Dan is rocking slightly. He smooths the bird's feathers. "He won't know what to do in a hospital. He will flap."

I can't argue with this logic. I look at the nurse again and she shrugs. "Your friend has been so stubborn," she hisses, loud enough for him to hear. "He insisted that we put a bandage on the poor bird before we were even allowed to touch his own wound. It has all been most awkward. Luckily Dr. Fribbs was prepared to bend the rules in the interests of stopping your man bleeding to death. But really, we do have to get rid of the pheasant now — one way or another."

She looks at me meaningfully. Dan turns his eyes upon her. They are flaring. "Don't kill him," he cries. He clutches the pheasant a little tighter. It lets out a plaintive squawk.

"Two questions," I say, beginning to take control of the situation. Clearly somebody has to. "Is Dan well enough to leave the hospital and is the pheasant . . . well enough to leave the hospital?"

The nurse consults her clip file and clears her throat. "Dan should be able to go home in a while, once the doctor's been in again. He'll have to keep his leg up as much as possible, and the dressing will have to be changed daily. As for the bird, I'm in no position to say. It was bleeding plenty too, but it's been disinfected and bandaged. If I was to take a bet on it I'd say it'll live." She adds as an afterthought: "If, that is, it can still forage for food and get away from predators with its broken wing, and avoid getting shot again, which I doubt."

Dan winces.

"Dan, I'll take the pheasant." I reach out my arms to receive it, not quite believing what I'm doing.

Dan is still reluctant. "Where will you put him?" he asks.

"Safe and sound in my car," I answer. "He will be warm, he will be comfortable. We'll return him to Exmoor just as soon as we can."

At last Dan seems satisfied. He delivers the long-suffering, feathery bundle into my arms.

15
DAN

Phineas is extremely handsome. He has a rich green sheen on his head and a white ring round his neck like a vicar's collar. His cheeks are a deep red, which makes him look permanently embarrassed. He has feathers of brown and russet and luminescent rose all over his rounded frame. His tail is long, beautifully tapered and elegantly striped. His eyes are round and bright, very. How could anyone want to shoot him?

He has been through a lot. He was terrified. We both were. I don't think he enjoyed being threatened (neither did I) or manhandled (neither did I) and he did not like the car journey one bit (neither did I), he did not at all like the man with the gun (neither did I), he did not enjoy being inside the hospital (neither did I), he did not like being bandaged (neither did I) and above all he just wanted to escape back to the peace and quiet of Exmoor (so did I).

He was nestled in a tartan rug at the back of Ellie's car when I next saw him. It was the same rug that I put her harp on top of when I first gave it to her. Phineas looked quite comfortable in the rug, but I took him onto my knee for the journey because he doesn't like engine noises. That's another thing we have in common. Ellie put the passenger seat right back for us both because my leg would only go straight out and there wasn't much room for it. My leg and Phineas's wing are going to cause us both some problems, I can see that.

There are always reasons for things. It's a good thing I gave Ellie that harp, not only because it was on her before-forty list but also because if I hadn't given her a harp then Phineas and I wouldn't have had anyone to take us home after we got shot. My girlfriend Roe Deer or my sister Jo might have been prevailed upon to give me a lift back, but they wouldn't have cared about Phineas, I know that. They would have said he is only a pheasant, why didn't you just let him get shot and eaten like other pheasants? And Roe Deer would have left him behind in Taunton because she would never permit a pheasant to be anywhere near her. I know this because she once said birds were fine from a distance but up close she didn't like them on account of their scratchiness. She has never actually been scratched by a bird, it is just some strange notion that she has. She has a lot of those.

On the other hand if I had asked my sister Jo to bring Phineas home to Exmoor she would have told me I made her scream and tear out her hair because Jo says that a lot about nearly everything I do or say. (She does not really tear her hair out, though, because if she tore out a single tuft of it every time she said that she would have none left. And just to be clear about this, Jo is not bald. Not at all.) I don't know what Jo would have done with Phineas. I somehow don't think she would have been sympathetic to his needs.

Ellie is different in that way. That is why it was Ellie's name that I gave to Lawrence Burbage.

"Why do you call him Phineas?" Ellie asked me as we drove out of the hospital car park.

I told her I had to call him something and it seemed to suit him. He had the look of a Phineas. And besides, I was partial to alliteration.

"Phineas the Pheasant," she said, emphasizing the *ph*'s. She glanced across at him. "Yes, you're right. It does seem to suit him somehow."

Phineas opened his beak and a sound midway between a sigh and a squawk came out.

"And what are you planning to do with him when we get back?" Ellie inquired.

I said I thought Phineas was likely to be hungry after his ordeal. I wasn't sure Phineas would like sandwiches very much, but I had a seed and grain mixture that I sometimes put out for the garden birds. Perhaps Phineas would deign to partake of some of that.

"But will you release him back into the wild?" she asked. "With that bandage round his wing he's a bit vulnerable, isn't he?"

I answered that indeed Exmoor was a place fraught with dangers as far as Phineas was concerned. In his injured state he was unlikely to fly again, certainly for a while. Knowing the way that human beings often acted irresponsibly, one of them (to be more specific, a hooray henry) might try and shoot him again, and at present Phineas was poorly camouflaged. The white bandage would show up very plainly against the green grass — or the brown moorland — or the purple heather — or indeed any kind of background except for snow, and I didn't think snow was forecast for some time yet.

Bearing these things in mind, I said I would do my best to look after Phineas and keep him in the orchard, which has a stone wall around it and a high hedge at the back, so hooray henrys probably wouldn't go in there; and also it has a woodshed where he can take shelter when it rains. I hoped he would be satisfied with these arrangements.

I stroked Phineas gently on the head and neck as I was outlining these ideas to Ellie, and he made quiet chuntering noises to express his approval.

When we arrived back home Ellie helped us both out of the car. I couldn't walk very well and progress was slow. The people from the hospital had lent me some crutches and the crutches helped, but I couldn't manage them and carry Phineas at the same time so I entrusted him to Ellie. She was gentle with him and he seemed to know that he was all right with her. We went out the back first, into the orchard, and she placed him under the plum tree. He flapped off a bit but not very far. His eyes were upon us, beady and bright.

"I'd better go and get the birdseed," I said, starting to hobble back to the barn.

"No, stay here, I'll get it," said Ellie and dashed off. She dashed back a moment later. "Where do you keep it?" she panted.

I told her it was in the kitchen cupboard next to the coffee jar. She now knows where the coffee jar is because these days she helps herself to coffee. (This is a good thing. The more coffee aromas around the barn, the happier I and my nose tend to be.) She raced off again to fetch the bird food.

Phineas trotted round while we were waiting. I told him to make himself at home. He put his head at different angles and stuck his beak into a lot of things and looked as though he was doing exactly that.

Ellie returned, brandishing the packet of seed. "Phineas!" she called and threw a little in his direction.

He looked at it sideways, then darted forward and pecked it. We watched him for a while.

"He's quite a character, isn't he?" said Ellie.

"Yes," I said.

"And he's not the only one," she muttered. Then she said (slightly louder): "After everything he's put you through, I do hope he'll be safe tonight."

I was hoping that too. I told her about another plan I had just been conceiving. My new plan was this: to make Phineas up a bed in the barn, on the ground floor, with the harps. I had decided this would be a

good idea because, although we had established that hooray henrys probably wouldn't
be prowling around in the orchard, what
might be prowling around the orchard was
foxes, and they were also very likely to take
advantage of his disability. Phineas would
have to sleep in the barn for the time being,
for his own safety. I hoped he wouldn't
mind being among harps. Harps are very
peaceful and not unlike trees, so it probably
wouldn't be a problem for him. What might
be a problem, though, was the feeling of
restriction that being indoors would place
on him. I was therefore also planning to
install for him a pheasant flap with top
hinges; a new design, bigger and better than
a cat flap. This way he could come and go
to his heart's content. I probably wouldn't
manage to get it made by bedtime tonight,
but I would do it as soon as I possibly
could, for Phineas's well-being and comfort.

"Lucky Phineas!" Ellie said.

Ellie and I then went round and into the
barn ourselves. I showed her the place in
the corner where I would make up Phineas's
bed and the place in the back door where I
would install his pheasant flap. After she'd
expressed her amazement at my ingenuity
and devotion, she suggested it might be a
good idea for me to see if I could get

upstairs. I tried it. I discovered that, with one crutch and the help of the banister, I could still get up the seventeen steps to the kitchen, the bedroom, the bathroom and the little room where Ellie practices, which is a very lucky thing indeed.

Ellie then got me a glass of water and made me some sandwiches, cheese and pickle, rectangular, in super-quick time.

"Do you need me to help you make up Phineas's bed?" she asked, surveying my leg.

I told her no, I could manage. I still had my hands.

She moved from one foot to the other in the way she does sometimes. "The doctors gave me a big bag of extra dressings for your leg. They said your wound needs to be washed and dressed regularly. I thought I could easily do that and check up on you when I come for my harp practice . . . or will Roe Deer be coming round to help you . . . ?"

I told her I doubted Roe Deer would be changing my dressings because Roe Deer has a particularly strong dislike of blood, and that it would be very kind of Ellie to do it if she didn't mind such things.

She answered that of course she didn't mind at all, that I had given her a harp and it was the least she could do. And if there was anything else she could do, I must just ask. She said I could ring her if there was ever anything I needed. She stopped and added but please — unless, of course, it was an emergency — would I never ring her during the weekend or on weekdays after five thirty?

Then she said she really had to be going because her husband would be badly needing his dinner. She would find a way to call in on me tomorrow, although it was a Sunday. And she would bring a meal because it is difficult to cook and things when you have to keep your leg up. And then she pecked me on the cheek and said Dan, do take care. Her hair flew as she dashed away downstairs and out of the barn. I watched her from the window. She dived into her car and drove away very quickly indeed.

16
ELLIE

"Christina, will you do me a favor?"

"Yes, of course, Ellie. Anything you like. Anything at all!"

"I want you to lie to my husband." It's hard to hear my voice saying this. I've always thought of myself as a straightforward, open sort of person. Now it seems I'm not only capable of deception, I'm totally immersed in it. Dragging my friend into the sticky mire too. Honorable. Admirable. Nice one, Ellie.

"Sorry, the line's bad. Did you say you want me to lie with your husband?"

This is deliberate, but I'm not in the mood for her messing around. "No, Christina! Lie *to* my husband. Lie to Clive."

"Lie to Clive? Certainly. It'll be my pleasure. What about?"

"It's to do with the harp playing. I'm afraid I was put in a bit of a spot yesterday."

I outline Dan's mad heroics for the sake

of a pheasant. I describe my trip to the hospital and the flustered excuses thrown at Clive.

"Wonderful!" she cries. Christina is a vegan and animal rights campaigner. Her idea of heaven would be to live in Donkey Sanctuary or Lost Panda's Home or such-like. In the past she's owned rabbits, chickens and a colony of guinea pigs (all classed as dearly beloved family members), but now there's just her and Meow. "I like this Dan guy more and more!" she declares. "He risks his life to save a pheasant, he's creative *and* he's good-looking. You'll really have to introduce me to him. Unmarried, you say?"

"Yes, but with a girlfriend. My harp teacher, remember?"

"Oh yes. And you say she's a sex bomb?"

"Absolutely."

"Shame. Oh well. If he shows any signs of getting tired of her, just send him along to me, will you? Or have you still got designs on him yourself?"

"Christina, I'm a respectable married woman!"

"Sorry, the line's buzzing again. What was that about being a repressed married woman?"

I snort. "Troublemaker!"

She cackles at me. At least one of us is

having fun.

"Have your birch trees grown yet?" she asks.

"No, of course not! They take time to germinate. But Dan and I do go and look at them most days just in case. That is, we go and look at the seed trays and the compost and we hope that the seeds are OK. And we keep them well watered."

"We, we, we!" she chants. "Dan and I this, Dan and I that!"

"Christina, stop it!"

"OK, OK! Untwist your knickers! I've stopped. So you want me to lie to Clive. So I've cut my hand on a can opener, have I?"

"Yes, you slashed it really badly. Just in case he ever answers the phone and asks how you are."

"Can I elaborate? Say I got gangrene and nearly had to have an amputation —"

"No!"

"Spoilsport!"

"This is serious. I'm relying on you," I tell her.

"Calm down, Ellie! Clive won't suspect anything. What sort of can was it?"

"I don't know. Baked beans?"

"No, let's go for chickpeas. More realistic."

"Chickpeas it is, then! And Christina,

something else. You find it really difficult to manage shopping bags and stuff like that. So I have to come and visit you and help out with things every day, OK? Saturdays and Sundays included."

"Right you are. It'll be nice to see you."

"But actually I'll be at the Harp Barn, helping Dan."

"Message received and understood. It would be nice to really see you sometime, though."

Christina can put on a good act, but I sense a bout of depression looming. I gather Alex has stopped coming home every weekend and when he does his treasured visits are mostly used up in phone calls to his new girlfriend rather than quality time with his mother.

"We'll get together soon, I promise. So sorry to put you in this position. Sorry about everything. And, Christina — thanks for being such a star."

When I replace the receiver I feel urgently in need of fresh air. I scramble into my jacket and pound along the road. At the far end I veer off onto a footpath that leads steeply up the fields alongside the wood. A strong wind is buffeting the trees and scooping leaves up from the ground. I can't take my eyes off those frantic leaves. They're scurrying like gnats, spinning wild patterns with every gust.

Oh, what a tangled web we weave,
When first we practice to deceive!

I just can't shake those lines out of my head.

I'm kicking myself. Why didn't I just tell Clive how much I wanted the harp in the first place? Now everything's escalated and I can't see a way out. The two most important things in my life — my husband and my visits to the barn — are clashing. Clashing like different tunes played in different keys at the same time.

Clive is my rock. Clive is my rock.

I must hang on to that. It's true, so true. I don't know how I'd manage without Clive. The other day when he came home from work he saw at once that I'd been crying, even though I'd washed my face four times.

"Ellie, hon-bun, what's wrong?"

"It's nothing," I said.

"Clearly it isn't. Hon, tell me what's the problem. I'll try my best to fix it, whatever it takes."

"It's just — Mum again. I phoned her today and she didn't know who I was. Not for ages. Then, when she finally clicked that it was me, she said, 'Ellie? Oh, *Ellie!*' in such a scornful way. Then she muttered, 'Useless!' I know I shouldn't let it get to me, but it did."

Clive held me tight. I breathed in the comforting bergamot and leather tones of his aftershave.

"C'mon, El. Your mother has no idea what she's saying. You know that. The 'useless' was probably referring to something else altogether."

"It wasn't." I sniffed. "She's always thought I was useless."

"Well, she's always been wrong."

Once I'd recovered he went out again, even though he must have been exhausted from his day's work. He returned three-quarters of an hour later with a spray of chrysanthemums and a beautiful little pair of silver earrings for me, "Just because." Then he lit the fire, made me sit by it and massaged my feet. We ended up making love on the hearth rug, the firelight glowing on our naked skin. How precious it is to be loved.

I don't deserve Clive.

Yet the harp playing is crazily vital to me. It isn't just the dreams-coming-true thing, or even my strange bond with Dan. I've made an astonishing discovery: I can make music. It's like a rich seam of gold inside myself that I never knew was there before. If — when — I tell him, Clive is going to resent the fact that he has nothing to do with this new seam. He'll take it personally, see it as an act of rebellion. He may even try to make me stop.

I can't stop now. I won't stop now.

Dan submits to my peeling off his dressings, cleaning the wound and rebandaging him without complaint every day. Torn flesh, seeping blood and puss — not something I'd normally relish. In this case, though, I don't mind at all. It feels deliciously intimate. I'm flattered that Dan puts his trust in me, even while he winces with pain. He's not as patient as I would have expected, though. He's in a hurry to get better. I suppose he's missing his daily walk.

It's just as well Dan has Phineas for company. He seems to have bonded with that bird in an extraordinary way. Phineas sleeps in the barn every night. He comes and goes through his new pheasant flap. Great big bird though he is, he even leaps onto Dan's knee at times, when Dan is resting on one of the wooden chairs. Dan wraps his arms around him, talks to him and strokes his feathers. It's a surreal sight, the two of them cuddling up together so tenderly, surrounded by harps.

It struck me that Dan might be interested in Thomas Hardy's poem "The Puzzled Game-Birds," so I took a copy up with me and read it out to him last time I was there:

> They are not those who used to feed us
> When we were young — they cannot
>   be —
> These shapes that now bereave and
>   bleed us?

Dan nodded sagely. "That's the thing exactly! Those are the exact words Phineas would say to the hooray henrys if he could speak — and if they would stop shooting for a moment and listen."

He petted Phineas on the head and Phineas nestled into him, smiling as much as a bird can smile.

Later, after I'd finished my harp practice, I watched from the window as Dan hobbled around the orchard on his crutches. He gazed up at the trees and the golden smudges of clouds, and heaved a great sigh. Doubtless he was missing Rhoda. I sighed too.

"How do you feel about Dan's new pet?" I

asked Rhoda during our last lesson at her house in Taunton.

"Oh, *that*!" She laughed in a way I didn't quite like. "Yes, he told me about the pheasant."

"So you haven't met Phineas yet?"

She shook her head. "Nope. Nor do I want to, particularly. I'm not megakeen on birds."

"I'm surprised you haven't even seen him, though," I said. "Phineas is hard to miss. He virtually lives in the barn."

She flicked a lever on her harp. "Well, I don't get out there that much."

Hadn't she even been to visit Dan since his accident? I knew for a fact that he couldn't drive at the moment, so it was up to her if she wanted to see him. Surely she'd want to check he was all right? Comfort him, bring him treats?

I looked at her curiously. She continued fiddling with harp levers, her lips pressed tightly together.

I wanted to slap her. However unbelievably good-looking and talented she is, she shouldn't take Dan for granted.

"Dan's still really suffering with his leg, isn't he?" I said. "It's a horrible injury."

"Well, if he must run out in front of guns, what does he expect?"

17
DAN

I juggle with two crutches, a bag of birdseed
and a harp. It is important to carry all these
at the same time. Into the orchard, whatever
the weather, four times a day. I am getting
quite good at it. Sometimes I also manage
to bring a peanut butter sandwich, as a
special treat for Phineas. I've discovered he
has a penchant for them.

Phineas and I have become firm friends. I
don't speak his language and he doesn't
speak mine, but we've worked out a very
satisfactory means of communication. When
it's time for his meals I use the smallest lap
harp (the *Lapwing*) and I play a chord. For
breakfast I play a B-flat major, for lunch I
play an F minor, for tea I play a C7 and for
evening snack I play a G arpeggio. Phineas
knows exactly what they all mean. He
comes running each time, bounding across
the grass with his wing (the uninjured one)
unfurled and his beak open in a great flurry

of excitement. He likes the harp so much I am beginning to wish I could play it properly. But I have never learned to play because making harps takes all my time and energy. Perhaps I could get Ellie to play for him sometimes, as she's here so much. She's quite good on the harp now. When concentrating on technique she stops and starts a lot, but when she knows a piece well she pours expression and feeling into each note. She and the cherrywood harp are as one. Through it, she sings. I love it when this happens. I think Phineas must love it too. I feel he is a musical bird. Hugely brainy, no; musical, yes.

Ellie and I could be like a mother and father to Phineas. Except that we'll never tell him what he's supposed to and supposed not to do. Phineas is a free agent and if he wants to flap his wings and make strange noises that's fine by me.

Phineas is also welcome to poo in the woodshed if that's what makes him happy. Washing pheasant poo off my carefully seasoned harp wood is no chore. In fact, I find it quite soothing.

I think I will name my next harp the *Phineas*. He can select which wood it is made from in his own inimitable manner.

Roe Deer rang this morning, just after I'd given Phineas breakfast. "Dan," she said.

"Roc Deer," I said.

"Are you any better?"

"Better in what sense?" I asked.

"Your leg, you lemon!"

I told her my leg was much improved and called her a banana. Two can play at that game.

She gave a huffy sound down the phone. "Are you up to making harps?"

I said of course I was.

"Good, glad to hear it," she said. "Dan, you haven't phoned Mike Thornton yet, have you?"

I confirmed that I hadn't.

"Dan, I try to help you, but honestly! He is really, really keen for you to make a harp for his wife, for Christmas, but you do actually have to ring him and talk about it."

I am not good at phone conversations with anyone, let alone people I've never met. I pointed this out to Roe Deer, even though I would have thought she knows it already.

"Yes, but Dan, Dan, Dan," she said. She does that repetition-of-my-name thing sometimes. "You have to make an effort. I

169

was the one who recommended you, so it'll reflect badly on me otherwise. And unless you get on with it soon, Christmas will be over and my student still won't have her harp."

I can be pretty quick making harps if need be. Still, perhaps she had a point. So I promised I would ring the man straightaway, without further ado.

"Hang on a mo!" she said before I could put the phone down. "Have you actually got his number?"

I reminded her that indeed I did. She had told it to me when she first mentioned the subject. "I suppose you remember it still after all these weeks, do you? Tell me what it is."

I told her. She laughed and said I was dead right. She said I was superefficient in some ways and completely hopeless in others. She said to be sure and ring him straightaway. So that is what I did.

Mike Thornton wants me to make a harp for his wife Fifi out of an old apple tree that was cut down three years ago and is now sitting in chunks in a shed near Bridgwater. That is fine. What is not so fine is that he wants me to carve the word "Fifi" on the side of the harp. I informed him that this was not a good sort of a name to carve onto a harp. He said what did I mean? I said it was not a musical and mellifluous name, not a name suited to harps. He said in a much louder voice that he considered it to be a very musical and nice name, it was his wife's name, and if I took that tone with him he would take his business elsewhere. I told him it was up to him to take it where he liked. I was about to put down the phone when he said well, perhaps I could make the harp first and then after that we could talk about the issue of the name. There was no hurry to decide. But there *was* a hurry to get a harp made out of the apple wood by Christmas. I said all right, I could get a harp made out of the apple wood by Christmas. But in order to do this I would need the apple wood. My leg was not yet OK to drive; otherwise, I would drive in my Land Rover to collect the apple wood from his shed near Bridgwater the following day. He asked what was wrong with my leg, so I told him a hooray henry had shot it. He said was I joking? I said no, I wasn't. He said well, that was damned inconvenient. There was a gap in the conversation, so I waited for him to fill it. At last he did that and he did it in a voice that sounded as if he was trying to swallow a hedgehog, and what he said was this: "I suppose that means I have no choice, I am going to have to bring the wood over to your workshop . . . ?"

I said I supposed so too.

"Hi, Dan, what's up?" Ellie said the next time she came. Her cheeks were pink and her hair was windswept. She was wearing her blue scarf. One of the tassels had got loose and tangly.

"*Is* something up?" I asked her.

"Well, yes, presumably. You look traumatized. And your hands are twitching."

I said that was maybe the look that I wore and the twitch that I twitched when I had just met a stranger and the stranger was called Mike Thornton and Mike Thornton had come to the barn with a load of apple wood and Mike Thornton wanted me to make that wood into a harp by Christmas and Mike Thornton also wanted me to carve the word "Fifi" into the harp and Mike Thornton was being pushy. I did not mind the apple wood, but I did mind Mike Thornton.

"Dan, you should get out more," is what Ellie then said to me.

I replied that it's difficult to get out with my leg bandaged up, but I will certainly get back onto my daily walk as soon as I can.

"No, that's not what I mean," she said.

172

She sat on the bottom step of the seventeen steps that lead to the upstairs of the Harp Barn. I came and sat next to her. It took some time to do this because my leg didn't like it, and it would take even longer to get up again because my leg would like it even less, but it was what I wanted to do so I did it. Ellie budged up to make room for me, but we were still close, very. We sat for a long while without speaking. Then the closeness began converting itself into a hotness and a trembliness, so I asked quickly what she'd meant when she said I should get out more.

"What I mean, Dan, is that maybe you need a bit more variety in your life."

I informed her that my walk gives me all the variety I need. Even though it is always the same walk, it is always different. How the trees and the bracken are always changing. How the sunshine, shrinking behind a cloud, suddenly mutes the colors, but then it sails out and sets them ablaze again. How I like it especially in autumn when the leaves are all painted in copper and bronze and scarlet and ocher and rust. Even if I limit myself to looking down at the path, there are different worlds to explore. Sometimes a pattern of pebbles, sometimes a procession of ants, sometimes a chip of eggshell from a tiny egg, sometimes a shiny green beetle, the skeleton of a leaf, a slip of silver water snaking through the stones.

"Dan Hollis!" she cried, and her eyes were bright with a brightness that made me want to dive into them. "There is so much poetry in you."

I was pleased when she said this.

But after that she said: "Still, it's good to go to lots of different places and see lots of different people. You can't really expand your horizons on just that one walk every day. You hardly see anyone except for Thomas the postman and me . . . and Rhoda." She then patted my arm. "Not a criticism, just a thought."

I pointed out that every so often I also see my sister Jo, and the people who buy harps.

She glanced over at my notice board. "But that's not exactly a huge variety of people. And you do need variety, Dan; it's the spice of life. Don't you long for a bit of spice sometimes?"

I had to think about this.

"Tell you what," she said. "As your leg's so bad and you can't get out much at the moment, I'll take you into Minehead or Lynmouth to see a show or something."

I said no thanks.

"OK, then, how about somewhere different in the countryside? I could drive you up one of the moorland roads. I'm sure you wouldn't regret it."

I told her I almost certainly would regret it, as new things never feel right to me, especially en masse. They make me short of breath. A long time later they might begin to be right, but by then they are not new things anymore, they are old things.

She sighed deeply. "You have a lovely life, Dan, but it's not real."

How is my life not real? To me it is very real. I didn't say this, though. I looked at her shoes, which had a small shred of mud on the toe, and her socks, which were olive green. It occurred to me that maybe Ellie thought I was boring. I didn't want her to think this.

"Dan," she said, stirring to action. "I'm insisting. We'll just go for a short drive. You need to get out."

She helped me to my feet. We walked outside together and she put my crutches in the back of her car. I got in. She was insisting, so what could I do? She got in too.

I asked where we were going.

"Not far. I want to show you the local church. It's really pretty, with some gorgeous stained glass. Nobody will be there.

It's a lovely, peaceful place. I'm sure you'll like it."

I watched the scenery sliding by. The hills were smooth and pale. The trees were bare and spindly. The bracken was ragged, nice, brown and orange. The sky was blue with little bunches of gray and white cloud.

We drove past a farm and through a cluster of cottages, then she pulled in at a lay-by beside a mossy lych-gate.

"The ground is quite level here. Do you think you could manage without your crutches if I help support you?" she asked.

I tried it and found that I could, provided she took my arm and I leaned on her a bit. I leaned on her possibly a bit more than I really needed to. She leaned back into me. We went through the lych-gate in this fashion. Ahead of us was a sandy path and at the end of it a small white church was peeping out from behind some holly bushes. Ellie was right, it did look pretty.

Just as we were getting to the church door it opened and a woman came out. She was gray-haired and wore a hat that, like herself, was small and pot shaped. She was carrying a watering can and pruning shears. Ellie let go of me very quickly. She then grabbed me again as I started to topple sideways.

"Hello, Ellie!" said the woman in a voice

curling with questions.

"Hello, Pauline," said Ellie. "What are you doing here?"

"I've just finished arranging the church flowers. I'm on the roster, didn't you know? What are *you* doing here?"

Her look went from Ellie to me, from me to Ellie.

Ellie's face had turned a strange shade midway between crimson and beetroot. "I was . . . we were just coming to look at the church. This is my friend Dan. He's injured his leg, so I have to support him. Dan, this is my next-door neighbor, Pauline."

I said hello and so did she.

"Are you local, Dan?" she asked.

I said I was.

"And how do you two know each other?"

I was about to tell her that Ellie had visited the Harp Barn one day and I'd given her a harp, and she was now always coming up there to play it, and that she had rescued me and my pheasant from the hospital after we'd been shot, and she helped change my bandages for me every day, but Ellie cut in.

"Dan's a friend of a friend," she said.

I tried to think whether this was true or not. As far as I could see it wasn't. But before I could say anything else she had pulled me into the church, calling, " 'Bye,

177

Pauline," over her shoulder.

It was an ancient church with fine wood-work and a very pleasing stone font. The windows showed saints and birds and fish, all with similar vacuous expressions on their faces. I looked at their faces for a long time. Seldom have I seen such complete and utter vacuousness. But the colors were good. Amber and sapphire blue and sea greens. Sunlight shone through the stained glass and made glowing patterns on the floor, and glowing patterns are something I like very much. I was glad I'd come after all. But Ellie was not as enthusiastic as she had been earlier.

18
ELLIE

She welcomes me to her lounge, a large, square room, tastefully color coordinated in blue and gold. Her three harps stand majestically side by side in the center of everything.

The lesson always follows a similar format. Rhoda demonstrates something on the largest of the harps and I try to copy it. The harp I use is similar to my own, but it's made of beech wood and boasts a set of forty-two strings. It was made by Dan some years ago and she tells me the sound has changed and mellowed over time.

Rhoda gives me a cup of tea. I plant it on the floor by my feet and settle behind the harp. Today's issue is the problem I keep having with my left hand. It can't seem to stick to the correct rhythm, either lagging behind or leaping just ahead of the beat. Rhoda takes me through some exercises.

"See if you can get this bass pattern under

your fingers," she suggests, zigzagging up and down the strings to a jaunty rhythm.

I try to imitate. It sounds quite effective, but I'm getting some of the notes mixed up.

"No, your index finger goes here. Do you see how it's based around the D minor and C chords? Once you've got it, you can improvise over the top, like this."

She adds her right hand, playing it much faster to create a sparkling cascade of sound. Her hair hangs down in golden waves and she rocks backward and forward fractionally to the rhythm of the music. Mesmerizing. For both the eyes and ears. I wish — I can't help wishing — she wasn't Dan's girlfriend.

Her phone bleeps at us just as she approaches the climax. She stops dead.

"Sorry, do you mind if I take this?"

"Go ahead!" I prepare myself for a long wait.

Rhoda's harp lessons are disjointed because of the number of phone calls she gets. Sometimes she switches them off and sometimes she whisks away into the next room to answer. The door between the two rooms has a habit of drifting back open once it's closed, so I get to hear bits and pieces of her conversations.

There seems to be a large fan club. She

plays in a duo with a guitarist and a lot of the calls are from him. I've never met him, but it seems he's besotted with her. I bet she relishes the fact. Whenever it's him on the phone she puts on a sugary, simpering voice and plays with her hair. I've been the unwilling witness to various flirtatious fragments of conversation. It makes me cross and bothered on Dan's behalf.

"Keep practicing that left hand," Rhoda instructs me as she hurries into the other room. I hear a "Hi, Mum" as she pushes the door closed behind her. This will be one of the less interesting conversations. I pick at the harp quietly.

The door is slowly performing its reopening trick. It makes eavesdropping not only easy but almost compulsory.

"No, Mum," she's saying. "We've been through all this before! . . . I feel strongly about it. I don't care if he's asking questions. You'll just have to change the subject. I really, really don't want him to know!"

The mother says something and then Rhoda replies: "That may well be the case, but I'm simply not prepared to deal with it at the moment. He's not ready, I'm not ready! I've got my career to think of and that comes first."

A short answer.

"No, I didn't mean more important than *him,* of course not! Just more important than him having to know."

A longer answer.

"You said before you were more than happy to do it. Are you changing your mind?"

Something else from the mother.

"No! Bad idea! And yes, of course it would be traumatic. He's happy as he is. You'd only upset the apple cart. Next he'd insist on being introduced to his father and I don't want that. There'd be no end of repercussions. It would be a nightmare trying to handle it all."

I sit up straight. His father. Whose father? Who are they talking about? A suspicion launches itself straight into my guts. I strain my ears, but at this point she lowers her voice even more and I can't catch anything else.

It's impossible to halt the swift course of my imagination, though. It's bounding ahead and assuming things. I just can't stop it. I pluck harp strings in a desultory fashion, thinking, thinking. Then I hear Rhoda speaking, slightly louder again:

"Anyway, just don't say anything yet, Mum, I beg you! We'll talk more later. I can't now, I'm in the middle of a lesson. I'll call this afternoon."

She comes back into the room looking peeved and pouty. She seems distracted for the rest of the lesson, I would almost say impatient to get rid of me.

The garden looks as bedraggled as I feel. At least it's quiet. I start cutting back the dead flowers in the border. A damp, brown heap gathers in the bottom of the wheelbarrow. I keep wondering about Rhoda, wondering if I can be right, telling myself it's none of my business and trying to focus on something else. Then I start wondering again. It's driving me insane.

Pauline looks over the fence and hails me.

"Ellie, you haven't been up the hill today on your usual jaunt."

She's an awful curtain-twitcher.

"No," I explain. "Clive is off work, suffering from a bad head cold. I'm sticking around to look after him."

I haven't made it up to the barn yet today. I can't put it off much longer. Dan will be wondering what's happened to me, and those dressings won't change themselves.

Pauline waves her trowel in the direction of the Harp Barn. "Where is it you go so often anyway?"

I see straight into her thoughts. She's

remembering how close Dan and I were when she saw us at the church the other day. Her gossipmongering mind is fast putting two and two together and making five hundred.

I try to smile. "Oh, just, you know, walking."

"You're very keen," she comments wryly, a gleam in her gray eyes. "Bad weather never seems to put you off. I saw you go out the other day and it was coming down in buckets!"

"Well, I enjoy the exercise," I answer, squirming inwardly at my lies. "Anyway, better get in now and see if Clive's OK."

I practically run inside to escape from her.

"Is that you, back in, hon-bun?" Clive's voice calls from the sitting room.

"Yes, it's me, of course. Feeling any better?"

"Not really."

"Another lemon?"

"Well, if you don't mind . . ."

I put the kettle on and fish a lemon out of the fridge, squeeze it and add a spoonful of honey. I'm exhausted.

I take the steaming mug into the sitting room. Clive is lounging on the sofa. As I present him with his drink, he takes my hand. He raises it to his face and rubs his cheek against it. "Mm-mm, your skin's nice and soft. But you've cut your nails short. Why did you do that?"

I'm blushing again. I wish that didn't keep happening.

"I just thought I'd try a new look."

"Since when have you cared about your look?"

"Well, long nails aren't exactly practical for gardening and stuff, are they?"

He sniggers. "Gardening? What is it about gardening all of a sudden? I thought you'd forgotten the meaning of the word!"

I glance out the window. My attempts with the border are pathetic. Brambles are sprouting up everywhere and there's still a forest of decaying brown stalks demanding attention. "Well, I'll do some more tomorrow." I hope that, if I do, Pauline won't be around again.

Clive coughs. The TV is still on with the sound turned low, but Bristol City aren't doing well today. He takes a noisy slurp of lemon. "How's the poetry going, hon? Written anything recently?"

The last poem I wrote was a love song to my harp. Thankfully Clive never asks to read my poems. "I've been dabbling," I answer. "This and that, you know. Nothing worth writing home about, but it's always fun fiddling about with words. I find it therapeutic and —"

"You complete stupid, sodding cretin!" Clive shouts. Not at me, at the television. The shooter has just missed a crucial goal.

I consult my watch. "Clive, I'm just popping out to see if Christina's OK."

"What, now?"

"Yes. It's really hard for her trying to use her left hand for everything and she's still in loads of pain."

"In case you hadn't noticed I'm not exactly a hundred percent myself."

"I know, hon, I know. I won't be gone for long."

"Why does it always have to be *you* playing Florence bloody Nightingale? Where's that sodding son of hers when he's needed?"

"Clive, he can hardly come up all the way from Exeter every time she needs a hand!"

"I thought he was *always* coming back to see her, bringing a ton of dirty laundry with him."

"Well, she did say that, yes, but that was a while ago and things have changed. He's getting more and more involved in uni life now."

"Don't go, El. Christina can cope. It's only a cut, for Christ's sake!"

I wish I'd given Christina a more serious injury.

"I've just got this feeling she needs me. I'll be back soon."

Clive glares at me. "I don't know what's got into you recently, El. You never used to be like this. One minute you're all ditzy and dreamy, the next you're stubborn as a mule." His voice is getting louder and louder. The conversation is going to erupt into a full-scale row if I'm not careful.

"See you soon," I say quickly and leave him to stew.

I'll get the silent treatment when I arrive back, but what can I do? Dan needs me.

19
DAN

November is sucking the color out of Exmoor. Only the hollies and pines have stayed green. The beeches cling to their coppery, curled leaves and some of the oaks are snuggled in thick yellow-green sweaters of moss. But all the other trees stand naked, the last gray tatters of leaves drifting about their ankles. They are resigned, patiently waiting until the year turns again. They'll have to wait a long time.

The air has begun to bite. I don't feel it much because I'm made like that, but the harps aren't keen on cold air. It's bad for their strings. Phineas isn't keen on it either. Pheasants are not native to Exmoor, they are native to Asia, which must be substantially hotter. They must therefore be prone to winter chilliness. The people who breed pheasants and feed pheasants and then let pheasants out into the wild to be shot don't think about this. Not at all. They consider neither the feelings of the ones that are shot nor the feelings of the ones that aren't.

When I asked Ellie the Exmoor Housewife if she thought Phineas might be too cold, she said, "Glad to see you are so concerned about your pheasant." She had a little sharp tang in her voice. She was blowing on her fingers, which were slightly blue. I wondered if, underneath his feathers, Phineas was also slightly blue.

Phineas dislikes cold, but he dislikes the noise of machinery even more. I know this because whenever I am using the electric band saw he heads for his pheasant flap in double-quick time. I have therefore made him a second bed, in the woodshed, so he can still be warm when I'm using loud machinery in the barn. Phineas is pleased about this, very.

Today Ellie arrives at four fifty-six. She's booted and wrapped in a cardigan (moss colored like the ones the oaks are wearing). It hangs a long way over her jeans and has eleven buttons. She is plucking at the hairs of her right eyebrow.

"Sorry, I couldn't get away! My — Oh, never mind. How are you?"

I tell her my leg isn't in the best of health, but the rest of me is very well. "Good," is what she says. I then ask if she is well too because that's a question you are supposed to ask and also because I want to know the answer. She answers: "I'm fine, thanks, fine." Then she adds, "Although . . ."

I wait for more of this sentence, but it doesn't come.

As she takes out the clean bandages from the cupboard she is muttering something about rocks and limpets, however. I ask her to please repeat what she said.

Her mouth twists a little, then she unrolls the bandage and lays it flat on the table. "I said that even limpets have to stand on their own two feet sometimes."

This is interesting and unexpected. I point out to her that I am no expert in marine biology, but I am pretty certain about this fact: Limpets do not have two feet.

"Metaphorical ones do," she says.

I consider metaphorical limpets for a while. The subject fascinates me. I ask her what else metaphorical limpets do apart from standing on their own two feet.

"Well, they can drive," she tells me.

I express my astonishment. I ask what else.

"They enjoy a good weepy film on TV," she says. "They can make a damn good curry. Also they've been known to make rather good jam. And they read a lot — and write poetry."

I comment that I would very much like to read a poem written by a metaphorical limpet.

"Would you?" she says.

I tell her yes.

"That just shows . . ." she says, doing her tailing-off thing.

I don't ask her exactly what it shows. Instead I inquire what other artistic pursuits the metaphorical limpets pursue.

"Well, I know that a metaphorical limpet once made a papier-mâché unicorn for her nephews and nieces."

I remark that metaphorical limpets must be very clever. Very clever indeed.

"They do their best," she answers. She pauses, then adds, "They love the harp. They practice harp playing whenever they get the opportunity."

I am increasingly impressed with these limpets. I ask if they can make harps as well.

"No," she says. "Metaphorical limpets can't make harps. That's a job for . . . for metaphorical oysters."

Then she bursts out into one of her snorty laughs. Her whole body is jolting so that she can't hold the bandage straight. I laugh too.

"I love that I can have this sort of conversation with you, Dan," she says when she's able to speak again.

She looks completely different to how she looked when she came in. Less stiff. More smiley. Lighter. I am glad.

But all of a sudden, without any reason that I can fathom, there's a reversal. She's stiffer. Less smiley. Heavier.

She gets up slowly. Normally after doing my bandages she goes upstairs to practice the harp, so that is what I'm expecting her to do, but she doesn't. She walks over to the middle of the three big windows in the barn and she looks out at the great gray sky. Then she picks up a bright penny, one of the ones I've polished and placed on the windowsill, and she plays about with it in the palm of her hand. Then at last she says, "Do you mind if I am a bit nosy, Dan?"

I tell her I don't mind a bit.

Then she asks, "Do you mind if I am a bit nosy about Rhoda?"

I tell her again that I don't mind a bit.

Then she starts asking me questions. They come slowly at first but then gather momentum and roll out one after another as if hurtling down a hill. Her first question is this: Have you known Rhoda a long time?

My answer is this: Yes, six years.

Her second question is this: And has she

been your girlfriend for a long time?

My answer is this: Yes, six years.

Her third question is this: So, I'm just wondering — did you used to be closer to her than you are now?

My answer is this: No. She's always lived in Taunton and I've always lived here.

Her fourth question is this: Oh, all right, then, did you, by any chance, ever go through a phase of not seeing her?

My answer is this: Yes, for most of 2012.

Her fifth question is this and the words are strung together so fast I can hardly catch them: Um, strange question this one, but do humor me. I'm a woman and interested in these things. Do you mind telling me: Has she always been as beautifully slim as she is now?

My answer is this: No, not always. She did get a little plumper in spring 2012.

There is then an "I see" and a bit of a pause. I wonder if the questions have finished, but then she comes out with this one: Would you say, Dan, that it ever seemed to you that Rhoda wanted to tell you something but couldn't quite manage it?

My answer is this: I have no idea.

Her seventh question is preceded by another pause and is this: How much do you . . . do you, well . . . trust her?

My answer is this: What do you mean?

I know it's bad to answer a question with another question, but I am not clear exactly what she means when she asks if I trust Roe Deer.

Ellie doesn't seem clear either. She just says: "Oh, never mind! I have to get back home now." She puts the penny back on the windowsill and looks at her watch. "I must dash. Take care, Dan. See you tomorrow."

She has not practiced the harp today, which is an odd thing. Her smile has not come back either. Not at all.

20
ELLIE

I close the front door and smooth down my hair. There's a great deal of coughing and spluttering coming from the sitting room.

When I go in, my husband is still sprawled on the sofa. My favorite picture — a Yorkshire landscape painted by my grandmother — is lying in smithereens on the floor.

"Oh no! What happened?" I cry.

When Clive has finished coughing (which takes some time) he explains: "It went crashing down. Must have been a weak nail. I'd have cleared up the mess, but — well, not quite up to it."

He has the injured-blame thing down to a T.

I run and get the dustpan and brush. I feel his eyes on me as I'm sweeping. Does Clive sense I'm not being honest with him?

The frame is obviously destroyed, but I would have thought the painting would still be redeemable. Yet somehow the surface of

195

the picture has got horribly scratched as well. I'm gutted. I loved that picture.

I chase the fragments of glass round the floor with the brush. A painful headache hovers just behind my eyes.

I can't stop thinking about Dan's relationship with Rhoda. He calls her his girlfriend all the time, but they *can't* really be together, can they? Surely I would have witnessed something — a romantic kiss, a mushy phone call, any indication that they are intimate — by now? I harbor suspicions that it's all in Dan's head, but is that just wishful thinking? Just because I find Rhoda shallow and selfish doesn't mean he does. Men — even Dan — always have a very different perspective.

What about her? What's she hiding? And who is she hiding it from?

A shard of glass drives into my finger. I yelp with pain.

Clive isn't sympathetic. "Looks like Christina will have to come round and look after *you* now."

I suck my finger. "It's nothing, it's nothing!"

It won't help with playing the harp, though, I think as I head upstairs to fetch a plaster.

■ ■ ■ ■

"Rhoda, may I use your bathroom?" I ask the minute I've stepped over her threshold on Tuesday morning.

I'm granted a bright smile. "Of course, Ellie!" She is in a scarlet jersey dress. Her hair is scooped onto the top of her head with a few blond locks prettily straying over her brow. "It's up the stairs and straight ahead of you."

I dash upstairs, then slow my pace and look back over my shoulder. She's disappeared. An instant later the soft sound of harp arpeggios starts drifting up from the living room. I am safe. It's time for a good snoop.

I push open the door next to the bathroom. The room is quite small, furnished with only a bed and a chest of drawers — perhaps a spare room. I scan the walls. No photos. Just a watercolor of an elephant in an African landscape and another of trees by a lake.

I close the door softly and try the next one. This is clearly Rhoda's bedroom. The bed is unmade with a pair of tights strewn across it. My eyes quickly take in the silky crimson covers, a pine wardrobe, a bedside lamp in the shape of a curved crocus flower, bookshelves, a CD player. And exactly what I'd hoped for. Hanging in pride of place opposite the window is a huge wooden frame full of photos. I creep into the room, hungry for details. My heart is thumping.

The photos have been arranged in a montage. Many are professional photos of Rhoda herself together with her harp, and I recognize the same one that's in Dan's workshop — the one with the cleavage and the come-hither look. Nobody could accuse Rhoda of false modesty. Another photo shows her posing with her guitarist friend, the edges of their instruments just in view. He sports a goatee beard and one of those crooked smiles that's actually quite attractive. He looks smug, the cat that got the cream. I wonder. I feel disturbed. I'm not quite sure what I'm hoping.

Then my eye falls on another photo and I know this bears no resemblance to what I was hoping. Dan and Rhoda together. Slightly younger than they are now, standing under the plum tree in his orchard. Dan has a hazy, romantic look in his eyes, which are directed straight at her. Her smile is radiant. The sunshine is picking out the gold in her hair as it tumbles loosely over her shoulders. She is in a saffron-colored dress that flows around her in the breeze. She appears to be all made up of honey-colored light. She looks utterly beautiful.

There's a sharp tug in my guts. The plum-picking day is sacred in my memory, something I want to wrap in tissue paper and fold away tenderly and take out often to gaze at before I fold it away tenderly again. But now it's been polluted. Rhoda was there first, before I ever knew Dan or he knew me, before he even knew I existed. My doubts about their relationship are suddenly looking flimsy in the face of this new evidence. I fight with the feeling and push down the pain. It will have to wait until later.

Now my other suspicion looms larger. I scan the other photos. Some seem to be family snaps, many quite small. Are there any children among them? I step closer. There's a little girl looking sweet and coy in a bridesmaid's dress, but if my deductions have been correct, it's a boy that I'm looking for.

"Ellie, what are you doing?"

I jump. Rhoda is peering in at me from the stairs. Frowning. I was so intent on my search I didn't even notice that the harp sounds stopped a few moments ago.

"Oh!" I cry, leaping out of her bedroom covered in blushes. "I'm sorry. I somehow lost the bathroom . . . and then I noticed your beautiful photos and had to have a closer look."

She's not amused.

"That picture of you in the green dress is so stunning!" I gush.

She thaws slightly. "Yes, it's my favorite." A pause. "The bathroom's right there at the top of the stairs, like I said."

"Sorry, Rhoda. I shouldn't have been so nosy."

I see from her face I'm not forgiven.

"I wasn't expecting to find you in my bedroom."

I rack my brain for excuses. "It's just that . . . I'm feeling a bit hassled today because . . . because I had a row with Clive. It's still going round and round in my head. I'm in a bit of a daze. I wasn't thinking straight."

"Oh?" She looks at me curiously. "Do you want to talk about it?"

"Just money matters. I'm spending too much on petrol. He doesn't like it." This is very true.

"Are you all right?"

"Um, yes, I suppose so. I just get upset about these things."

"It's hit you quite hard, hasn't it?" she says, suddenly sympathetic. She comes a step higher up. "Have you told him you play the harp yet? Perhaps that would be a lovely surprise for him and make everything better."

"I don't think so," I mumble.

"Are you sure you're OK? You look quite shaken. We can postpone the lesson if you like."

"No, I'll be fine. I'll just . . ." I gesture toward the bathroom, then dive into it, shutting the door behind me with more of a bang than I'd intended. My reflection gawps at me from the mirror, shame painting it crimson. I splash my face with cold water to try to reduce the color. My hands are actually shaking. I am furious with myself. What's more, the mission has been a complete failure.

Perhaps I've been completely wrong. But then, I reflect, the bedroom might be the very place where Rhoda is most anxious to conceal her secret, assuming she is visited there by Dan . . . or anyone else. I'm no longer sure what I can assume and what I can't.

I glance at my reflection again. I am biting my lip.

I hurl a bottle in and listen with satisfaction as it shatters. Then another. Breaking things is great therapy. Thank God for recycling centers. Thank God Clive drinks lots of beer these days. There are plenty more bottles to go.

I hate her. I shouldn't. But I do.

I feel like a caged animal gnawing at bars. My eyes are raw and watery. I pause to take a deep breath, then reach inside the polythene bag for another bottle. I smash it into the bin with all my force. Three more follow, blasted to smithereens, the noise roaring painfully through the air. Then I stop and breathe again.

Late shoppers are scurrying past on their way to the car park. I glance upward and suddenly notice the sky. It is a vast, gleaming landscape above me. Bright tiers of copper-edged clouds drift across the deep, silky blue. I let myself imagine for a moment that I'm swimming among those clouds; I'm bathed in light, gliding along to the sounds of harp music. Dan is gliding by my side. Guilt, my constant companion, tells me to stop being an idiot, to banish the romantic image. I don't want to banish it, though, I want to keep it treasured right here in my heart. I let my eyes linger on the sky for another few moments, then remind myself of Rhoda. I smash another bottle.

I am desperate to get to the bottom of

Rhoda's secret. If my theory is correct it has monumental significance for Dan, and he has no idea. But I'm lacking proper information. If I was closer to her I could come straight out and ask Rhoda, but I'm not close to her and don't think I ever will be.

I head back to the car, lost in thought. I'm a slave to my own curiosity. It just keeps on thrashing away at the same questions. Until I get answers I'll have no peace.

Meow looks calm and thoughtful. Christina doesn't. She's fluttering about the kitchen like an anxious butterfly.

"She's Swiss, so will probably want to eat funny things. Do you think I can get away with nut roast for Christmas dinner? Alex says she's easygoing, but Alex is not the greatest judge of character. And he's seeing her through love-struck eyes."

I try to reassure her. It's surely a good thing that her son wants to bring his girl-friend home for Christmas.

"But what if I hate her? What if she hates me?"

"Nobody could hate you, Christina!"

"I so wish that was true!" She reaches for a cigarette, a slight puckering in her face. Underneath her cheerfulness I sense there's a thick, dark lump of sorrow. She recently tried online dating and met up with a string of unsuitables and losers. Then, to try to fill the emptiness, she managed to get in touch with one of her exes — only to be presented with the words: "Christina, I don't want you in my life. Get lost!" I don't know why she's so unlucky with men. She's attractive, exotic even, and fun to be around. Perhaps she's just too much for them to handle.

"Anyway, let's talk about you!" she cries, settling into a chair at last. "Have you told Clive about your harp yet? Do you still want me to lie about my very dangerous can opener?"

"Yes, please keep lying," I say. "And no, I haven't told anyone about the harp except you."

She looks flattered. "Meow," she says, scooping the struggling creature up in her arms and nearly singeing it with the cigarette, "she hasn't told anyone except me!" Then she eyes me suspiciously. "Not even your sister?"

"No. Vic would tell her husband and it might get back to Clive somehow."

"And if it did?"

I take a deep breath. "I need to tread carefully. You know what Clive's like!"

"Yeah, I know: sweet and sour. Good

when he's good, but when he's grouchy . . ."
An extra note of worry leaps into her eyes.
"Ellie, you're playing with fire, you know.
Clive isn't going to like it. And you can't
keep it a secret forever."

I don't want to talk about this. I don't
want to think about consequences.

"Talking of secrets, I've found out something about Rhoda," I tell my friend. "Well,
I *think* I have."

"What sort of something?"

"Something big. But I've got some investi-
gating to do. I may need your help."

"Tell me more," she says.

21
DAN

I make eight sandwiches. I cut them into diamond shapes because Ellie says variety is the spice of life.

Over the sandwiches she asks me if I know about Roe Deer's concert next week.

I tell her yes.

"Are you going to it?" she asks.

I give her this answer. I say that in the past I used to go to all of Roe Deer's concerts because she was keen to have my support, and that she made such wonderful music it was always a pleasure to listen. However, the thing that was not such a pleasure was the fact that there were always lots and lots of other people at her concerts too.

Other people are fine when they are sitting in rows and quietly listening to harp music. But they are not fine when they surge around everywhere in a cacophony of roaring words and sentences, as happens during intermissions. I get shredded by it. So whenever I went to Roe Deer's concerts I always used to reserve the seat nearest the back if I could. I nipped in at the last minute, nipped out just before the intermission to go and sit in my Land Rover, nipped in again just when the second half began, then I nipped out as soon as the concert had finished. All that nipping was quite exhausting. And I had to be very exact in my timing, and so did she. Only sometimes she wasn't. Which led to a problem or two.

Eventually Roe Deer said not to bother. It was costing me a lot of effort and she explained that she didn't actually need me there anymore. In fact, my presence was beginning to stress her out. It was not good for her to be stressing just before going on to perform with her harp in front of an audience.

So I haven't been to any of her concerts for five years now.

Ellie contemplates one of the diamond-shaped sandwiches. It has hummus inside. She picks it up. Then she says an odd thing. What she says is this: "Tell me, Dan, is Rhoda really your girlfriend?"

I blink.

"Don't be offended," she hastens to add, "but you don't see very much of each other, considering you are geographically not that far apart. And she doesn't even seem to want to come here for my harp lessons; it's always in Taunton now. I would have thought it would be nice for her to have another excuse to come and see you, but no. And when you were shot she didn't come to see you at all to check that you were all right." Her eyebrows are drawn very close together. "I just wondered. Boyfriends and girlfriends usually make a bit more of an effort to meet up." She waves her sandwich in the air and a bit of hummus drops out and lands in her lap. She gets a tissue out of her pocket and scrubs at it. "Sorry, Dan, it's none of my business really, but I can't help wondering."

I do not say anything, but I put down the sandwich I am holding and I start thinking.

"Another thing," Ellie says, then she stops. I am too busy thinking about Roe Deer to lend her much attention, but I sense she's examining my face intensely. "No, that's enough for now," she mutters.

Twenty minutes later I hear her say that she has to be off now and take care, Dan, and she pats me on the shoulder and off she goes. I am still sitting there, thinking.

I think for a while longer.

After this I get myself downstairs. I am

supposed to be starting on the *Fifi* harp because the pushy man called Mike Thornton has brought the apple wood to the Harp Barn now and he wants me to give him weekly progress reports. But I don't feel in the mood for starting a new harp. I thread twelve strings onto my nearly completed *Kestral* harp instead and tighten them bit by bit and I carry on thinking hard. I think especially about boyfriend and girlfriend definitions.

Two hours later I ring up Roe Deer and ask her if she is still my girlfriend.

"No, Dan," she says. "No, I'm not." And her voice sounds very clear, clear as hailstones. "Not for many years now."

I was sad. Sad with a sadness I'd never felt before. The sadness chewed me up and swallowed me bit by bit. I was so sad I wanted to spend the whole day walking and looking at trees and gathering pebbles, but I couldn't. My leg wouldn't let me.

I also wished that Roe Deer had told me this news before. If she has not been my girlfriend for many years, why didn't she inform me of the fact earlier? As far as I remember we did not go through a breakup and I'm sure I would remember something like that. I don't watch TV except when I go and visit my sister Jo, but when people on TV split up, they shout and throw plates at each other. Roe Deer has never once shouted or thrown plates at me. I have never shouted in my life at all, or thrown anything. That is, I have sometimes skimmed stones across water, and I did throw a tennis ball once when I was a boy, but I don't think that counts. I didn't know Roe Deer then anyway.

Roe Deer said, when I asked her on the phone why we weren't together anymore, that relationships weren't my forte. That it wasn't my fault. That I was just made of the wrong ingredients.

Perhaps I should have noticed there was a problem. I should have gleaned. But gleaning isn't my thing. I'm not good at gleaning, not like other people. Harpmaking, but not gleaning.

I wonder if Phineas has such problems with his love life. I doubt it. A few lady pheasants come round from time to time and Phineas always seems to get on with them just fine.

I managed to get myself as far as the woods today and I leaned my crutches against the trunk of a great, tall pine tree and I leaned myself against it too. I thought about Roe Deer. I thought about our relationship that I had been wrong about for so many years. I wondered exactly how many years I'd been wrong about it. Three? Four? Five? There was a massive brown anthill just in front of me, but I was wondering so hard I didn't even bother to count the ants.

My head was full of the time Roe Deer and I first met, when she came to the barn looking for a harp. Her hair was primrose yellow, shining and plentiful. Her eyes glinted bluer than any eyes I'd ever seen before. She was dressed in a jacket, cream colored with eight buttons, and navy trousers, very tight. She flashed her blue eyes and flicked her primrose hair around and kept on saying my name.

"Oh, Dan, I've never seen such beautiful harps," she said.

"Oh, Dan, what a place to live!" she said.

"Dan, you are amazing!" she said.

"Dan, I'm so glad I've discovered you!" she said.

She played all my harps, one by one. She played them very beautifully, every note perfectly placed. Every note, as it was plucked, plucking in turn at something deep inside me. It seemed as though my harps and her fingers were made for one another.

After I'd thought about this for a while I thought about how she came back day after day to look at my harps, and every time she came she stood very close to me, much closer than I was used to anyone standing. I made sandwiches for her: egg, cress, Gorgonzola cheese and marmalade alternately. And she laughed. She ate some of the sandwiches, but I ate most of them. She spent a long time choosing a harp because, she said, they were all such good quality. Even after she'd finally bought one (I didn't think of giving it to her at the time) and taken it back to her house, she still came back every day to visit me and stand close and laugh at my sandwiches.

Sometimes we used to go into the orchard or a short way up the lane together, even though her shoes were not very practical for lumpy, bumpy ground because they had spindly little heels. Then one day (it was a hot, bumblebee-filled Wednesday in August and we were under the cherry tree) she pressed her lips against mine. I pressed mine back; otherwise, I would have fallen over. After quite a lot of lip pressing, there was some tongue exploring. After quite a bit of tongue exploring she took my hand and led me back inside the barn. She led me right up the seventeen stairs and through the little room and into my bedroom. In my bedroom she started taking off her clothes until she had completely nothing on. I wasn't sure at all what I was supposed to do, whether I was supposed to look or not, whether I was supposed to touch or not. But she soon made it clear that I was very much supposed to do both. So that is what I did.

I did it plenty of times after that.

After a few months of plenty, there was suddenly a lot less. She did not come and see me so much and said it was inconvenient whenever I offered to go and see her. She started to talk about needing a change of scene. I said on Exmoor scenes were changing all the time and asked what more of a change she could possibly need. To which she sighed and replied that she was going away for a bit. In fact, she would not be around for quite a while. She told me not to worry about getting in touch because she'd be traveling in different countries different days. But she'd come and see me when she came back.

I waited. And I waited.

After a long, long while she did come and see me.

"Hello, Dan," she said when she stepped into the barn. She had shorter hair and extra makeup.

"Hello, Roe Deer. Here you are," I said.

"Yes, here I am."

Thinking back, I probably should have asked her all about her holiday, but I didn't. I was too busy wondering if she was now going to take off all her clothes.

Her clothes remained on, however.

She hung around for a while, wandering through the harps, plucking strings a bit in a thoughtful way. Then she gave me a little, light, odd sort of a kiss, more pecklike than her usual (no tongue exploring at all) and said she'd better be going. Her parents had cooked a casserole for supper and were waiting for her.

Possibly, in retrospect, this might have been the day on which we split up. But there was definitely no shouting or throwing of plates. I therefore presumed she was still my girlfriend.

As I leaned against the pine it occurred to me that Roe Deer and I have not been in bed together for five years. Perhaps that's what the problem is. It was nice being in bed with her, but the opportunity does not seem to have arisen recently. Perhaps if I offered . . . ? What is a man supposed to do? If my father was still alive, I could ask him, but he isn't so I can't.

When I got back to the barn I rang my

sister Jo and asked her instead. She said: "Aha!"

I repeated my question about what was I supposed to do.

She said, "You are supposed to stop moping and think, 'Good riddance!' "

This, although possibly good advice, was not quite as helpful as I might have hoped. The what is very different from the how.

I thought of Thomas. He is always having arguments with his wife Linda but has managed to never actually split up with her. He is clearly an expert.

I gave him a call.

"Roe Deer isn't my girlfriend anymore," I said.

"Oh, boyo, that's bad luck," he said. "I'm sorry, mate." Then he said, "But I have to be honest with you, I did think you were a lucky bastard to have it so good for so long."

"We apparently split up many years ago. Five years ago, I think."

There was a low whistle down the phone. "Stag's Head?" he suggested.

"Good plan," I said.

"But you are driving this time," he added. "You can drive now, can't you, mate?"

I said I could. I got out the Land Rover.

22
ELLIE

That photo. I can't stop thinking about it. Dan and Rhoda looked so lovely together, so romantic and so . . . *right*. I can't deny it: As a couple they do make sense. He the handsome harpmaker, she the beautiful harpist. Both creative, both charming, yet with differences that complement each other. He more straightforward and stubborn, she more practical and ambitious.

Ignoring my own feelings for a minute, I see that I've been willfully prejudiced against Rhoda. Hasn't she been kind to me during all the harp lessons? Hasn't she helped me patiently and painstakingly with my harp playing? Hasn't she been good about the fact that I've been hanging around her boyfriend every day? I've wanted so much for her to be undeserving of Dan, callous and nasty, that I've fitted everything she says or does into my own interpretation. Because I've wanted *me* to be the nice one. She can have all the beauty and talent, but can't I at least claim that? Evidently not.

I'd hoped that Dan's relationship with Rhoda was all in his head, but over the past week I've dwelled more and more on the photo and I've come to the conclusion I must be wrong. There are all sorts of relationships in this world. Just because Dan and Rhoda don't follow the normal rules doesn't mean they don't have something very strong.

I catch myself biting the inside of my mouth so hard that I can taste blood.

I can't and I mustn't be so involved. Maybe it's music that's done it to me. Music brings out such strong emotions. It makes us feel things we shouldn't feel. The loveliness of the harp has wafted me into magicland and the boundaries of reality have become blurred. I've allowed myself to get carried away. I'm a married woman. I've got Clive and we've promised to be together for better, for worse and all the rest of it until death do us part. I think back to the days when Clive supported me over my library job. We're not as close now as we were then, but he's provided me with so much over the years. He's given my life a framework and I'd be lost without it. I have to try and put myself back on track.

I'm doing it as a favor for Clive. He's doing it as a favor for his colleague Andy. Andy is doing it for himself. Andy's met a girl who won't go out on a first date with him alone. She's insisted that he invite a couple he knows to come along too. For some reason Clive and I have been appointed as that couple.

I have some sympathy for the girl. I don't know Andy very well, but he does come across as rather big and boorish. She may be scared or she may be wise. No doubt she'll get more insight into his character by seeing him interact with friends rather than partaking in a flirtatious one-to-one.

Intrigued though I am, I'm not looking forward to it.

"Thanks, hon-bun! You're such a star!" calls Clive, pulling his best shirt over his head without unbuttoning it.

I don't feel like a star.

I'm not sure how much to dress up. Obviously the evening isn't about us, but it might be nice to make a bit of effort for Clive. It'll be a chance to discover a little more about his life at the office as well. Apart from complaints about his evil boss, he doesn't fill me in much. He likes to keep his work in a separate compartment from me, just as I keep my harp playing in a separate compartment from him.

I go for a boho-chic look in the end: smart beige trousers with a patterned chiffon top and scarf.

They've chosen a seaside pub in Minehead. The windows look dirty and there's a heap of lobster pots outside the battered blue door. Strong smells of fish and vinegar assault our nostrils the minute we step inside.

"What'll you have, hon?" asks Clive, marching up to the dimly lit bar. I ask for white wine. There's a newspaper lying on the bar stool.

"Oh, look! *The Fishing Wire!*"

I pick it up and leaf through. Every page seems to display at least three pictures of large bearded men holding up ginormous trophy fish. One of the men bears a striking likeness to Andy.

On cue a voice bellows behind us. "Hey, Clive, me ole chum! And if it isn't the lovely Ellie-wellie! How's it going, Ells?"

I'd forgotten how annoying he was. I immediately become extra stiff and formal. "Very well, thank you, Andy."

He grasps Clive by the hand. "Good man,

thanks for coming. Allow me to introduce the exquisite Sandra!"

"Exquisite" is pushing it a bit. Sandra has several chins, sharp little eyes and a nose that looks as if it has spent a lot of time pressed against things. Shop windows, presumably. Her hair has been lavishly lacquered and curled. She has squeezed herself into a skimpy dress that can't quite deal with her ample proportions. Acres of smooth, shining flesh are on view. It's clear why Andy likes her. It isn't because of her brains.

Not that such a display means she has no brains, I hasten to remind myself. For all I know she may have a degree from Cambridge in astrophysics. After my prejudice regarding Rhoda I'm not going to let myself leap to any unfair judgments. I sense, though, that Sandra has no such qualms in passing judgment over me. Later, when reporting the evening back to her girlfriends over a G and T, she'll call me words like "square" and "stuck-up." We smile sweetly at each other.

At least we have something to talk about straightaway. "Look, Andy! I found a picture of you." I hold out the page of *The Fishing Wire* for them both to look. Laughter spreads around our foursome and the ice is broken.

"Well, I'll be f— flipped backward by a flying kipper! It does look like me, doesn't it!" He holds the picture next to his own face and pulls a similar expression. "If only I was holding a fish, you wouldn't know the difference."

"Perhaps Sandra will be your fish," suggests Clive, who has slipped into laddish mode.

"Will you be my fish, Sandra?" Andy asks pleadingly.

She puffs out her cheeks and opens and shuts her mouth. I have to hand it to her, it's a fair imitation.

But from then on everything slides downhill. I do my best, but the evening only provokes in me a stronger and stronger yearning to be somewhere else. We position ourselves at a table in the corner so that Sandra gets the view of the sea and Andy gets the view of Sandra. The meal arrives and we forge our way through it. I find it too big and a bit tasteless. Sandra shovels cod and chips into her mouth and gabbles on and on about the time her cousin was on *X Factor* (". . . and Simon Cowell was, like, *OMG*"). Andy leers at her and interjects dry comments. She shrieks with laughter. I ask the odd question and try to maintain polite interest. Clive alternates between competing with Andy for double entendres and grinning at me. But no matter how hard I try not to, I'm still thinking about Rhoda and what she may or may not be hiding.

"You're very quiet, Ellie-wells! What's up?" asks Andy eventually.

"I'm fine, just a little tired, that's all."

"I'll take you home soon," Clive promises. Then he gets up and buys another round of drinks. I try to keep a pleasant smile anchored to my face.

Twenty minutes later Andy and Clive are trading insults about their boss while Andy plays footsie with Sandra under the table.

Then Clive stands up. "Gotta go and take a leak. Won't be long. Guard my beer!"

Andy starts wheeling out fish-related jokes.

"What do you call a fish without an eye?"

Sandra doesn't know and it doesn't matter whether I know or not.

"A fsh!"

Her laugh tortures my eardrums.

"There's two parrots sitting on a perch. And the first one says —"

A waitress is passing. "Is this finished?" she asks me, indicating Clive's beer glass.

"Yes," I say before I can stop myself. She

balances it on the corner of her tray and disappears.

Andy looks at me. "You're brave," he says.

Sandra leans across the table and brushes a crumb from his beard with her manicured fingers.

He looks gleeful. "I think there may be some more in there, if you wouldn't mind checking . . . ?"

At that moment Clive arrives back.

"What the . . . ? Who took my beer?"

Sandra points at the waitress, who is now wiping down a neighboring table.

"Why the hell did you let her take it?" he thunders.

Andy smirks and Sandra giggles.

"There was only a tiny bit left and it's getting late," I tell him. "Clive, let's go home. I'm sure Andy and Sandra can do without us." Andy gives me a sly wink and thumbs-up while Sandra looks at Clive hopefully. But he's fuming.

"God, El, I bloody wanted that beer. I can't believe you did that!"

To take a man's beer from him is to let loose a Pandora's box of demons. I cower under the hailstorm of swearwords. The blood has rushed to my face with the humiliation of it. Even Andy and Sandra look uncomfortable. Part of me wants to buy my husband another drink to atone for my sins, but part of me just says no. I can't always let him win.

Clive drives us back, even though he's over the limit. It isn't worth protesting, but I cling to my seat belt as he screeches round the lanes. He'll be like this until morning, possibly tomorrow as well. I don't feel as full of remorse as I'm meant to, though. In there somewhere is a naughty, stubborn little strand of triumph. I was desperate for some headspace for my own thoughts, and now I have it.

No matter how much I've tried, I am still obsessing. I need to decide whether to pursue a line of inquiry or whether to leave well enough alone. I should probably leave well enough alone . . . but I know I won't.

23
DAN

How could I have been so wrong? So wrong for so long? Rhoda says I am made of the wrong ingredients. Perhaps I am just not cut out to have a girlfriend. Perhaps I don't fully understand the way girlfriends' minds work and therefore girlfriends get fed up and don't want to put up with me. Perhaps I am destined to be always alone. This seems likely.

Roe Deer is not, not at all, my girlfriend. I say the sentence over and over to myself. There is now a big hole in my life. I am listening to music a lot every day, not just because I want to but because I have to. Music helps fill up the holes that people leave behind.

The Roe Deer hole reminds me of the other two largest holes in my life, one mother-shaped and the other father-shaped. It is the father one that I think about most. Maybe this is because my father and I discovered harpmaking together. Unlike my mother (who was more concerned with fitting me into a mold that I couldn't really fit into no matter how hard she tried) my father always wanted to do whatever made me happy. I have discussed fathers with Ellie the Exmoor Housewife. Ellie agrees with me that fathers are very important. We are both sad that our fathers aren't around anymore.

After my father was killed in a car accident I had a problem with my hands. They refused to do what I wanted them to do. They wriggled about all over the place. Whenever I tried to draw or to saw or to drill or to glue anything, my hands wouldn't let me, they were flapping and thrashing around so much. I cut the third finger of my right hand quite badly on the band saw. It became impossible to make harps. The situation went on for exactly three weeks and four days, which is a long time not to make harps, very. So what my sister Jo and I did during that time was this: listen to music.

We listened and we listened. We listened to orchestras and string quartets, operas and jazz trios, reggae and hip-hop. We listened to Vivaldi, to Beethoven, to Fauré, to Palestrina, to Joan Baez, to Sting, to Led Zep-

pelin and the soundtrack of *Star Wars.*
Some pieces of music were hard to listen to
at that time. Others were soft and soothing.
They were all necessary. Otherwise everything inside us would have turned to dust.
We listened together and we listened sepa-
rately. My sister Jo cried for hours, then
listened some more. I went on walks, then
listened some more. That is how we survived.

After all the music my hands eventually
calmed down again. So what I did next was
to make harps continuously for six months,
stopping only to eat and sleep. I made my
most exotic and experimental harps at that
time: tiny little delicate harps and huge great
clomping harps and harps of all sorts of
peculiar shapes.

I was in the middle of making peculiar
harps when my mother went and died too.
When this happened, exactly the same thing
followed as with my father. My hands
wobbled and flapped around for three weeks
and four days. So I listened to large doses
of music and after that I made a load of
harps very quickly indeed. Odd, exotic,
strange harps.

Jo sold the peculiar harps as quickly as
she could. She said we needed money, as
we were waiting for a thing called probate.

Probate was in no particular hurry, so it was just as well I was in such a manic harp-making mood. One of the women who bought a peculiar harp (it had seven crescent moons carved in a falling formation all down the pillar) put a film of herself playing it on YouTube. Jo brought her laptop computer into the workshop and showed it to me. She said the harp sounded peculiar as well as looking peculiar. She said you could hear the grief. I don't know about that, but I think she may have been right.

The evening with Thomas was helpful, in that he did a lot of head shaking and pint buying and uttered the word "Women!" many times. However, the girlfriend-to-not-girlfriend switch was still problematic and hard for my brain to grasp. So the following day I went back to the woods and leaned against the pine tree again and carried on thinking about Roe Deer. I thought about all the things that had happened between us over the last six years. The memories were as clear as ever in my head, but now it was as if I was viewing them through a different lens. Or as if somebody had come along and altered all the colors.

I stayed thinking among the pine trees for a long time.

Pine trees are very beautiful and they have a scent that never fails to beguile my nose. They have made their home here, but they do not absolutely belong on Exmoor. They were planted in the 1940s because people needed wood to build ships so they could fight each other more effectively, it being wartime. Then wartime stopped, so people were not so bothered about building ships and killing each other, but the pines still kept on growing.

Although I like pine trees, they have two clear disadvantages. Disadvantage number one is that they create a lot of darkness. When you are sitting under pines, you cannot appreciate the sky, as it's all blocked out by their dense shade. Disadvantage number two (which is a result of number one) is that other plants won't grow under pine trees. Not at all. Under pine trees the forest floor is nothing but old, brown pine needles, thousands and thousands of them.

However, if you go to an area where our native deciduous trees are growing — the oaks, ashes, birches, hazels, hawthorns, beeches — then you see that all sorts of things thrive under their branches. There are the magical greens of the mosses and ferns, the bright white of the wood anemones, the acres of shining bluebells in May, the foxgloves in early summer. And every autumn the trees create their own rich carpet of dazzling colors.

After a bit I found I was wanting to move on from the pine tree where I was leaning, so I gathered up my crutches and move on is what I did. I walked a little farther along the woodland trail. Soon the birdsong grew louder and the path came out of the pines and lightened and there were birches and oaks flanking my way. They had lost their leaves but were still beautiful because you could see the intricate tracery of every twig. The birches were shining silver-white. Just a few were hanging on to little twists of yellow leaves that lifted and spiraled in the breeze. The last time I focused in on birches was the day I planted birch seeds for Ellie the Exmoor Housewife. Birch is her favorite.

What happened next was that I found the birches had got right in there, into my thoughts, and I wasn't thinking about Roe Deer anymore. Not at all. I was thinking about Ellie.

First I thought about the way Ellie walks. It reminds me of a young colt; sometimes hesitant and leggy, unsure of quite where to place the feet, but then breaking suddenly into a trot or canter, tossing the mane, as if no longer caring. A sort of clumsiness combined with a sort of grace.

Next I thought about Ellie's face. The way her hair curls around it in different ways on different days. The gentle slope of her nose. Her lips, and how they curve sometimes up and sometimes down and sometimes she opens them and words come out. The words have a singsong sound, a bit of a lilt, with an inflection like questions even when they are not questions. When Ellie speaks, all of her face is animated, her cheekbones, her dimples, the flesh of her forehead, the line of her jaw, the arch of her eyebrows. Her eyes.

Her eyes, the color of bracken in October. Sometimes Ellie focuses them on my own eyes and sometimes she focuses them into the distance as if she is looking for something and sometimes they are shielded from view by her eyelids. Then they will come back and focus on my face again, and I see all sorts of things reflected in them.

Next time I see Thomas I ask him what is his opinion of Ellie's eyes.

"Why you asking me that, mate?" he demands.

I tell him it's because I want to know the answer.

"Well, in that case I'd say they're a good

231

pair of eyes. Yup, good ones. No question, boyo. Ellie Jacobs — new girlfriend material, deffo. But she's hitched already, isn't she?"

I confirm that Ellie Jacobs is indeed hitched.

Ellie Jacobs is hitched and I am made of all the wrong ingredients.

At least we still have music.

24
ELLIE

Clive pauses with his fork halfway to his mouth. "What sort of concert?"

I pour a bit more gravy onto my chicken. I've worded the proposition carefully and modulated my voice to sound as if I was hoping for the answer yes, while all the time I am in fact praying for the answer no.

"Harp music," I tell him. The word "harp" is loaded with risk and tight emotion, but I do my best to make it sound carefree and trivial. I rush on before he can make any sarcastic references to Exmoor eccentrics who dole out harps to women they've just met. "Christmas music mainly, I think. Carols and stuff."

"Christmas seems to start earlier every year," he comments. "Not sure I'm ready for carols yet."

I say nothing but set to work carving the chicken on my plate.

"Hmm . . . In Taunton, you say?"

"Yes, in one of the churches. I'm taking Christina too, as she hasn't been anywhere for ages." I cut a potato into small pieces and mop up some more gravy with it. "I expect it'll be quite mushy, but it's the sort of music she enjoys. Well, the sort of thing both of us enjoy, really. I expect you'd enjoy it too, if . . ." I carefully insert a note of pleading as I tail off. Exploiting Christina again is a stroke of genius. She has happily agreed to come with me, but her presence is calculated to guarantee Clive's absence.

He sniffs. "Think I might give it a miss if you're sure you don't mind, hon-bun."

I breathe a sigh of relief. Although I know Dan won't be there I'm intending to go and speak to Rhoda afterward and it would be tricky pretending to Clive that I've only just met her.

"No, I don't mind," I tell him with an air of resignation. "It'll be nice to have a girly chat with Christina at least" — a comment that clinches it.

"How's her hand these days anyway?" he asks, tucking more chicken into his mouth.

I'd almost forgotten about that particular lie.

"Oh, much, much better."

I'll need to keep him away from Christina for a good while longer in case it occurs to

234

him to inspect her hand. "Apparently she won't even have a scar," I add, mentally congratulating myself on my foresight.

"Oh, good. Seems a crazy kind of accident anyway, cutting open your hand on a can opener. Only Christina could manage something like that."

"Yes, I suppose it *is* a bit bizarre." I ponder for a moment, then add: "But it was one of those old-fashioned can openers that takes a lot of brute force. She was using it for a can of chickpeas and something made her jump — I think it was her smoke alarm suddenly going off — so she ended up jabbing herself. Nasty. There was blood all over the kitchen, she said."

Clive wrinkles his nose. "Too much information."

He is right. I'm only setting myself up for future problems. I'm now going to have to brief Christina about the specifics of her can opener and her smoke alarm.

The night is raw, starlit and frosty. The roads are covered in a thin film of white. They haven't been salted so I drive with utmost care until I reached the edge of Christina's village, where they are a bit clearer. She comes out to meet me, swathed head to toe in pashminas, scarves and boots.

She looks colorful and stylish. She makes me wish I'd made more of an effort. Still, my agenda tonight isn't to try and impress anyone, just meet a couple of people if I can.

Slow traffic crawls around the outskirts of Taunton. We're running late and it takes me some time to find the church, then there's nowhere to park nearby. I eventually leave the car four streets away and Christina and I end up running. We arrive at the church, panting, just as the concert is about to start.

We slip into a pew near the back. I take a brief look around. There are plenty of elderly couples, but I can't see any small boys at all.

Rhoda's harp is placed at the front. The lighting glistens on its strings and sweeps over its frame with glowing amber brush-strokes.

"Wow!" cries Christina. "Is yours like that?"

"Smaller. But similar, yes," I boast.

When Rhoda steps onto the stage the audience lets out a gasp. She is svelte and stunning in a golden dress that hugs the curve of her hips then drops in shimmering layers to the floor. Her hair hangs in a single perfect coil over one shoulder. Her slinky black gloves reach up to her elbows. She smiles graciously and makes a show of sliding them off finger by finger before she sits down at the harp.

From the moment she begins playing we are all transported. Notes call to each other, flutter and echo across the arches of the old building. Arrangements of folk melodies, classical pieces and familiar carols ring out, each enhanced by the fey quality of the harp. We drink them all down with relish.

"God, I think I'm in love with her!" whispers Christina in my ear.

"Shut up and listen," I hiss.

The intermission arrives in no time. The audience moves en masse to the back of the church, where mulled wine is being served.

Rhoda is some time joining the throng, but when she does I aim myself straight at her. She's already deep in conversation with a small, sharp-nosed man. Her guitarist friend hasn't come for reasons I can only guess.

I butt in. "Rhoda, that was fantastic, fabulous! Really moving!"

She inclines her head. "Thank you, Ellie."

"May I introduce my friend Christina, who is a great fan of yours." Christina darts an arch look at me but shakes Rhoda's hand, her bangles jingling.

"And this is Pete." Rhoda indicates the

diminutive man. "He plays the cello." I shake his hand, then let him talk to Christina for a minute while I ask Rhoda if her parents have come to support her this evening.

"Yes, of course. That's Mum over there in the navy skirt and jacket, and Dad with her, with the bald head."

They look amiable enough, but they're not talking to anyone. They're standing stiffly and sipping their wine in a slightly awkward fashion. Rhoda catches her mother's eye and waves. The mother mouths, "Well done!" across the room at her.

Rhoda is clearly keen to resume her conversation with Pete the cellist, who is now being monopolized by Christina, so I leave the three of them to negotiate and edge over to the parents.

"Your daughter is very talented," I begin.

They look pleased, as parents would.

"I'm Ellie, one of her harp students."

We shake hands. The mother is tall and slim with a fine bone structure, similar to Rhoda's. Her hair is neatly curled and she is wearing glasses. The father is slightly shorter. He has a shiny bald patch but rather heavy eyebrows. The only physical trait he seems to have passed on to Rhoda is the bright blue of his eyes.

"Have you been learning the harp for long?" he asks.

"No, not long," I reply. "But I must say Rhoda's an extremely good teacher. I've only had a few lessons with her, but — well, I think I'm improving quite fast."

They make polite noises of interest and appreciation.

"I've got a harp very similar to hers. It's made by the same man, Dan Hollis, the Exmoor Harpmaker. I expect you know him?" I prompt.

I watch their reaction, a little exchange of glances passed furtively between them.

"Yes, we've met Dan a few times," says the father.

"Yes, he's a very fine craftsman," adds the mother.

"Oh, isn't he? And a dear man!" I insist. "He's been so sweet to me. And he thinks the world of Rhoda, of course . . ." I let the sentence dangle.

"Oh, does he?" the mother says in a noncommittal voice.

I nod enthusiastically. "He adores her!"

The pause is awkward. I need to throw in a casual comment to encourage them to share more information, but my brain isn't functioning very well.

"They're such a lovely couple!" I blurt

out at last, and immediately regret it. I always resort to crass clichés when stressed.

The father's eyebrows have shot upward. The mother puts her lips tightly together and views me through narrowed eyes.

The father says: "Another glass, dear?"

"Yes, that would be nice," she answers, handing him her empty.

"Can I get you a second, er . . ."

"Ellie," I remind him.

". . . Ellie?"

"No, no, I'm fine, thanks. Driving back home. Must be careful."

He disappears into the crowd for refills.

"I live some way away," I explain. "But I expect you're local to Taunton, are you?"

"Yes, we live quite close," replies the mother. "Not too far from Rhoda, which is nice. We get to see her whenever she's not too busy with all her harp activities."

"Ah, how nice to have family close by. I hardly ever get to see my mother; she's up in Yorkshire, much nearer my sister."

"Ah, is she?"

"Yes. It's a shame we can't both be close to her. That bond with parents is so vital, isn't it?"

She gives a forced smile and glances over in Rhoda's direction but says nothing.

"It must be nice to be near shops too, here

in Taunton," I babble on. "I have to drive for miles just to buy a pint of milk. It's lovely scenery where I live, mind you; I do love Exmoor. But sometimes I think it would be so great to be nearer a bit of culture."

"Mm-mm, yes, I'm sure." She's looking bored now. "If you'll excuse me I must just go and have a word or two with my daughter."

She makes her way toward Rhoda and her cellist friend. Christina has vanished. I guess she's gone outside for a cigarette. I return to our pew to await the second half of the concert. I sit pulling at my eyebrows. There has to be a way of finding answers to my questions; otherwise, I'll obsess forever. I'll have no eyebrows left at this rate.

"Did you find out anything?" asks Christina, plopping down next to me.

"Not enough."

I cross my arms. Bit by bit my anxiety is hardening into stubborn determination.

"But the car's *that* way. Isn't it?" Christina is forever doubting her sense of direction, usually with good cause.

"Yes, but we're not going to the car yet," I reply, sotto voce.

"What? Why?"

"I'm following them." Rhoda's parents are ahead, strolling arm in arm. "I need to know where they live."

"Can't you just ask them?"

"Well, I would have done, but the opportunity didn't arise, and I need to be subtle."

Christina shoots me a glance. "Why the urgency, Ellie?"

"It seems crazy, but I can't deny the facts. Rhoda and Dan have been together for years. At one point she put on weight, then she disappeared for a while. And now she and her parents are hiding something from him. Christina, Dan is my . . . my friend, my kind, lovely, good-hearted friend. It's not fair on him. And it's driving me insane. I need to know the truth. Stop!" I put a hand on her arm. The couple are getting into a white Toyota.

"Christina, wait here!"

"Eh?"

"Remember the number plate and tell me which way it goes!"

I turn and run back along the streets to where my own car is parked. I leap in, breathing hard, rev up and drive at top speed — thank God the roads here are clear of ice — to where she's waiting. I can only hope that Rhoda's parents are ditherers. As

I reach the spot, I lean over and open the door for Christina. She hops in.

"They went straight down and turned left at the end!" she cries. "And I don't remember the numbers, but the letters were *BLT*. At least that was memorable."

I shoot down the street. As we round a bend we see the tail end of a white car disappearing up another side street. I turn after it. The number plate has a *BLT*.

"Well done, Chris! Great detective work!"

"Thank you, my dear fellow! But — ?"

"I'll tell you later . . . I may have to indulge in a little light espionage first."

She gawps at me. "Who the devil are you and what have you done with my friend El- lie!"

I tail the Toyota through a few more twists and turns of Taunton and down past a smart row of detached houses. It eventually swerves into the driveway of one of the houses near the end of the row. There's a big willow tree in the front garden, which slightly obscures something else that piques my interest. The sign on the gate reads *Swandale.*

"Swandale. I'll remember that."

Another trip into Taunton, this time alone and in daylight. Clive said he was stopping by at the gym on his way back from work, so hopefully he won't realize I've been out again.

The drive seems to take forever. So does the wait.

Visions pass before my eyes.

Then, suddenly, it's over. I know what I wanted to know. What I cannot now unknow. What touches me and worries me and terrifies me. And I have to decide what to do about it.

25
DAN

Ellie the Exmoor Housewife was wearing a woolly hat, green, when she came to the barn this morning. She took it off and her hair crackled with electricity and stuck out sideways. She ran her fingers through it and it calmed down a little and allowed itself to be tucked behind her ears.

"Morning, Dan," she said. "How are you?"

I told her I was very well, thank you. I said this because it is what you are supposed to say, not because it was strictly accurate. If I had been strictly accurate I would have said my leg was full of grinding pain and my hands were numb. The numbness was due to the fact that I had just come in from a frosty walk (or actually, a frosty limp) and I had collected twenty-three pebbles from the stream. The water of the stream is sparkly clean but ice-cold, not designed for finger comfort. They were nice pebbles,

245

though. They were mottled, red-brown and silver streaked, the color of rain clouds, the color of autumn sycamores, the color of dolphins. Some smooth, some rough. Some flat, some rounded, some jagged. Each will be assessed in due course and viewed against different types of wood to see which ones will end up embedded as jewels in the bodies of harps. The others will just be used for admiring independently.

Ellie didn't seem to appreciate them at all when I showed her. Neither did she go up the stairs to her harp, but instead she did her pacing, hovering, shuffling thing. I left the pebbles on the end of the workbench and started to plane a piece of apple wood for the *Fifi* harp.

Ellie stood by my shoulder. She lingered. And lingered. Seldom have I seen so much lingering. I stopped planing and turned to look at her. She opened and shut her mouth a couple of times. Eventually words started trickling out in a random monologue.

Roe Deer. She brought up the subject of Roe Deer. So I held up a hand to stop her and I told her Roe Deer was not my girl-friend anymore. I wanted to be clear and I wanted Ellie to know the Truth of the Matter. (I like things to be clear, and I very much don't like the fact that it took me so long to find out the Truth of the Matter myself.)

"Oh!" Ellie said on receiving this information. Her voice was stiff and fragile like a beech twig. "Oh." The corners of her mouth looked as if they couldn't decide whether to go up or down. "So . . . so when did that happen?"

I told her that it had apparently happened five years ago but that Roe Deer had only informed me about it last week. Possibly, if I had not asked her about it, she would never have informed me at all. If Ellie had not requested confirmation on this matter, it would never have occurred to me to question it, but she had, so I did, so there we were.

"I see," is what Ellie said. She put a hand on my arm. I moved her hand off my arm again. I did not want any hands on my arm at that moment.

"So . . . so are you OK?" she asked.

This was a difficult question to answer. Over the last four days my levels of OK and not-OK had been yo-yoing so much I didn't really want to think about it. Talking about Roe Deer had made me focus on something that felt very sore, though, and I was now far closer to the not-OK end of things than I had been when Ellie came in. I therefore said nothing and hoped that she would go upstairs and play her harp.

But she still didn't go upstairs to her harp. She leaned against the workbench and started mumbling stuff about life being unpredictable and how you never know what is just around the corner. As she went on, she gathered momentum and suddenly a great gush of questions came whooshing out at me. She has always been somebody who asks questions and normally I don't mind it, not at all, but today it grated. However, Ellie is special and I did not want to offend her even when my levels of OK-ness were plummeting. I therefore did my best to answer.

I told her no, I was not lonely. If ever I felt lonely I could have a chat with Phineas and that would sort it out. I agreed that it was important to have support in times of crisis and that friends were helpful. Yes, Thomas was a good friend, and so was she, Ellie. Very. And, yes, it would be nice to have more family around, but as both my parents were dead and my sister Jo did not live that close, there wasn't very much I could do about it. No, I had not particularly considered ever having children, but yes, I did like children. So long as there weren't too many of them at once. Yes, if I ended up with any one day that would be fine. It was not looking very likely, though, the way things were going.

I didn't answer her question about how I saw myself in the future. But she then asked the same question again but slower and louder and in slightly different words. So I told her I did not see myself in the future at all. I did not possess a crystal ball, and even if I did I doubted whether it would work. I lived in the present. I lived bit by bit, as I went along, and that suited me fine.

She twisted her mouth to one side and she picked up one of my pebbles and put it down again. Then she started pulling out the hairs of her left eyebrow.

At that moment there was a scuffling sound and Phineas came in through his pheasant flap. He looked at us both sideways, then he looked at the harps, then he looked at us again. I don't know what he was thinking, but obviously it was an exhausting thought because next he put his head down and aimed himself straight for his bed. We watched his tail disappearing through the archway.

"Dan," said Ellie, still picking at her eyebrow, "I'd really like to meet your sister sometime. You talk about her so much and she sounds . . . nice. She lives in Bridgwater, doesn't she?"

I confirmed that this was the case.

"Do you think it would be all right if I called in on her one day? Or . . . is she coming here at all in the near future? Could I possibly meet her then?"

I was quite surprised, as people don't often ask to meet Jo, but I told her yes, that would no doubt be possible. In fact, somebody was intending to buy my *Starling* harp so Jo was coming over to fetch it on Friday and if Ellie wanted to coincide with her then, she could. Only, I added, it might be a good idea for Ellie not to mention to Jo that I had given her a free harp, as Jo would not take kindly to that, Jo being my chief accountant and business consultant and a little bit inflexible about financial matters.

Ellie said she promised not to tell Jo about the free harp, but that she would quite like a woman-to-woman chat with Jo.

A woman-to-woman chat? What does that involve?

"What does that involve?" I asked her.

She cleared her throat. "That involves just me and her. Alone," she said, underlining the words.

It must be a particularly private female thing she wants to discuss, the sort of thing that I wouldn't understand.

Anyway, I said I was sure that wouldn't be a problem.

26
ELLIE

Rhoda isn't that much younger than me, but she has two parents who are still alive and well. She has no idea how lucky she is.

I ring Vic. "How's Mum?"

"Oh, you know."

I do. I know only too well.

"And you?" I ask.

"Busy sewing name tapes into socks."

Vic has four children who are forever losing items of gym kit and a mother who cannot recognize her own clothes. Sewing on name tapes is one of life's necessary evils for Vic.

"Ugh, poor you!"

My sister is a great ally, although our lives have gone different ways. These days Vic is all about family. (I don't actually know what I'm all about, but it's not that. I sometimes wish it was, but try not to think about it.) I'm longing to confide in her. She knows nothing of my harp playing, let alone Dan and Rhoda and my recent discovery. But I'm sensing a need for caution.

"Is it still all right if Clive and I come up for Christmas?"

"Of course!" she cries. "I'm relying on you to help with the dinner, not to mention everything else!"

"What's the plan?"

"The usual: turkey, presents, tree, everyone running about."

"I bet the kids are getting excited."

"Oh yes, uncontrollable!" She laughs.

I can see them now, the little flock of terrors I love so dearly: two boys, two girls; all enthusiasm and noise and mess. "I'm really looking forward to seeing you. Will Mum be joining us for Christmas Day?"

"Yes, one of us will go and pick her up."

"Do you think we can make her enjoy herself?"

"We'll certainly try."

I sigh. "Vic, thanks so much for everything you're doing."

"Ellie, it's OK. I know you'd do more if you could."

"Just let me be grateful, will you?"

"All right, then. Off you go. Be grateful."

"Vic, you are *fabulous*!"

"Yes, I know. Fabulous me! Fabulous, patient, long-suffering, resentful me!"

I know exactly the face she's making as she says it. We're so alike.

I try to soothe her. "Resentful is allowed. Mum resented us first."

"Not half."

A stream of memories runs through my head. Mum disliked any show of emotion, punished any hint of self-interest, clamped down on any flights of fancy. She didn't even like it when we, as little girls, gave names to the bees and slugs in our garden. (Bertie Bee was my favorite. And when I burst into tears on finding Bertie dead one morning — I was sure it was him, although all the bees looked similar — Mum said: "Ellie, grow up! You're so silly to let things like that affect you.") I never once saw *her* cry, even when my father died. She didn't radiate warmth as mothers are supposed to do. The only thing she radiated was disapproval.

"Do you think we totally ruined her life?" I ask Vic.

"Well, if she didn't have us, where would she be now? Rotting away in some dire council-run place with smelly loos. And zilch visitors."

As the dementia set in, Mum's few friends dropped away. Only Vic and I come to see her now, and my own visits are infrequent.

Yorkshire is just too far away from Exmoor.

I sigh. "I wish Dad was still with us."

Not many people would have put up with Mum the way he did. He never went against her, but he provided Vic and me with that quiet encouragement we so much craved and needed. It was Dad who made childhood bearable.

"I miss him every day," says Vic.

"Me too."

I ring Mum. "How are you, Mum?"

"Who are you?"

"It's me. It's Ellie."

"Ellie who?"

I nearly say, *Ellie Jacobs, the Exmoor Housewife.*

"Ellie your daughter," I tell her.

"Ah, the older one."

This is promising.

"Mum, can I ask you something?"

A slight pause. "She's very likely to, whether it rains or not."

"Mum, listen! Do you . . . Do you wish you'd never had children?"

"Children? Children?"

"Yes. Children."

Has she forgotten the meaning of the word?

"Children," she repeats. "Yes, I did have

children. I had two."

I take a breath and try again. "Mum, tell me: Are you glad at all, ever . . . that you had children?"

"Why, yes, of course! It was the best thing I ever did!"

Her voice conveys a fervor I haven't heard in months.

"I'll ring again later." I put the phone down. My body is racked with sobbing.

Jo is shorter and stumpier than Dan, but she has the same jet-black hair and round, dark eyes. Her hair is cropped close to her head and she's wearing jeans and a scarlet sweater. Her face is completely free of makeup, but she's one of those women who don't need it at all. Her features are strong and speak for themselves.

I feel a little threatened by her at first, and not sure I've made the right decision. But she comes over and squeezes my hand warmly.

"And how did you and Dan meet?" she asks.

"A coincidence," I tell her. "I stumbled across the Harp Barn and then I started having harp lessons with Rhoda." I notice her scowl at that word. "I come up here to practice. I'm borrowing one of Dan's harps," I add.

She glances at his face. I can see that she's assessing the probability of my buying a harp and warning him to stay out of the transaction, should it occur.

Dan has bits of sawdust in his hair and his shirtsleeves are rolled up. He stands close to his sister and I observe a sort of tolerant affection between them.

Dan mimes a little harp playing. "Ellie is a very fast learner."

There's something like pride in his voice. My heart swells. "Rhoda has put me through a lot of technique in a very short space of time."

I'm not sure if the topic of Rhoda is still horribly painful to Dan, but his smile gives me a gleam of reassurance.

"Shall I get sandwiches, then?" he asks. "And while I'm making them you two can have your woman-to-woman chat."

Jo looks as alarmed as I feel. I laugh nervously.

"Oh, it's nothing important," I bluster. "Just something I was wanting to ask you."

She relaxes again. She evidently thinks I'm going to question her about harp prices, too delicate a matter to discuss in Dan's presence.

"Right you are! Lots of sandwiches, please,

then, Dan," she says briskly.

He heads upstairs to the kitchen, his leg delaying him slightly. I watch him all the way to the top, wondering if this was such a good idea after all.

Jo folds her arms. "Fire away!"

There's no easy way to say it, even though I've rehearsed a thousand different versions in my head.

"Go on, spit it out. I won't bite!"

I brace myself. "Sorry to spring this on you, but is there any chance that . . . ah, some years ago, Rhoda might have had a baby? Um, Dan's baby?"

She sits down abruptly. I stay standing. I'm too nervous to sit.

"What makes you say that?"

"Well, the first thing is that her parents seem to be looking after a little boy. I've seen him. He would be about the right age. And the resemblance to Dan is striking."

She stares at me, her eyes penetrating. I can see thoughts chasing each other around in her head.

"It's possible, it's possible," she mutters.

It's a relief to share it. I rapidly tell her about the phone calls I've overheard during harp lessons, how my suspicions grew, how I engineered to meet Rhoda's parents at the concert and followed them home.

"There was a child's swing in the front garden, so it was obvious a child lived there," I tell her. "I knew the child was Rhoda's, but I couldn't be sure about the father. So I went back the following day and sat in the car by the road, watching. At around three, I saw Rhoda's mother leaving the house. She walked down the road in the direction of the local school. About half an hour later she returned to the house. She was hand in hand with the little boy. He had jet-black hair and eyes that . . ."

Now that I see Jo's wide eyes fixed on me, I feel a fresh certainty. I carry on. "I watched him stoop and pick up a pebble from the driveway. He showed it to his grandma and then stuck it in his pocket. There was something about the gesture . . ."

"Holy shit!"

"I'm sorry. I may be wrong, but . . ."

I know I'm not.

Jo shakes her head. "No. No, you're . . . I bet you're right. It makes sense, thinking about it. Dan and Rhoda were so close for a while and then she suddenly distanced herself. Now I see why. Conniving little cow!"

"She was trying to keep it a secret from him."

"And still is, I take it."

"Yes, so it seems," I reply. I can't believe how calm my voice is sounding. "But why? If she didn't want Dan to be involved as a father, why keep seeing him at all? And why did she let him carry on thinking she was his girlfriend for so long?"

"She's not stupid. She stood to gain quite a lot from Dan. Didn't you know two of her harps were gifts from him?"

"Oh." I didn't know that. I try not to let my face register my dismay.

"And he's always sending harp students her way. She earns a lot of money through them."

"I suppose that's true."

"And Rhoda loves to be doted on. Dan dotes on her. He did, anyway, when he thought she was his girlfriend. Rhoda just sopped up all the admiration. She's one of those people who are fueled by the admiration of others."

Jo is much clearer in her convictions than I am. I've been muddled about Rhoda all along, not trusting my own instincts. I see it now.

"She seems to be very good at hiding the fact that she's a mother," I comment. "I'm not sure *anyone* knows about it apart from her parents."

"And the lad himself?"

I shrug. "Goodness only knows what they've told him! I don't know how much of a mother Rhoda is to the poor boy. It seems to be her parents who run his life."

"Unbelievable! I suppose she thinks having a child might get in the way of her glam, independent, everyone-has-to-admire-me lifestyle."

"Maybe. I don't suppose getting pregnant was ever part of her plan."

There's a slight pause while we both try to construe Rhoda's thought processes. "Well, she didn't get rid of the baby," says Jo. "At least that's something. But she's been incredibly devious to hide it — him — from Dan for all these years."

I grimace. "Yes, it's horrible, isn't it?"

Jo's fists are clenched. "I'd like to wring her neck!"

We can hear Dan clunking about in the kitchen upstairs.

"I didn't know what to do," I explain. "I probably should have spoken to Rhoda about it, but I just couldn't. I don't think she would have taken too kindly to the fact that I'd been spying on her parents."

"She'd kill you!"

"I know," I whisper. I can't pull my eyes away from Jo's face. I'm terrified about the consequences of my revelation, but I can't take back what I've told her. I've transferred the responsibility now.

"I thought about just doing nothing, but that seemed wrong too. I'm sure the boy needs a father in his life. God, I certainly did! And, Jo, I haven't known Dan for that long, but I'm very fond of him," I confide. "I can't help feeling that if he's a father he should know about it. He'd *want* to know about it, for sure. I know parenthood is no easy task, but, from what I gather, it does enrich your life in all sorts of ways." I permit myself a little sigh. "But there's no way I could tell him. And, well, as Dan's sister, I thought you might have the best idea what to do."

I gaze at her helplessly.

"Are you certain the boy is Dan's son?"

"Yes. I am. Ninety-nine point nine percent."

She stands up, steel in her eyes.

"Well, in that case, I know exactly what to do," she says.

"What?"

"We tell him."

"What, now?"

"Now."

"But . . . won't it be rather a shock?"

"It will be a shock, yes. But my brother is strong. Sensitive, but very strong. He'll deal

262

with it his own way."

"Shouldn't we . . . well, wait a bit? Maybe you want to check it out first?"

"You said you were ninety-nine point nine percent sure. That's good enough for me. There's no way you'd come and tell me like this unless it was true."

"But for his own sake . . . ?"

Jo is having none of it. She is filled with righteous indignation. "Think about it, Ellie: Hasn't it been kept from Dan long enough? Isn't he the first person who should have known? What right have we got to treat him like a mug, hide it from him an instant longer? He's a father, for God's sake!"

27
DAN

I made thirty-three sandwiches. This is the same number as my age and also means that we could eat eleven each. I did wonder whether thirty-three might have been on the overgenerous side, but Ellie and Jo seemed to be talking earnestly in hushed voices and I guessed that they probably weren't ready to be disturbed yet and they wouldn't want a male person barging in on them while they were in the middle of discussing lingerie, even if he did have a mountain of triangular, crust-free sandwiches. The fillings of the sandwiches were these: seven with peanut butter, seven with hummus, four with blue cheese and cucumber, four with cheddar and pickle and eleven with plum jam, the jam that Ellie made from my plums.

Once the sandwiches were completed and arranged on the plate in a tall tower I made coffee for the nice smell. I wafted it around the kitchen a bit, then poured some out for Ellie, who likes to drink it. I also poured out three glasses of my favorite: water.

Normally when I make sandwiches it is to the strains of harp music, but there was no harp music today. It was a very unusual day.

My sister Jo marched into the kitchen.

"Aren't those sandwiches ready yet?" she thundered. "I'm starving!"

I said that the sandwiches were indeed ready if she and Ellie were ready to receive them.

"Of course we are!" she cried. "And where's the coffee?"

I told her I had poured out a mugful for Ellie and, having wafted the rest around the room, I'd tipped it down the sink.

"Aaargh!" she screeched. "I wish you wouldn't do that! How many times do I have to tell you, coffee is for drinking. Hang on! How come Ellie gets a mug and I don't? Here, give me the pot. I'll make another."

While she was wrestling with the coffee I took the sandwiches down to Ellie. She was pacing round and round. Today her socks were navy blue, but her sweater was a nice deep shade of russet. It looked good with the walnut-colored glossiness of her hair, I thought. Her skin was pearly white.

"Dan!" is what she said.

"Ellie," I said back to her. It is reassuring that we know each other's names so well.

I put the sandwiches on the table and I told her about the different flavors, adding that there were thirty-three in total.

She accepted one without seeming to give much consideration as to which flavor it was, and took a bite out of it.

"Don't say anything!" Jo called from the kitchen. "I'll be with you in two shakes of a lamb's tail!"

Ellie and I did not say anything. When Jo issues a command, you follow it. However, she did take a long while. I would estimate that a lamb could have shaken its tail possibly up to four hundred times before she came in with the brimming coffeepot. I thought of explaining to Ellie that my sister Jo is given to such exaggerations, but I didn't because I was forbidden to say anything.

When Jo came back in she poured out two more coffees, even though she knows I don't drink it.

"You may actually want something stronger," she said.

I asked her why.

"Ellie and I have . . . news. Stop dithering around, now. Stop twitching your hands, sit down and pay attention." Her voice was even louder than usual and set off a bit of an echo effect in all the harps.

I did what I was told.

"Now, this is all about Rhoda."

"Roe Deer?"

"Rhoda," she confirmed. Jo always looks as though she is having her teeth extracted when she talks about Roe Deer. I waited. Over these last days I've been experiencing a sore, raw feeling whenever I think about Roe Deer, but today the feeling was neither quite so sore nor quite so raw.

"Six years ago you and Rhoda were very involved, right? I mean, not like now but *on an intimate level.* Right?"

I studied my sandwich. It was peanut butter, with rather too much peanut butter in it. The bread was nice and thin, though, the corners of the triangles good and pointy.

"Right?" she urged.

I told her yes, even though I had a feeling it was the wrong answer. I do pretty much always tell the truth, even though I know you're not supposed to. I can't seem to help it.

"And then, soon after you got together, she disappeared out of your life for quite a long time, didn't she?"

I told her yes again.

She fixed her eyes on me. "Dan, listen.

We've got something very important to tell you, something that you ought to know. Ellie here has made a discovery. In that time that you didn't see her, Rhoda was having a baby."

I heard the words, but the meaning slipped right past my brain and scuttled out of reach.

"Your baby," said Jo.

Something started yanking deep down inside me. The yank was strong, very, as if my heart was on the end of a bit of string and somebody had tugged the string and hauled my heart right up through my rib cage. It made it difficult to breathe. The two faces were swimming before my eyes.

"Do you understand me?"

I told her yes, then added no.

"Listen, Dan. Rhoda has been keeping it a secret from you all this time, but Ellie has found out and we think it's time you knew."

My mouth moved, but words wouldn't come out.

"You have a five-year-old son," she said.

I don't know how long I sat there or what they said after that. But I know that at some point Jo left because she had to go to work. And some time after that I took myself outside to feed Phineas. And some time later I came back in and picked up various harpmaking tools one after the other, but my hands were shaking so much I couldn't hold them. There was a mug of cold coffee and a great heap of untouched sandwiches on the table.

Ellie was still there, pulling her hair and eyebrows into tufts. When she saw I was back inside, she went into the kitchen and emerged again with a fresh cup of tea. "Drink this," she said.

My hands couldn't get a grip of it and I spilled it down my trousers. My bandage and everything was tea soaked. I sprang to the tap and sloshed water everywhere.

"Stop, Dan!" cried Ellie. "That's way too much water! You'll drown yourself!"

My hands were flapping and weaving patterns in the air. My eyes wouldn't stop blinking. Strangulated noises were coming from my mouth. I had no control over any of it.

Ellie put her arms around me and held me close. She was very warm and I could feel her heart beating through her russet-colored sweater. "It's all right, it's all right," she repeated. "Dan, calm down! Everything's going to be all right."

Phineas has eaten lots today. He had all the leftover sandwiches. I will have to put him

269

on a diet next week.

I cannot make harps, I cannot eat and I cannot sleep. I'm already feeling that what I am supposed to do and what I want to do are probably not the same thing. My mother would have very clear ideas on that, but she is not alive now, so she can't help me. I am sure my sister Jo has very clear ideas too. The phone has been ringing constantly over the last two hours and I know it's her. I haven't answered it, though.

Ellie has gone home to cook supper for her husband. Phineas has come in and settled in his bed.

I'm going out. It's dark out there. I'll have to take a flashlight, but luckily a flashlight is a thing that I have. I will walk among the trees in the dark and have a think because now, suddenly, I have a son and, although I don't believe it a hundred percent — probably only about eight point five percent at the moment — the percentage is rising all the time. When I get to a hundred I will have to decide what to do because you can't suddenly discover you have a son of five years old and not do anything.

I put on my boots and tramp down the lane. I walk and I walk and thoughts come and go. Overhead are thousands of stars. There is a wispy fragment of moon and a sharp frost. The air bites into me. An owl hoots, pauses, then hoots again. Something rustles on my right in a hedgerow. The flashlight beam glints in the frozen puddles on the lane. My footfalls thud like a drumbeat in the stillness of the night air. I walk and I walk and eventually I realize my leg is hurting, very, very badly. I ignore it and carry on. There is not much sky now; the branches of the pines are crowding out the stars. A twig snaps underfoot. I keep going uphill until I have a sense of opening as the trees give way to moorland. The breeze is cold on my face.

I have a son I have a son I have a son.

I sit on a stone and switch off the flashlight. How many stars are up there? I start to count, beginning at the left-hand edge of the sky and working my way across inch by inch. Some are nearer and some are farther, some are brighter and some are so dim I'm not sure if they're really there or if I'm imagining them, so it's tricky. Normally I'm good at counting and don't lose my concentration before a few thousand, but tonight I can't seem to keep track.

I have a son I have a son I have a son.

An animal, light of foot, rushes across the ground in front of me. It is a deer, a stag. I catch the glow of the eyes, the branching of

271

the antlers against the glimmery sky. The deer senses my presence and gallops off in the darkness. Exmoor is full of deer, but they see you more than you see them.

I have a son I have a son I have a son.

I start counting again, this time starting from over the sea and dividing the sky up into rectangular sections, but it is no good. Stars keep popping up out of nowhere and then vanishing again. They are playing games with me.

My son is five years old.

I have missed five years of my son's life.

There is a whooshing sound in my ears, like wind in the trees or the sea.

Why didn't Roe Deer tell me? I feel anger like I have never felt before, like thunder and lightning hammering inside my skull, trying to get out.

It is cold and I have been sitting on this stone for too long. I get up. I am stiff and my muscles groan with the effort. I ignore them. I walk and I walk until the first smudges of dawn are beginning to appear and the ghosts of trees are emerging from the gloom.

I head back for the Harp Barn. I know what I'm going to do.

28
ELLIE

"El, do leave your eyebrows alone!"

"Sorry!" I whip my hand away. I hadn't realized I was doing it. It leaves little bald streaks — not an attractive look. I'm going to have to invest in an eyebrow pencil.

Clive has lit the fire. It gets dark early now and we both feel the need of that cheerful, chuntering presence. We've just consumed vast quantities of pizza. I didn't leave myself time to cook properly because I stayed so long at the Harp Barn. I cut the pizza into slices so we could eat it with our fingers, plates balanced on laps in front of the warm blaze. Now we're sprawling on the sofa, toasting our toes.

I wish I could have stayed with Dan longer. His level of shock has left me shocked too. And I feel scared. Scared about what he might do short-term. Scared about the consequences long-term.

Why did I go and spill the beans? Was it

273

because I believe in honesty and transparency, because I support a father's rights? Or was it because I secretly hoped Dan would hate Rhoda for her deception? And (possibly, just possibly) transfer his love to me because I'd discovered his beautiful son . . .

It seemed a good idea at the time, but now I'm terrified it's all backfired.

Dan will find a new love in his son and will be too busy to think about me at all. And what about Rhoda? Jo said he *doted* on Rhoda. Envy is coiling around my heart. The image of them in the plum orchard keeps flashing before my eyes. I add a small, stubby, black-haired little boy to the picture and see them at once as a gorgeous, happy family. Isn't that something Dan will strive for?

I'm struggling. It's hard to imagine how he must feel. One good thing about being a woman is that at least you can't have a baby without knowing about it.

Rhoda must have gone through a lot those five years ago. Presumably the baby was what people call "an accident." What were her feelings when she realized? Horror or delight? Surely she must have wanted the child? Or maybe it was just that she didn't like the idea of getting rid of it. There's a difference. I think I know Rhoda well enough to know which it was. I can see why she didn't say anything to Dan at the time. But now that he knows, they'll have to work something out together. I remember Dan's hurt when he realized she wasn't his girlfriend. I remember how tetchy he was the day he told me about it and I attempted to soothe him.

Dan has incredible powers of persuasion, as I well know! If he is still keen on her . . .

Rhoda will want to go back to him and make a go of things, won't she? Won't she? I would in her shoes.

I hate myself sometimes. I shouldn't have spied on Rhoda's parents. I shouldn't have said anything to Jo. I shouldn't have let Jo tell Dan. But then . . . then Dan would never have known he had a son. How could I have kept that from him?

"Penny for your thoughts."

I scowl and throw my hands into my lap. "Oh, I was just thinking about Mum."

Clive's expression changes from amusement to sympathy. "Oh, poor old honeybun! Never mind. You'll be seeing her soon."

It is small comfort. But he means well. I force myself back into the role of concerned daughter.

"I have no idea what to get her for Christmas. Chocolates, I suppose."

"Sounds like a plan," he says. "We'll have to buy lots of expensive rubbish for all your nephews and nieces as well, I suppose?"

I nod. "Yup. I'll have to ring Vic again and find out what gimmicks they're into this year."

"Why don't you give her a ring now?"

I sigh and stroke my tummy. "Too full to move. Later."

He picks up the TV remote and starts channel-hopping. I watch the screen, retreating back into my thoughts.

29
DAN

I rang Roe Deer.

I said that I was now possessed of the fact that we had a son and, this being the case (I paused to give her an opportunity to deny it, but she didn't), I thought it was high time I met him. Ideally this would have happened at his birth and I couldn't pretend to understand why she'd kept it from me all these years, but still, that was then and now is now. You can't do anything about then, but you can do something about now. And the thing I was proposing to do was to come and see him.

What she said was this: "Who told you?"

I told her that my sister Jo had told me, but the person who told her was Ellie Jacobs the Exmoor Housewife.

"I thought as much," was what she said, and her voice sounded short and hot.

I gathered (because I can sometimes gather things) that Roe Deer had not wanted her secret to come out. She had wanted it to stay in the bag, like a cat. But, like the cat, the secret was getting extremely cramped and uncomfortable in the bag and wanted very, very badly to get out. And now that it had got itself out, there was nothing Roe Deer could do about it.

I also gathered that Roe Deer was cross with Ellie. She was so cross with Ellie that she couldn't find the words to express it. She was so cross with Ellie that her crossness was seething and bubbling inside her. Her crossness with Ellie was volcanic.

30
ELLIE

The phone made me jump.

I was propelled into sudden panicky action, but Clive, who was sitting right beside it, picked up the receiver first.

"Hello . . . ?"

He smiled across at me. "Yes, I'm Ellie's husband. Would you like to speak with her? Who's calling, please? Her — excuse me, what did you say? Her *harp teacher*?" His eyes bore holes in me across the room. "I wasn't aware she was having harp lessons."

I waited, transfixed, heat rising up my neck and into my face.

"No, not at all. It's not your fault. What did you say your name was? . . . Rhoda . . ."

Oh God, what was she saying?

". . . No, I'm afraid she never even mentioned you. But I expect she had her reasons."

I felt an interrogation coming on.

"No, don't feel awkward . . . The Exmoor

Harpmaker? . . . Actually, I have."

There was a long gap in which Clive's face steadily grew darker and darker.

"I see . . . Well, thanks for filling me in. This is all very interesting."

I scarcely dared look at him. He was looking at me all right, though. "Would you like to talk to her? She's here now."

I wobbled to my feet, but he shook his head at me, glaring. "No? You wouldn't? . . . Yes, you're absolutely right. My wife and I do need to talk . . . No, you haven't. I would have found out sooner or later anyway . . . OK, then. It's been very — nice talking to you, Rhoda. Good-bye."

He replaced the receiver oh so slowly and carefully. I was in for it now.

"Clive . . ." I made an attempt to hug him, but it was like trying to cuddle a stone.

"Apparently," he snarled, "apparently you have been having harp lessons. For quite some time. Apparently you have been playing a harp made by the so-called Harpmaker of Exmoor. Apparently you go and visit him often — almost every day."

"It's not like that," I whimpered.

"Well, what is it like, then?" he said through his teeth.

"It's because of the harp!" I gulped. "You remember. The one he gave me . . . tried to give me. I loved it so much and he meant so well and . . . I was in an impossible situation. He made me play it. And the sound was so . . . All I wanted was . . . I only didn't tell you because I knew you would disapprove. But — Clive, you have to believe me! He's a lovely person, that's all. It's quite innocent, I swear. It's not about him, it's about the harp."

The blood was beating in my cheeks all the more because I knew I was being economical with the truth. The truth had become a complicated tangled mass of feeling that couldn't easily be put into words.

"What the hell's going on?"

"Nothing. Nothing but a little harp practice." I tried to laugh.

"If it was *nothing but a little harp practice* why the hell didn't you tell me?"

"Because you would have argued me out of it and I wanted the, the harp so, so badly."

"You wanted the, the harp so, so badly!" he mimicked.

"Sorry," I whispered.

I could hear my heart thumping in the grim silence that followed.

He took the poker and jabbed at the fire. "I don't think I know you at all," he said.

I had never heard such venom in his voice.

31
DAN

He is smaller than I am expecting. He has hair the color of coal and eyes the color of the midnight sky, with stars. He is wearing blue trousers and green socks and a thick sweater, green with blue stripes. Roe Deer's mother shows me into the sitting room, where he is perched on the sofa, a wooden truck clutched in his hands.

"Edward, this is a nice man who has come to see you. His name is Dan Hollis and he is a harpmaker." Roe Deer's mother has a voice that is very stiff and controlled. She has artificial waves in her hair, equally stiff and controlled. She is too thin. She walks in a very upright way, as if somebody has pushed a ramrod down her back.

The boy stands up and comes toward me. He transfers his truck to his left hand and puts his right hand out to me. I shake it. It is a small hand, very, but warm.

According to Roe Deer and Roe Deer's

parents I am not supposed to tell him I am his father. But sometimes I do things I am not supposed to do.

"Hello, I'm your father," I say.

His mouth shapes itself like an O. I can feel the thing in my heart yanking at me again, very hard.

"Are you?" he asks.

"Yes," I tell him. "I am. Which means that you are my son."

We contemplate each other for a while. Roe Deer's mother did a gasping thing when I said the word "father" and my son and I are aware of her hovering in the background, wringing her hands, but neither of us pay her any attention.

"This is my truck," he says, proffering it. "Do you like it?"

I examine it, run it along on the carpet a little way to try out its wheels, then pronounce it to be a good one.

"I've got a train too," he tells me.

I declare my delight and astonishment.

"It goes around on my bedroom floor."

"Does it really?" I ask.

"Yes!" he answers. Then he says: "Would you like to come and see it?"

I say that I would.

He takes my hand and leads me past his gaping grandmother and upstairs.

Perhaps I should point out here that Roe Deer is not happy about my visiting Ed. She told me on the phone that I must not on any account visit him. I told her that, no matter what she said, visiting Ed was exactly what I was going to do. I had not visited him for five years and it was high time I did. Moreover, I knew he was living with her parents and I knew where they lived, so if she tried to prevent me, she would find it difficult.

"Oh, all right, do what you like!" She sighed. "But don't blame me if it all ends in tears!"

I promised not to blame her. I might blame her for other things, but I wouldn't blame her for that.

"I'll tell my mum you are coming. After school tomorrow should be all right."

I said that suited me fine.

"I won't be there," she said, and her voice was acidic.

I said this was probably a good thing, as various strong forces were now battling inside me and if I saw her again right now the forces might get the better of me and I might not be responsible for my actions. And I did not want the first occasion that I set eyes on my son to be a scene of physical violence.

She laughed. "Physical violence! Dan, you wouldn't hurt a fly!"

I said this was true, I wouldn't hurt a fly, but I was more and more inclined to hurl my fists at *her,* which I suspected might hurt rather considerably.

She was quiet for a bit then. I was going to put the phone down, but then she said, "Look, Dan. I can't stop you going to see him, but remember he's my child too. I do have a say in things. And I don't want him to know right now that you're his father. Perhaps when he's older, but not now. OK?"

I didn't really think that it was OK, so at this point I did put the phone down.

Upstairs in Roe Deer's parents' house in Taunton, in the room that my son Edward sleeps in and calls his bedroom, I am making some important discoveries. I've found out that Edward my son likes pebbles, wooden trucks, trains, airplanes, trees, music, football, feathers, mud, sandwiches, animals, snow and puddles. Ten of those things are things that I like too. Ten out of thirteen is over seventy-six point nine percent, which is a good proportion. We have agreed that we should be friends.

Edward's train is a good train, as trains go. It has green, red and blue carriages and makes a satisfactory clicking sound as it goes round the track. It is not noisy and crowded like real trains. In fact, there seems to be nobody on it at all.

I mention this fact to my son Ed.

"I sometimes sit my rabbit on the top of it," he tells me.

I say what a good idea that is.

"Do you have a rabbit too?" he asks me.

I inform him that sadly I have no rabbit, but I do have a pheasant. My pheasant is called Phineas and he likes peanut butter sandwiches and harp music. I do not think he would like to ride on a train, though. He did not much like being in a car, but on that occasion he had just been shot, so the circumstances were unusual. Ed nods as if he absolutely understands these things.

I then ask Ed if I might be introduced to his rabbit. He reaches up to a shelf where various animals are assembled. The rabbit is orange and has spiky whiskers and one ear that is floppier than the other.

Ed takes the rabbit down and strokes its nose. "Rabbit, this is my father. Father, this is my rabbit."

We shake hands/paws earnestly.

I ask Mr. Rabbit which of the train's carriages is his preferred carriage for sitting on. Mr. Rabbit looks down at the train and then answers me in a squeaky voice: "The front one, of course!"

I state that clearly he is a very brave rabbit, if this is true. Perhaps he would like to demonstrate?

So Mr. Rabbit hops on and the train starts off again. Mr. Rabbit has wedged his bottom in, and he manages to balance quite well when you bear in mind the speed at which he is traveling. But then the train goes round a bend and he suddenly flops over to one side. He continues at right angles to the carriage for another fifteen centimeters or so, then he and the train part company.

"Don't worry, he isn't hurt. He sometimes does that," explains Ed. "He sees a bit of carpet that he likes the look of, and he just has to get off straightaway. He can't wait for the train to stop."

Mr. Rabbit is now examining his favored bit of carpet very closely, so we leave him to it and concentrate on the train again. We make it go round another twelve times, then take the track apart and put it together again a different way and run the train round it twenty-five times, then take the track apart and put it together again a different way and run the train round thirty times.

Edward asks me a question while we are

driving his train around. His question is this: "If you are my father, then are you married to my mother?"

I tell him no.

"Why not?"

My answer is this: that his mother used to be my girlfriend but that she changed her mind about it some time ago. Which is a pity in some ways, but there isn't much I can do about it. She has only recently informed me of the fact. I apologize to Ed for not getting in touch sooner, but his existence is another fact that I have only recently become aware of.

He pulls one of the carriages off the train. "Why am I living with Nan and Gramps and not with you and my mother?"

I pick Mr. Rabbit up off the floor and tell him his whiskers are very fine indeed.

Ed firmly takes Mr. Rabbit and sits him facing me. "You haven't answered my question," he says.

He is an astute boy. I tell him this.

"What does 'astute' mean?" he says.

"Clever and wise and able to see through things and people."

"Is it good to be astute?" he asks me.

"It can be," I say. "Sometimes."

"So what's the answer?" he asks.

I sit cross-legged on the floor beside him.

Normally I do not hesitate to tell the truth because normally it seems like a good idea. I want him to know the truth very much, just as I want to know it myself. However, I suspect that the truth in this matter is an unkind truth. Also I know that Roe Deer is already cross with me, her parents are cross with me and I have done a lot of things that I'm not supposed to do. Probably quite enough for one day.

My son is looking at me, his face all wide-eyed and shaped like a great big question.

I pat him on the head.

"You will find out one day," I say.

32
ELLIE

"Been playing the harp today, have you?"

He makes it sound like a crime.

"Yes," I confess.

It's been three days now and Clive hasn't said a word to me except "Pass the salt." Pointedly, with no "please." A proper question is at least a step in the right direction. It gives me hope that he might be getting lonely on the moral high ground. He takes a swig of beer from the bottle and throws another log onto the fire. A few sparks fly out.

I normally enjoy our cozy winter evenings reading or watching TV with the fire lit and the wind raging outside, but now the atmosphere between us is so taut it's impossible to relax even for a moment.

I wouldn't have ventured back to the barn at all, but I was worried about Dan and desperate to know what he's decided to do about his son. I tried ringing, but he didn't answer my calls. Eventually I drove up to the barn while Clive was at work to find out what was going on and offer support if I could.

Dan has already been to see his son in Taunton. It sounds as though Ed was pretty pleased to have found his father, just as Dan was pleased to have found his son. I couldn't bring myself to ask how things are between him and Rhoda, but I noticed a transformation in Dan. Unlike the last time I saw him, his eyes were brightly lit and seemed even huger than usual. He went about all his normal harpmaking and sandwich-serving routines with a new briskness and bounce. He seemed too absorbed in his own thoughts to talk much. I went upstairs and attempted some harp practice, but my fingers seemed to have got rusty and I couldn't focus. The notes sounded jagged and disjointed, not like music at all.

I'm sure Rhoda rang Clive to get me into trouble. She must know it was me who let her secret out. She doesn't want me anywhere near her son . . . or the father of her son. I'm longing to see Dan with his little boy, but now, caged in as I am by Clive's suspicions, I'm not sure that is ever going to happen.

Clive picks up the poker. "My harp-playing wife," he growls. "I suppose you fancy yourself as an angel or something."

"No, of course not!"

Is he ever going to forgive me? But I can't really blame him. I haven't even forgiven myself. I should have told him long ago. My life is full of should-haves.

I battle with my regrets, rally a little and realize I've missed a trick. I muster what's supposed to be a charming smile. "Clive, I wanted it all to be a lovely surprise for you once I'd learned to play properly. I thought I'd . . . I'd serenade you or something."

My attempt at humor falls flat.

"Nice try, but that's not what you said before. You said you thought I'd disapprove. Why would I do that, I wonder?"

I am such an idiot. Why can I never think of the right thing to say at the right time? I close my eyes.

When I open them Clive is standing in front of me, the firelight casting patterns over his face. He looks utterly miserable. I curse myself. I ought to be working out how to mend the hurt I've caused him, but even now half of me is elsewhere, worrying about Dan, worrying about Rhoda.

Clive addresses the flames. "That harp teacher told me you were getting really good at it. Thanks to your many, many visits up the hill to the harpmaker's place."

"The Harp Barn. Yes. That's where the harp is," I point out. "Although —" I am about to say I could actually bring the harp back home, but realize that absolutely isn't what I want to do, so I shut my mouth again.

"I suppose that's where you've been going on Saturdays and Sundays too? When you said you were visiting Christina."

"Yes," I whimper. "But only because Dan was injured. He needed help with his bandages."

"Dan." He draws the word out torturously, as if examining all its implications. "Dan was injured?"

"Yes, very badly. He was shot in the leg. It was a silly accident when he was out on the moor. There wasn't anyone else to help him." I think of Jo, of Rhoda, of Dan's friend Thomas the postman and I wonder again how much I am stretching the truth in my anxiety to defend myself.

"So I presume Christina never cut her hand? The whole thing about her and the can opener was entirely made up?"

"Yes. I'm sorry, I just couldn't find a way to tell you. It was all so complicated."

He stabs a log with the poker. Orange reflections flicker in his eyes. "God, Ellie. I never would have believed you capable of such lies."

There is bitter disappointment churning around with his anger. I've never felt so bad in my life. If only he would just hit me with the poker and put me out of my misery.

"So do I ever get to hear your harp playing? Or is that only for other, more important people?"

Tears spring to my eyes. "Oh, Clive!"

He stands up, propping the poker in the corner of the fireplace. Finally he looks at me. "What's the matter?" he says icily.

"I'm sorry," I sob. "I'm just so, so sorry! I can't tell you how sorry I am!" I hate my tears. I wish I could get a grip on myself.

He sits down in the chair opposite me, takes another swig of beer and picks up the newspaper. He starts turning pages. I wonder whether to go upstairs and bite my pillow or whether to sit it out. I decide to go for the latter. I gulp down my emotions and pick up a book. The words dance in front of my eyes, which are in any case too full to read them.

"Where is this place, anyway?" he asks suddenly.

"The Harp Barn?"

"No, Timbuktu!" he sneers. "Of course the Harp Barn. I googled it, but there was no address. I saw the photos of your fancy man, though. Very pretty."

I gasp. If he's been digging around for information behind my back it's even worse than I thought. "Clive, you have to believe me. He's not my fancy man! If you knew Dan, you'd understand."

"Well, I don't know Dan, do I?"

I view him sorrowfully. "I'd be happy to drive you up to the barn anytime you like."

He scowls and retreats behind his newspaper.

Five minutes later he is out of it again.

"OK, then. Take me there now."

I look at my watch, alarmed. "Well, it's getting rather late. I don't know what time Dan goes to bed. Perhaps . . ." The words die on my lips. "Whatever you like," I tell him.

33
DAN

I'd made coffee and wafted it around a bit so that the aroma hung pleasantly in the air. Phineas was nestling comfortably in his bed. Soon I would be off to bed too, but I was doing a little extra work on the *Fifi* harp, as it is not so long until Christmas now and Mike Thornton keeps ringing me to ask if it's nearly ready. The *Fifi* harp is not nearly ready, but the nearly stage will be soon now because I have finally got some momentum going.

Apple wood is dense and has fine pores, but it glues, stains and turns well. Mike Thornton's wood is grayish with a regular graining and some darker streaks. Its scent is sweet, calming, just a little fruity.

As I was shaping the apple wood for the soundboard I was not thinking about the *Fifi* harp, though. What I was thinking about was my son Ed. Him and his train and his rabbit and the things he said to me.

In the middle of those thoughts there came a very quiet knock at the door. I was surprised because it was dark and frosty outside and people do not normally come out here to buy harps in such conditions. So I assumed it was just a twig that had blown against the door in the wind. But then the knock came again. I went over and opened the door. And there in front of me was Ellie Jacobs the Exmoor Housewife.

"Ellie!" I cried, seizing her hand. I was feeling enthusiastic and excited with all the things I had been thinking about Ed my son, which is the reason I did this. Also because I was glad to see her. But Ellie's hand was rather cold and limp. Her face looked cold and limp too.

"Hi, Dan," she said in a voice drained of color. She moved to one side slightly and I saw there was a man standing in the gloom behind her. He was large. He had a square sort of face and not very much in the way of hair. He was in a big, dark coat.

"This is Clive, my husband," said Ellie. "He wanted to meet you and to see the Harp Barn. Sorry, I, er, hope it's not too late in the evening . . ."

I assured her that it wasn't, not at all. I put on my biggest smile because that was the way I was feeling and, besides, she

297

seemed to need cheering up. I put out my hand again and shook the hand of her husband, even though the hand had a bit of a lackluster feel to it, as if it did not want to be shaken much. I said I was pleased to meet him, as that is what you are supposed to say. I then invited them both to come inside where it was warm — well, warm*er.*

They came in.

Clive the husband of Ellie turned his head round and round to look at the barn and all the harps. He stuck his lackluster hands into his big black pockets.

Phineas is not too keen on meeting people he doesn't know. He got out of bed, flapped his wings and made a hasty exit out through the pheasant flap. Clive the husband of Ellie stared after him.

I offered my guests a drink. I offered coffee even though I'd just recently made some and tipped it down the sink, because I know Ellie likes to drink coffee and maybe her husband does too. I also offered sandwiches. I mentioned the fact that the sandwiches I was offering would be good ones. The sandwiches that I was offering would be filled with excellent jam, the jam Ellie made from my plums, as there was still a bit of it left.

The Clive man swiveled on the spot and

looked at Ellie. His eyebrows were very close together and his mouth was a straight line.

I repeated my offer.

"Not for me, thank you," Ellie then replied very quickly. A little lump was moving down her throat.

I asked Clive if he would like some sandwiches made with the jam that Ellie his wife had made with my plums.

There was silence.

"Would you like coffee or sandwiches?" Ellie said to him. She seemed to be acting as an interpreter, even though I had spoken in plain English.

"Yes, a cup of coffee would be nice," he said finally. "And a sandwich with some of the jam Ellie made from your plums, Mr. Hollis. Funnily enough I've never tried it. I never even knew Ellie was capable of making jam."

I told him she was certainly very capable. Just as she was with so many things.

I then told Ellie to make herself at home as she always did, and to show her husband around everything as she liked, and I bounded off up the seventeen steps to make coffee and sandwiches. I was still thinking about my son Ed.

From the kitchen I heard that Ellie and

Clive had also ascended the seventeen steps and were now in the little room where Ellie practices. They were not talking very much, though.

I spread the jam thick, as it is such good jam. Today the bread was wholemeal, with seeds. Cut into rectangles. I'm not sure Clive would like triangles.

When I came into the room and handed the sandwiches (there were six) and the coffee (it was strong) to Clive Ellie's husband, he was standing by the window. He was scrutinizing Ellie's harp from a distance.

"You remember it from before, don't you, Clive? Lovely, isn't it?" said Ellie in a mouselike voice.

"So this is where you play every day?" he asked.

"Um, yes, often I do," she said. "While Dan makes harps downstairs in the workshop." She said the words "downstairs" and "workshop" louder than the rest of the sentence.

Clive walked up to the harp. In one rapid movement he raised a hand over the harp. I saw Ellie flinch. Clive then moved his hand down again and rested it for a second on the curve of the harp's neck.

"Very lovely," he said. His voice somehow did not seem to echo the sentiment, though.

His voice was all snagged up with brambles.

Ellie made a little noise at the back of her throat. I informed Clive that Ellie's harp was one of the best harps I'd ever made. I told him I had made it out of cherrywood. I had selected it especially for Ellie because, although cherry was not her favorite tree (that was birch) she sometimes wore cherry-colored socks and I thought she had an affinity with the wood. Also because the harp had a very lovely and unique voice and resonance that seemed to fit Ellie particularly well. As had been proved by her learning to play it so fast.

Clive fixed his eyes on Ellie.

"Play it!" he said.

These are the exact words I had said to Ellie to persuade her to keep the harp when I first gave it to her. However, I had not said the words in the way that Clive Ellie's husband said them now.

Ellie pulled up the chair behind the harp and perched on it. She took a deep breath. Then she started to play "Scarborough Fair." Normally she can play it pretty well, but she was having some problems with her fingers. They seemed to be shaking violently and hitting all the wrong strings.

Clive stood with his arms crossed over his chest and listened. "Very good. Very lovely," he said when she had finished. "I am proud of you." He took a bite out of a sandwich. "The jam is good too. You have so many hidden talents."

I smiled at him. I did not feel a hundred percent comfortable in his presence, but it is good that he appreciates Ellie.

Ellie looked at her husband with shiny eyes. "I — er — the jam was to . . . I wanted to say thank you to Dan for letting me play his harp here so often."

"*Your* harp," I corrected.

"*Your* harp," Clive repeated, licking the jam off his fingers one by one. Ellie looked down at her socks. Today they were black.

Clive seemed to be enjoying the jam, so I offered him the rest of the pot to take home.

"I wouldn't dream of it," he said.

Ellie then turned to me and asked, "How's Ed?"

Ellie asked me about Ed only this morning, so I was a little surprised at this question. But before I had a chance to reply, she said to her husband: "Ed is Dan's son."

Clive turned to me. "Your son?" he said.

"My son," I confirmed. "Ed." I like to say these words. They are becoming my very favorite words to say.

I told them my son Ed was very well and was going to come out and visit me here at the Harp Barn soon, which was a fact that made me very glad indeed.

"With his mother?" Ellie asked quickly. "His mother is my harp teacher, Clive; the very beautiful and accomplished Rhoda — the lady who you spoke to on the phone."

Clive grunted. "She's your wife?" he asked.

I presumed this last question was addressed to me, although he was looking at Ellie. I explained that Roe Deer was not and nor had she ever been my wife, but she had once been my girlfriend. However, she was not my girlfriend at present. She had in fact not been my girlfriend for five whole years.

"I see," he said. "Not for five years."

Ellie looked as if she was about to say something, because her mouth opened just a little, but nothing came out of it. Her husband was still looking at her. I expect he likes looking at her a lot.

"Well, Ellie," he said at last. "It's getting late. And I have to be up early to go to work tomorrow. I think we had better leave your — friend — to his harpmaking." He paused, and then added: "Unless, of course, you want to stay?"

"No, no, of course not!" She shook her head and puckered up her face in a peculiar way. "Dan, we'll leave you to it. Thank you so much for your hospitality, and so sorry for the intrusion."

I said not at all and what a delight it had been to see them.

34
ELLIE

I got out of bed slowly. Clive had just left the house for work. He hadn't said good-bye.

I was feeling slightly sick. I wandered to the bedroom window in my dressing gown and looked out. He was still in the driveway, busily squirting deicer onto his car wind-screen, his breath a white plume in the cold air. His face had a yellowish tinge to it and, even from here, I could see the big bags under his eyes. He had silently poured himself out a whiskey when we got back home last night. Then another. Then another.

As he was giving the windows a final wipe I saw Pauline come out of the house next door with a shopping bag. She shuffled toward her own car, calling out a good morning to him, then something else. He walked across and handed the canister of deicer to her over the fence. They exchanged a word or two. She shook the canister, gave her windscreen a good spray and then walked back toward him. As she returned it she cocked her head to one side and said something. He seemed to ask her a question. I watched her giving a very full answer. As she was speaking, she pointed up the hill in the direction of the Harp Barn, waggling her head from side to side. Clive suddenly glanced up at our bedroom window and saw me there, watching. I lifted my hand to wave, but he didn't wave back. He scowled, threw another comment to Pauline, then got into his car, slamming the door. He revved up the engine and shot down the road at a ridiculous speed.

There are days and days of frosty silence. The only conversations we have are laced with snubs and cutting comments. I do all that I can. I cook all Clive's favorite meals. I make an effort with my appearance, applying lipstick and mascara, and wearing the prettiest clothes that cold weather will allow. I attempt the few seduction techniques I know about, but they fail totally. Even Sunday afternoon sex has been frozen out.

I have stopped going to the Harp Barn — to prove a point, I suppose — but that is making me even more miserable. Clive never asks about it, so it seems a vain sacrifice. In the end I decide to tell him.

"Just in case you're interested, I haven't been to the Harp Barn for weeks."

"Why?" he asks, as if it wasn't obvious.

"Because . . . well, because I thought you didn't like me going there."

He won't look at me. "Why should I care? You can do what you want. You do anyway."

"Look, I'm doing my best to make things right between us. I've said I'm sorry a million times. I've stopped playing the harp, even though I love it" — this is a mistake and I realize it the moment it has slipped out of my mouth, so I rush on — "and I'm trying to make up for everything because I know I was in the wrong. I do know it. I'm so unhappy when we're like this. But what more can I do?"

"If you *love playing the harp,* why don't you go and play it? You're being a martyr now as well as an angel, I suppose."

"No!" I cry. Being a traitor is quite enough for me. "Clive, please. I love you so much! Let's just go back to being the way we were before."

The "I love you so much" sounds high and false, more like desperation than affection. Clive raises his eyes and looks me in the face at last, but it is a look of disgust.

It's easy to see what he is thinking. The idea was planted in his head by Rhoda and fed by Pauline's insinuations and the wild whirrings of his brain. My own guilty behavior, my blushes, my picking at my eyebrows, my every word and move is interpreted as further confirmation. Our one joint visit to the barn made matters worse. Clive did not see what I wanted him to see — all Dan's peculiarities and eccentricities, his self-sufficiency, his other-worldliness. He saw only what he dreaded most — that Dan is devastatingly attractive and that he knows me inside out.

Clive has suffered betrayal before, from my friend Jayne all those years ago. He trusted her and loved her absolutely, and she walked all over him. She took delight in sleeping with other men whenever his back was turned. When he finally found out, he was wounded to the core. The scars are deep.

Now he thinks it is happening all over again. On the one hand I'm appalled that he could suspect me of such a thing, but on the other I feel for him. If only he would let me reach out to him, if only he would believe me! I can't think of any way to convince him of the innocent truth. It is tearing us both to pieces.

"Clive, I swear to you on whatever you like — on the Bible, on my father's grave, on all that is holy — I am not having an affair with the harpmaker."

He turns away. "Isn't it time for supper?"

The cold went on and on, inside and out. It was hard to bear. Part of me just wanted to die.

I rang Christina. "Can I come over?"

"Of course!" she said. "Still being horrible, is he?"

"Yes. It's his way of dealing with pain. I don't know what to do," I confessed. "Where will it end?"

"He'll come round. He adores you, Ellie. Always has done, always will."

I wasn't so sure.

"We'll talk it over. I'll see you in twenty. I'll get the kettle on!"

It was a bleak day. The trees were skeletal and dripped dankness and grayness. The hills were shrouded in mist. The car radio wasn't working so I couldn't put on any upbeat music to try and cheer myself up. I drove past a pheasant corpse on the road, bloodied and half-eaten by buzzards. It made me think of Phineas. God, I was even missing the pheasant!

What was going on up there, up at the barn? Dan and Ed were bonding . . . but what of Dan and Rhoda? I couldn't bear to think of it.

I'd had a short spell of happiness, of dazzling, uplifting joy to the soundtrack of harp music. I'd experienced the miracle of creativity. I'd started to see the world through new eyes. But now my own clumsiness had robbed me of it all. Not only that; I'd lost Clive's trust forever.

I drove through the villages and drew into Christina's lane. What a relief! I felt cheered seeing her little cottage ahead of me. There were fairy lights strung round the windows and a homemade Christmas wreath hanging on the door. I stepped up and rang the bell. My heart lifted at the prospect of some proper human interaction. But it sank again the minute I saw her. Her face was blotchy and tear stained. She grasped me in a tight hug.

"Christina, what's wrong?"

She wailed into my shoulder. "I'm so glad you're here, Ellie! I feel totally wretched. Alex has just rung and told me he isn't bringing his girlfriend home for Christmas after all! I won't even see him! They're going off to Switzerland, to her parents instead. I can't believe he's being so selfish!

And he knows how I get. He knows how low I always feel at this time of year."

I gave her another squeeze. "Maybe he'll change his mind." It was the only comforting thing I could think of to say.

"He won't," she sobbed. "I know he won't. He's in her clutches and that's what she wants, so that's what he does! Mum doesn't matter anymore. Anyway, come in."

I stepped into the hall and took off my coat. At least it felt snug inside. Christina's central heating is far more generous than ours, and she has an Aga too.

"It looks nice in here," I told her. She'd already got up a Christmas tree, twinkling with lights and her special red and gold handmade baubles.

"Thank you." She sniffed. "But what's the point? There's only me who'll ever see it."

"*I'm* seeing it," I said.

"OK, two people, then."

I prodded one of the baubles. "I'd bring Clive round, but I don't think you'd enjoy his company very much at the moment."

She gave me another hug, both of us crying now.

She pulled away, wiping her eyes. "Look at us!"

"Pathetic, isn't it," I agreed, wiping mine.

"Tea, tea, tea!" she said, heading for the

kitchen. I followed her. Jewelry-making odd-ments were scattered across the table. Meow was curled up on the chair nearest the Aga.

Christina grabbed mugs and biscuits. "It's bound to get us down. Seasonal affective disorder, Christmas and men behaving badly all at the same time."

I sank into a chair and started playing with a length of silver chain. "So Alex must be serious about this girlfriend."

"I suppose so. He won't tell me anything about her, though. Apart from the fact that she likes horse riding."

"Tell him to bring her down here to show off the Exmoor ponies."

"I've tried that. No good. Her parents obviously have something I haven't got. So I'll be here all by myself."

I wished I could do something to help. "Why don't *you* go away somewhere?" I suggested. "You could get one of those cheapo, last-minute flights. You could escape from England and go somewhere for a bit of winter sun. If Alex is going to be in Switzerland, why don't you beat him at his own game? Go somewhere better, brighter, sunnier."

She lifted the lid of the teapot to examine the color of what was inside. She gave it a vigorous stir. "I like your way of thinking, Ellie," she said. "Do you know, I think I might just do that." She glanced across at her cat. "Cattery for you, Meow! Sun, sea and sex for me!"

"I think I'll come too," I said, without thinking.

"Hey, do!"

I shook my head.

"I'm serious!" she cried. "Let's just take off somewhere and leave our troubles behind. I need sunshine and can't bear to be alone at Christmas. You need sunshine and can't bear to be with your husband at Christmas!"

I prodded her jewelry about the table. "Well . . . it's not quite as simple as that."

"It is! I wouldn't get in your hair, I promise. We could be quite independent once we arrive wherever it is. I might find some horny beach bum, after all — you never know! So might you! That would give that husband of yours something to think about!"

"Christina, my aim is to patch things up with Clive, not to make them worse."

She was silent for a moment. "Ellie, I admire your tenacity, but is it worth it?"

"What do you mean?"

"Your marriage. Is it worth it? Really?"

She doesn't get it. With her string of broken relationships, she can't see it. The way marriage works. The strength you need. I thought of my father. By example, he taught me so much about strength, about endurance, about how to weather the cold.

But it's easier for me than it was for him. Deep down I'm sure this winter of discontent can't go on for much longer. I don't believe it's in Clive's true nature, this terrible coldness.

"Christina, I love Clive. I do. I couldn't imagine life without him. And I believe in marriage. I don't think it's right just to give up the minute things get a bit sticky."

I knew as well that I'd be desperately lonely if I had to live by myself as she did. Perhaps even more lonely than her.

"You have staying power, I'll give you that," she said. "But Clive will soon learn to appreciate you if he's left to his own devices for a bit. A few days of arriving home to no dinner on the table and he'll be on his knees begging you to come back."

I shuddered. "I'd rather not risk it, if you don't mind. Besides, we're supposed to be going up to Yorkshire, to Vic's."

"Please, Ellie! Come abroad with me! I won't give you your cup of tea otherwise!"

I took the cuppa firmly from her. "Sorry,

Christina. I've told Vic we're going. I can't let her and her family down. And there's Mum."

I hoped being among family might smooth things over between Clive and me. But I was beginning to worry that he'd refuse to come up to Yorkshire. Although he gets on all right with Vic and Alan and their children, they are my family, after all, not his.

"Not tempted by the Bahamas? Or Mauritius? Or Thailand? I've always fancied Thailand."

"You go," I said. "Go and enjoy it for both of us. I can't just run away from the situation with Clive. It's all my fault it's got like this; it would be irresponsible and mean to take off and leave him right now."

"Oh, just be irresponsible and mean for a change!"

"Christina, I can't! And I won't!"

35
DAN

Roe Deer rang me and gave me what is called an "earful." My ears (both of them) were certainly full for a long time afterward. Full of words that were as scratchy as gorse bushes. Some were words I sincerely hope she will never use in front of my son Ed. The gist of those words was that she is cross. Cross that Ed knows I am his father, cross that I told him so straightaway without even consulting her. I wasn't supposed to do that. It has ruined everything.

"What everything?" I asked her.

"You really have no idea, have you?" she fumed. "You always were idiotic. Nonsensical! Head-in-the-clouds! You have no grasp of reality. Which is exactly why I didn't want you to mess about with Ed's life. He has enough problems without having the worry of a father like you."

I mentioned that Ed did not appear to be worried in the least. On the contrary, Ed was happy to have met me (I knew this because he told me so himself and he strikes me as being a truthful boy). I also suggested quietly that perhaps a father like me was better than no father at all. Just as I also suspected that a mother like her was better than no mother at all.

She did not seem to like this comment. At least, I presume that is why the phone cut off at this point in the conversation.

She rang back ten minutes later, however. "I didn't want to tell Ed about you until it was the right time," she said. "This is *not* the right time."

"For him or for you?" I asked.

"For him, of course. It takes sensitivity to handle an issue like this. As for me, it's actually the worst possible time for me as well. My feelings are unimportant, my career doesn't matter *in the least,* but I never asked to be a mother, did I? It was a mistake, but I didn't realize until it was too late. Now everything's so difficult for me. I've struggled with this for years. 'Single mother' just isn't me. 'Harpist' is what's me — and it's so much better if people see me that way."

Considering this was all about Ed, she seemed to be repeating the words "I," "my" and "me" an awful lot.

I waited to see if she had anything else to

317

add. She did: "And the last thing I needed was interference from *you* now, just when my own engagement is on the cards."

"Which cards?" I asked. "Engagement to who?"

"A man, OK? A guitarist. He and I are *made* for each other and I want to marry him. I have to do it before he finds out about Ed. I don't want this whole thing to put him off. He might think I'm more involved than I actually am; he might think there are too many strings attached."

I'd have thought that a harpist and guitarist would inevitably have plenty of strings attached.

I was about to tell her this, but Roe Deer started talking in a very loud voice about Ed's upkeep and how all the money she earned from harp playing went toward Ed's upkeep and how, morally speaking, I should be paying toward Ed's upkeep.

I pointed out that if she had informed me of Ed's existence as soon as it had happened, I would have been glad to pay toward his upkeep straightaway and keep doing it for the rest of my life — but she hadn't, so I didn't. If you don't know about things, you can't do anything to fix them.

Now, however, I knew of Ed's existence and of course I was more than happy to pay for as much of his upkeep as I possibly could. Upkeep was a bit of a mystery to me and I had no idea how much upkeep cost, but I would certainly start making extra harps, as many harps as it took. My sister Jo, I was sure, would help me sell them using my website. Jo had heard all about Ed and was keen to meet him soon. She would no doubt strive to improve my financial situation with all her business skills once she realized I was putting money toward such a worthy cause. I would churn out harps and every penny of my harp money would be spent on Ed's upkeep. From this point onward Ed's upkeep would be my priority in life. Perhaps this meant Roe Deer could marry Guitar Man and stop worrying.

"I'm still cross with you, Dan," she said.

Roe Deer's parents are not unkind people, I would say, even if they don't have much idea about what Ed needs. They seem to think what he needs is plenty of exams and money and computerized gizmos. They don't seem to realize that what he needs more is plenty of trees and fresh air and music.

I'll say this in their favor, though. Ed's grandparents have been helpful. When he asked them if they could bring him to the

Harp Barn to visit me, what they said was yes, they could. They did this on a Saturday morning at ten thirty-six.

Ed has big eyes anyway, but they grew even bigger when he came in.

"Dan — Dad!" he cried.

I liked that.

He inspected every harp in turn, plucking a few strings of each one and knocking the soundboard gently to see if it could double up as a drum. The grandparents stood around in the background. It seemed to be their role in life.

At last Ed turned to me.

"Can you make trains too?" is what he said.

The structure of a smallish train would be simpler than the structure of a harp. And the mechanism to make it run, once I had acquired the necessary bits and pieces, would not be difficult to install. Making trains could possibly become another branch of my business, under Ed's supervision. Although then I would have to rename the Harp Barn and call it the Harp and Train Barn. Or the Train and Harp Barn. Which would be better? I wondered. My sister Jo would know. Thomas would have an opinion too. So would Ellie, and that very quiet husband of hers who came to visit here the other week. I could also consult Roe Deer and Roe Deer's parents. Most of all, I could consult Ed. What a lot of people I now had to consult.

"Yes," I said.

I made coffee for the grandparents and sat them in the warmth by the fire, as Jo had told me that grandparents get cold and they like coffee and it is a good idea to keep them comfortable. Ed and I did not have coffee or sit by the fire, as we were far more interested in looking at harps. Then it was time to feed Phineas so we stepped outside, taking the medieval *Lapwing* harp with us. The air was sharp and there was a scent of pine trees, nice and tangy. I played an F minor chord on the harp and Phineas came scooting across the yard to meet us.

I introduced Phineas to Ed and Ed to Phineas. Both seemed delighted to meet one another. Phineas ate his lunch out of Ed's hand.

"Dad, will you teach me to play an F minor chord, please?" said Ed. Ed has seen Roe Deer play the harp and has tried it out himself a few times, but he wasn't yet able to play an F minor chord.

So I taught him there and then, out in the orchard. Our fingers were cold, but we were too busy to notice. Ed has very small fingers and they don't seem to want to go into the right places, so teaching him the F minor chord took some time. About twenty minutes. Phineas was going demented. I think he thought that each time he heard anything resembling the chord he should get another helping of lunch. He did get quite a bit more than usual because Ed was sorry for him. I had to tell Ed that Phineas needed to watch his weight. If he got much tubbier he would not be able to fly at all, and his flying was pretty lopsided as it was, with his injury and everything.

Then something happened and what happened was this: Because it was so cold and the *Lapwing* harp had been subjected to boy-force pressure for some time now, one of its strings (the second-octave C) suddenly twanged and broke.

I looked at Ed and Ed looked at me.

"Ouch!" he said.

I asked if he was hurt.

"No," he said, "but the harp is, isn't it?"

I said never mind, I had plenty of replacement strings and we'd soon have it sorted.

Ed pulled the broken string out of its socket. "Now I can play a harp, can I help you *make* a harp too?"

I said yes. Once I'd finished the *Fifi* harp we could make a harp together, like I did with my father when I was a boy. Ed could choose the wood and the design. We would go for a walk and find a suitable pebble together. And he could help me with sanding and threading through the strings. And he could design a motif.

"What's a motif?" he asked.

I told him it was a simple pattern such as could be carved easily in the neck or sides of a harp.

"Ah," he said. "I know what the motif is going to be!"

At that moment his grandmother and grandfather came into the orchard.

"Ah, there you are!" cried the grandmother.

I said yes, here we were.

"Thank you, Dan," she said. "It has been a very interesting time, but we really have to be getting Edward back home now."

They started dragging Ed toward their white Toyota.

But he broke loose and ran back to me and put his arms around my legs.

And he told me this thing: "I'm glad you are my dad."

I felt a peculiar pricking like dried teasels at the back of my eyes.

"Oh," is what I said.

I have finished the *Fifi* harp all except for the word "Fifi," which I have not yet carved into it. Mike Thornton has told me he will pay me an extra hundred pounds for doing this, so I will do it, even though I still think it is not a good word to engrave into a harp. I have to pay toward Ed's upkeep now.

Ed comes up to the barn every Saturday. Phineas is getting fatter and fatter. Ed likes to feed him, and plays the F minor chord quite competently. Phineas recognizes his style of playing and propels himself toward us even faster than usual because he knows he will get a massive quantity of pheasant feed from Ed.

We keep talking about the harp that we'll make together. I asked Ed if he wouldn't prefer me to make him a train, as he'd hinted he might like that, but he seems to have changed his mind. He said he already had a good train. But maybe we could make a harp with a train carved into it — as a motif? I applauded his brilliant idea and said that most certainly we could. He said it should be a steam train like the one that goes from Minehead to Bishops Lydeard and I could carve puffs of smoke coming out of its funnel to make it absolutely clear that was the type of train that it was.

I said I would happily do that. And (here I was being much more outgoing and adventurous than normal) we could also go together for a ride on a steam train to get inspiration. I am not so much a trains person, I am more of a trees person, but Ed's enthusiasm is infectious.

So one weekend we went down to Watchet together and took the train from there to Stogumber and we stopped and had tea in the station garden. That is, I had a glass of water and he had an orange juice. They didn't have sandwiches so I had a slice of cake and he had a choco-buzzle bar. We were the only people sitting outside in the garden because it was so cold. I asked Ed what he liked about steam trains and he said he liked the shiny funnel and the chuffing sound as they went along and the hoot was also good. The way he described it made me like it too, in spite of all the people and noise. I managed pretty well with the people and noise that day.

Ed is like a talisman. All the horrible things seem less horrible if I just think: "This is Ed. He is my son." So I have been thinking that a lot.

He talks about so many things, it is sometimes difficult for me to keep up with him, but he doesn't talk about his mother very much. I asked him in Stogumber if he saw her often.

"No, not often," he said.

I asked if he knew why this was.

Ed drew a pattern on the ground with his foot. "I *did* ask, but she just said, 'Reasons.' So I said, 'What reasons?' "

"Did she give you any?" I inquired. Ed told me she had eventually come up with the following:

Reason One: It is for his own good.

Reason Two: She is not a natural mother. It's just One of Those Things.

Reason Three: Gramps and Nan (her parents, Ed's grandparents) are much better at practical stuff, like cooking and organizing.

Reason Four: Gramps and Nan (her parents, Ed's grandparents) need a project to keep them going. Ed is now that project.

Reason Five: These days the family is different to how it was in the past. So long as Ed has a good place to live and a good school and good people around him, that's fine.

Reason Six: She, Roe Deer, is married to

her music and that means sacrifices have to be made.

Reason Seven: Of course she loves Ed, but the connection she feels is not as strong as she'd expected. Maybe it will be stronger when she has a more settled lifestyle.

Reason Eight: Everything is complicated.

Ed had memorized all these reasons verbatim and seemed to accept them. But I did not see that any of them was very convincing, particularly the last. And when I'd spoken to Roe Deer about it myself, the reasons she gave were quite different. They were all to do with a guitar man and strings being attached.

I asked Ed how often Roe Deer comes to visit him.

"About once a week," he answered. "She says she'd come more often but she's very, very busy."

I didn't say so, but I thought it was a bit similar when she was my girlfriend. After the first flush of excitement was over, it did tend to be about once a week, when she had nothing better to do. Maybe Roe Deer is not cut out to be a girlfriend or a mother. Maybe she is just cut out to be a really, really good harp player and so the other things get put farther down on her list. Perhaps that is OK, but perhaps it isn't. I can't help feeling that Ed should not be that far down on anyone's list.

Lists make me think of Ellie Jacobs the Exmoor Housewife, because she had a list too and harp playing was on it. She hasn't been to the barn to play her harp for a very, very long time. This worries me.

36
ELLIE

I try to write poems, but all my inspiration has dried up. I go for long wintry walks. I look at the bare trees, at the frozen patterns in the stream, at the poor birds hopping about, searching for food on the cold earth. I think of my harp, and of Dan.

I go nowhere near the Harp Barn. I can't risk it. Any wrong move could send my marriage over the edge. I wonder how Dan is doing, if he has finished his *Fifi* harp, if he is seeing much of his son. I wonder if he and Rhoda are together again. I need to let go, but I can't. I long more than ever to play the harp, to hear its soothing sounds. To lean my head against the soundboard and feel the warm touch of its wood. I wonder if I will ever go back to it. I know there will be no more lessons with Rhoda. She must hate me.

Not as much as Clive hates me at the moment, though. I'd thought that his rage would die down over time, but it just seems to be getting stronger. He stays at work very late. I put the dinner anxiously in the oven and wait, too tense to do anything. At last I hear the car engine outside. A few minutes later the front door opens. I run to meet him and try to kiss him, hoping that this will be the day the ice melts, but he brushes me aside. He dumps his briefcase in the hall and goes straight upstairs to change out of his suit. He comes down again in jeans and a sweater, goes into the sitting room. He scrunches up old copies of the *Telegraph* and his motoring magazines, places kindling round them in the grate, then strikes a match and sets fire to them in many places. He throws logs on the top, feeding the flames.

I bring his dinner through. He doesn't seem to want to eat at the table these days. We eat in complete silence, or else to the sounds of the TV. After dinner he opens the bottle of whiskey.

There are a lot of empty whiskey bottles lying in the recycling bin.

One evening about a week ago I lit the fire before he came back. I'm not very good at it, but I managed. I thought it might be warm and welcoming for him, a nice surprise. I had visions of us making love on the hearth rug as we'd done only a few weeks ago. I craved that intimacy again.

But no.

"What did you do that for?" he demanded.

"I thought I'd save you the trouble. I thought you'd be pleased."

He grimaced.

Whatever I did would be wrong. But while we were having a conversation of sorts I steeled myself to ask something that had been on my mind for a long time now.

"Um, Clive . . . are we still going up to Vic's for Christmas?"

"I'm not," he said. "You can if you like."

"But I promised Vic!"

He reached for the TV remote control. "Your problem, not mine."

"Please come with me," I tried. "They all love seeing us. They'll be so disappointed if we don't go. And . . . it's *Christmas*." I didn't dare add the season-of-goodwill bit.

"As I say, you can go. I'm staying here."

"Clive, I can't go on my own and leave you here all by yourself! That would be . . . and anyway, what would they think?"

He shrugged and switched on the TV.

I pulled out more of my eyebrows, watching him. I didn't relish the prospect of a long, solitary drive up north, but I hated to think of the crestfallen faces of my nephews and nieces, and all Vic's preparations gone to waste if I canceled. Clive was now intently gazing at a program about flatfish, so any further persuading was impossible.

"Well then" — I sighed, utterly dismayed — "in that case I'd better ring Vic and make an excuse. We'll have Christmas here, just the two of us."

I have to try. Sooner or later I'll get the old Clive back. He can't keep this up forever.

"Suit yourself," he said. "You always do, anyway."

Christmas Eve. Clive has gone out, I've no idea where. He has taken his car.

It is a bright, clear day. I open the back door and wander out. The garden is crystallized, every grass blade gleaming and glinting in the sunlight. I hug my jacket around me and breathe in the sharp air. It is invigorating. A ray of sunlight falls across my cheek. I begin to feel better.

Things have got to change soon. We can't carry on like this. And suddenly I'm sure: Clive is going to forgive me. He must. It's just the timing that matters. Of course! He is planning on leaving it until tomorrow morning, just to make Christmas all the more wonderful. Or tonight. Perhaps even now he is out shopping for some lovely present, some pretty thing that he knows I'll love. He will wrap his arms around me. He'll kiss me fervently and I'll kiss him back and everything will be all right again. We'll find a way to rebuild our relationship after these tribulations. It will be like it was before, when he bought me flowers and gave me foot massages and supported me when things went wrong. I smile as I feel a weight lift from my heart.

Since canceling the trip to Vic's I've done very little in the way of Christmas preparations, except for ordering the turkey. Now I launch myself into action. I grab the pruning shears and run down to the garden. There are holly bushes gleaming with tight clusters of berries, and there's ivy too. I cut generous sprigs, trim them to size and tie them with red ribbons. I tuck them into the bookshelves, over the pictures, along the mantelpiece, anywhere I can find to make the house look festive.

Next I pull out the Christmas box from the cupboard under the stairs. Inside is a tangle of glittering bits and pieces. I fish out streams of tinsel and string them up over the banister and around the fireplace. All our Christmas cards are lying in a heap on the kitchen windowsill. I arrange them on the cupboards and the dresser.

I notice the silver candlesticks are suffering from tarnish. I seek out the polish and buff them up till they sparkle. The candles have not been lit for a long time, but apart from a bit of dust they are all right. I survey the scene and laugh with excitement and anticipation. Perhaps it won't be the worst Christmas after all. Perhaps if we can talk things through, Clive will reconcile himself to my harp playing and I'll be able to go back to the barn sometimes. Just sometimes would be enough to get me through. I'd be happy with that. I'll aim for that.

There is no Christmas tree. Maybe Clive will bring one home today, but I'm not going to risk it. Last year's Norwegian spruce is still in a pot at the bottom of the garden. I rush out to examine it. It's a little straggly and bald in places, but nothing that a bit of tinsel won't fix. It will do. I start dragging it inside.

"Hello, Ellie!"

It is Pauline, calling over the fence, scarcely recognizable she is so bundled up in woolens.

"Hello, Pauline!"

"Everything all right, dear?"

"Everything fine! Merry Christmas!"

"Merry Christmas, dear!"

■ ■ ■

The tree, the house, the dinner — it is all perfect. I've put on my red dress. It looks good with the silver necklace Clive gave me on our last anniversary. I wink at myself in the mirror. For once I am feeling attractive.

The candles are lit and our favorite CD of Christmas music is playing. Surely he must be home soon?

I step over to the stove and give the curry another stir. Clive loves curry and this is a special recipe with saffron, raisins and almonds. Christmas Eve curry is a long-standing tradition of ours. I consult my watch, then add another few spoonfuls of stock. The curry has been on the stove so long it is beginning to dry out.

The music keeps jangling on and on. I press the stop button on the CD player and cut it dead. It's getting on my nerves.

I take the curry off the stove top. The smell is making me slightly queasy.

I blow the candles out. It is ten o'clock.

I wander into the sitting room. I've ventured to light the fire again just this once, but now it has died low. I sink into the armchair beside it and sit there, waiting and gazing into the embers.

At last I hear the front door opening. I shoot toward it.

"Clive, I was worried about you!"

One look at his face tells me that he is very, very far from forgiveness. He brushes me to one side and staggers upstairs. A whiff of whiskey trails in his wake.

I trudge upstairs. The curry is now in a Tupperware container in the fridge. Boxing Day lunch, perhaps. I am worn-out, but I somehow doubt I'll get much sleep.

Tomorrow is Christmas Day, and I'm not sure now what it will bring. I wonder if we'll be eating the turkey that's waiting, the potatoes and sprouts and parsnips, bread sauce and all the trimmings. Should I go to the trouble of cooking it all? I probably should. It will be worth it if it makes a difference. I need to keep showing Clive somehow that I care.

The light is on in the bedroom. I peer round the door. Clive's outline is illuminated. He is sitting up in bed, naked, a book in his hands. He stares at the pages. The book is my notebook, the book where I write my poems. I normally keep it tucked away in a drawer. Never, never has Clive shown any interest in reading it before. My heart rate quickens. Is there anything incriminating written on those pages? I know that there is. At least, according to Clive's already razor-sharp suspicions it will be incriminating.

I take a step forward. At once he clambers out of bed. He pushes past me without a word and heads for the bathroom. The book lies open on the pillow. I pick it up and see the poem I wrote only a few weeks ago.

Could this be it?
That thing we need,
We tremble and we ache for,
The one that haunts our every thought
The one we stay awake for?
All those years, those steadfast years
Of thinking it was mine
Of sharing laughter, sharing tears;
I couldn't cross a line.
But now I've found a warmer place,
With music, heart and breathing space
Unexpected, gentle, bright
It casts a very different light.
I seem to crave it more and more
I am not what I was before.

The back of my neck prickles as I scan the words. Why oh why did I write that? Why am I so, so dangerously stupid? Sometimes my poems seem to take on their own thoughts and breathe them out onto the page, while I myself am scarcely aware of them. Now the words floodlight all my feelings for Dan. And Clive has seen them.

A clod of dread is forming in my chest. What have I done, what have I done?

Footsteps sound behind me on the landing. I turn around. My husband is there. He comes to a halt and stands heavily by the door, trickles of water running down his face; a massive, naked mountain of a man. His eyes bore through me.

"A warmer place?" The words come growling through his bared teeth.

"It's . . . just a poem!" I stammer.

"You crave it more and more, do you?"

"Clive, it's not . . ." I hang my head.

He strides toward me, then stops abruptly. I can't look at him, but I can sense the anguish seething in every fiber of his body. He snatches the book from me. He begins tearing out the pages. I wince. My eyes fix on my creations as they are pulled apart one by one. The paper screeches out in distress as it rips. The noise runs through my teeth, to the back of my head, right to the core of me. Something inside me is ripping too.

As Clive reaches the final poem, I make a last desperate bid to grab the book back from him. For a second we are engaged in a tug-of-war, then suddenly he lets go. I hang on to it: one miserable, crumpled page. All that is left of my musings.

37
DAN

I spend a long time stroking Phineas, then finally push him off my knee. It is time for bed. I must be up early tomorrow morning to ring my son Ed and wish him a happy Christmas. I will not see Ed over Christmas, which is a sad thing. He will spend the day with his grandparents and his great-uncle and his great-aunt and Roe Deer and Roe Deer's guitar man. It will be the first time he meets Guitar Man.

Roe Deer has apparently now changed her mind and informed Guitar Man of Ed's existence. It was too difficult to keep hidden any longer. She wanted Guitar Man to meet her parents and her parents don't approve of hiding things like that from possible future husbands. Also, Ed himself couldn't be relied upon to tell the required lies at the required time, pretending he was a cousin and suchlike.

Much to Roe Deer's relief, Guitar Man

doesn't seem too bothered about the number of strings. Indeed he might still marry her. It is very important I contribute absolutely as much money as I can to Ed's upkeep, though.

I told Roe Deer I wasn't keen on Ed spending Christmas with his grandparents and his great-uncle and his great-aunt and Roe Deer and Guitar Man. I wanted him to spend it with me. I had already missed five Christmases of Ed's life, so this was only fair. But she said it was too late; it was all arranged now. I could have Ed next Christmas.

38
ELLIE

I lie awake for the rest of the night, cuddling my last poem. As I hold them close, the words I've written seem to seep deeper and deeper inside me.

But now I've found a warmer place,
With music, heart and breathing space.

It seems to me that those three elements are vital to life. Vital to *my* life, anyway.

Christmas morning dawns. Clive gives a loud yawn, stretches and climbs out of bed. Will he wish me a happy Christmas? Will he? Will he? I tell myself it all hinges on that. I lie there, silently. Looking at him, waiting.

He scratches his groin and takes a gulp of water from the glass on the bedside table. He meanders down the landing. I hear him having a shower, then he returns and starts opening and shutting drawers. He puts on jeans and a sweater. I am still waiting.

He disappears again. I hear him tramp downstairs, I hear the kettle and the radio and, half an hour later, I hear him go out.

I drag myself out of the bed. I stumble to the bathroom and slosh my face with water. Then, my heart banging in my chest, I run down the landing. I scramble into some clothes and throw some more into a bag. As an afterthought I rush back to the bathroom and add soap, toothbrush and painkillers.

Outside, the air stings my hot eyes. I dash the tears away and fling the bag into the car. The windscreen is all iced over. I return to the house to fetch my shoulder bag, find my wallet at the bottom of it, take out my credit card and scrape. At last there is a hole in the ice big enough to see through. Mercifully the engine starts up all right. I accelerate away, out of the village and along the winding roads of Exmoor.

My mind is in shock. I feel as if something inside me has been in the process of fraying, fraying, fraying. Now it has finally come apart and I am pinging off wildly in another direction. Is this moment real? Am I leaving my husband? Leaving Clive? Am I crazy?

I look down at my hands on the steering wheel. They appear to be my hands, purposefully driving the car away, farther and farther away from home. It must be true.

The hills and the fields are stunned and silent. The trees drip moisture. The world whirs past in a white blur.

I try to wrench my thoughts into some practical pattern. It seems I am creating a gaping hole in my future and I have no idea how it can be filled. Well . . . if I'm honest I *do* have an idea. Just as in Clive's head there's an idea, in my head — in that mushy, dreamy section of it, the section that writes poems — there's a version of that same idea. But there's no way I can act on it. I scold myself for ever letting such an idea in. It's simply not possible that anything similar can be in Dan's head. He's far too taken up with thoughts of his son and of Rhoda.

That wretched photo is haunting me again. I wish I'd never set eyes on it.

No, I will have to find some alternative future. I'm running away from substance and structure and I have only a dim mist ahead of me.

If ever I needed a friend the time is now.

When I arrive, something feels wrong. The wreath is still on the door, the fairy lights are around the windows, but nothing is lit up. I lean on the steering wheel, my head in my hands. Of course! Christina is in Thailand. I'd completely forgotten.

I realize with a pang how isolated I have become. I think of Vic, up in Yorkshire. But that is an incredibly long drive, and I'm not sure I am capable of it, mentally or physically.

I turn the car around.

39
DAN

She came to the Harp Barn today. Her hair
was the color of walnut wood. Her eyes were
the color of bracken in October. I did not
notice her socks because her face took up
the rest of my attention. It was full of tears
and lines of sorrow. Her eyebrows were
pulled together very closely as if they were
trying to squeeze something away. There
were purple-gray tinges under both her eyes.
They looked swollen.

"Dan, thank God you're here!"

Where else would I be?

"Can I come in?" she said.

I told her of course she could.

"I've left him," she said. And she held her
sleeve over her face for a long time.

I wasn't sure at all what I was supposed
to do, but I eventually decided it might be
all right to go over and hug her, so that is
what I did. She hugged back in a way that
was very tight and close. Her tears were

extremely wet. They trickled one by one down the side of my neck, inside my shirt collar and down my back.

Over her shoulder I watched outside the window the snow falling, little ashen fragments against a white sky. I thought about people leaving people and what a hard thing that is, under any circumstances.

At last Ellie took a deep breath, pulled a tissue from her pocket and blew her nose.

"Dan," she said, "what . . . what are your plans for today?"

I said the *Fifi* harp was gone now so the next thing was to cut up wood to make the *Phineas,* the harp that my son Ed and I are making together, and that was what I was planning on doing today.

"But it's Christmas Day!" she said.

I said I knew that.

"Aren't you doing anything with Jo? Or Ed? Or — or — or Rhoda? Aren't they coming round?"

I said no to all of these. Jo was doing things in soup kitchens to help those less fortunate than ourselves and Ed was spending the day with his grandparents and his great-uncle and his great-aunt and Roe Deer and Roe Deer's guitar man. He would come to see me on Saturday, as usual.

Ellie sank into a chair and blew her nose

again. "Dan," she said, "I have to be practical. I would have stayed with my friend Christina, but she's gone away to get some winter sun in Thailand. I'd forgotten. So I really don't have anywhere to go at the moment. I'll go and stay with my sister once I have spoken to her, but it's a long way to drive and I'm so tired! Would it be all right if I stayed here for a bit?"

I said of course she could.

She stood up and hugged me again. I was getting used to it.

"This is where I want to be right now," she said. "The harp is here and you are here and I feel . . . I'll be no trouble, I promise. I'll help with cooking and cleaning and things. I'll get out of the way if you want me to. It won't be for long, just a few days, till I get myself sorted. Would that be OK?"

I told her of course, of course it would. We held each other for a long time. My shirt was getting very wet.

"Sorry, I'm a bit wobbly. I haven't eaten yet today. How about a nice cuppa . . . and some sandwiches?" she suggested.

I said of course again. I was saying it a lot. Then I asked her how many sandwiches she would like, and what fillings she would like in them.

"You are a gem," she said. "Three, please!

348

Any filling will do."

After sandwiches (brie and tomato, whole-meal bread, three each) and tea (Earl Grey for her; I had a glass of nice, cold water), she brought a cushion (green, shabby) and rug (tartan, with a few pheasant feathers stuck to it) from her car and put them in the little room. I asked what she was doing. She said, "I'll sleep here, if that's all right?"

I said wouldn't she rather sleep in my bed, where it was softer and warmer? She looked at me in a strange way and there was a little silence between us. I said I would of course sleep downstairs and keep Phineas company if that was what she decided to do. She said no, no, she would hate to put me out, she'd be much happier on the floor in the little room, next to her harp. I said whatever made her happiest, that was the thing she should do. I put down some more cushions and rugs, though, because I thought that what she had wouldn't be enough to keep her comfortable. Not at all.

Then Ellie went out to look at the snow for a bit and she stroked Phineas for a bit and she played the harp for a bit. The harp playing soothed her. I could tell.

I did not wish her Happy Christmas, though. I guessed that, from her face, it wasn't.

■ ■ ■ ■

Ellie cooks with me, in the little kitchen. She makes curries and stir-fries and teaches me how to make them too, with ginger, garlic, lemon juice and stuff. I am learning all about cumin and coriander. She always did say that variety is the spice of life and I am beginning to think she is right. The spices keep our insides warm on these cold days.

There are white ribbons of snow outlining every branch and twig, and rows of icicles stuck along the roof of the barn like crocodile teeth. Drifts lie along the edges of the lane, very thick and powdery. It is deep underfoot too. I need to get the shovel and dig us out when we drive to Minehead or Porlock for supplies.

When Ed came to the barn on Saturday he was very excited. He likes snow, a lot. As soon as we arrived he launched himself into the snow, took great handfuls of it and flung it up in the air, jumping up and down. Then when Ellie came out he threw some at her, which she didn't mind a bit. She scooped up a load more and threw it back at him. This was their first encounter. I was glad it was going so well.

After that we compared footprints.

"Yours are biggest," said Ed to me, planting his small foot with flashing sneakers into my zigzag-ridged boot print. "Next are Ellie's," he continued, leaping into her narrower, smoother prints. She does not have her thick grippy boots with her because she left them in her house and doesn't want to go back and get them. Her feet get cold a lot in her not-very-practical shoes and she slips about. Ed and I had to hold on to her on both sides to support her. "Mine are smallest," said Ed, demonstrating the fact by making lots of footprints that ran round us in circles.

Then Ed told us that we had to turn and face the barn and count to a hundred while he went to hide, and after we'd reached a hundred we must follow his tracks and see if we could find him. Ellie and I obeyed. We trailed him across the white field, alongside the stream and up the bank, over the tumbledown stone wall, then into the woods. We searched for him under the laden boughs of the old oaks and beeches. We said, "Where can he be?" a lot of times. Loudly.

Then there was a sudden "Boo!" and he sprang out on us from behind a tree trunk. I collapsed onto the ground in shock. Ed laughed like a drunken hyena. His laugh is contagious. Ellie joined in. Which was a good thing, I think.

There is nothing Ed likes more than jumping out and shouting boo. I'm beginning to get used to such explosiveness. It seems to be a major feature of a small boy's life.

That same afternoon we made snowmen. We made a snow-Dan, a snow-Ed and a snow-Ellie in the orchard. We also made a snow-Phineas.

"We need carrots. Have you got carrots, Dad?" Ed asked. Luckily I did have carrots. We gave ourselves carrot noses and gave Phineas a carrot beak.

"We need lumps of coal. Have you got any coal?" Coal was something I did not have, but Ed was resourceful and found some dark stones. We carefully placed our eyes in our faces.

"What do you make mouths out of?" he asked next. "Twigs?"

I applauded his idea and said if there was one thing we were never short of on Exmoor that thing was twigs.

"I'll find some," said Ed and scooted off. A moment later he was back with three twigs. The curviest one he put on the snow-Dan's face to make him smiley. The second curviest he put on the snow-Ed. But on the snow-Ellie he put the twig upside down so she looked sad. I looked at the snow-Ellie and I looked at the real Ellie and I saw that Ed had got that right.

Ellie then said she'd like to take photos of the snow characters but she couldn't because she didn't have her camera with her. Then she went quiet. Ellie goes quiet a lot these days. I've noticed that. I don't mind it, though, and Ed doesn't mind either.

Later on Saturday my sister Jo came to join us. She brought hand-knitted gloves for Ed and chocolates in the shape of trains. She said that now she had her big opportunity to be an auntie. She patted Ed on the head and told him what a terror he was. She patted Ellie on the arm and told her she was doing really well, considering.

Ed likes talking. Ed talked all the time — to us or to himself or to Phineas. "You're cool!" he told Phineas. Phineas looked very pleased to hear this.

"You're megacool." Phineas looked even more pleased.

"You're the coolest pheasant in the whole world!" Phineas was so pleased at this that he took one of Ed's shirt buttons in his beak and pulled it off.

To me Ed asked lots of questions. I did my best to answer.

"Dad, tell me about *your* dad. What was he like?"

I said my dad was a big and gentle man.

"How big?"

I showed him where my dad came up to on the barn door.

With his arms outstretched Ed measured the distance between this and his own height, which was quite substantial. "And how gentle?"

I explained that my dad was so gentle he used to stop the car if a caterpillar was crossing the road. Even though my mother didn't like it. He stopped the car and then he got out and picked the caterpillar up and put it carefully on a leaf on the shoulder, where it would be safe.

Ed nodded. "That's much more gentler than my other granddad, Gramps," he told me. He meant Roe Deer's father. "Gramps doesn't like stopping the car even for schoolkids at the crossing."

He picked up a stick that he brought home from a walk earlier and waved it around. "What about your mum? Was she big and gentle too?"

I told him no, she wasn't, not at all. I told him she was quite small and I showed him on the barn door where she came up to, which was a little bit closer to his own height. I said that I wouldn't exactly describe her as gentle either. She was always too busy telling me all about what I was supposed to do and not supposed to do.

Ed said: "My mum doesn't tell me anything about supposed to and not supposed to. She leaves all that to my nan."

In the evening we sat together by the fire and Ellie read to us, bits from *Winnie-the-Pooh* and bits from Lewis Carroll, books I've kept from my own childhood. Ellie reads well. Ed was enchanted.

My friend Thomas has also been introduced to Ed. Thomas declares him to be a little monkey. Thomas lingers most mornings. He likes talking to Ellie about the weather.

It is strange when there are so many people in the barn at one time. My life is branching out into all sorts of new directions, like a hazel tree that resprouts after coppicing.

Weekdays are our quieter days. I make harps. Ellie sits wrapped up in a rug and reads or looks at the fire. She sometimes goes outside to wander by herself or sometimes comes with me on my walk and I show her all the things I like, from the frozen puddles to the iced tops of the pine trees to the shining structures that have formed over the stream like organ pipes. She gazes at everything and holds on to me so that she doesn't fall over.

But something is not right. Not at all. I would like very much to make it right, but I don't know how. I have no idea what a man is supposed to do under these circumstances. I am made of the wrong ingredients.

Ellie plays the harp in the evenings, but only sad songs. I listen and the sounds prod and poke at the tender places inside me. At times I am sorry that I ever gave her the harp because it seems to have led to so much pain, but at other times I think it is the balm that heals the pain.

40
ELLIE

Dan is busy embarking on a new harp. I wander out. It's not that late, but it's already getting hard to see. I can make out Phineas in front of the barn, pecking at something on the lane. I go back in, fetch some bird-seed, crouch down and hold it out to him. He runs toward me.

I'm getting fond of the bird. He's a wonderful listener and it's a huge relief to talk to someone who doesn't understand.

"Phineas, do you think I was right to leave Clive?"

He gobbles at the seed, ignoring the giver.

I have no idea if Clive has tried to find me, if he assumes I've gone to Vic's or Christina's. I wonder if he regrets tearing up my poems, if he misses me.

"I tried so hard to keep loving him. I did try! He didn't make it easy for me, though, did he? No, he didn't."

Phineas looks at me sideways.

"OK, so I wasn't blameless myself."

He finishes the last fragments of seed and looks at me again, hoping for more.

"I really, really don't want him to think I was unfaithful. But I suppose he's bound to think that, especially now I've run away. I hope he's all right. I mean, his drinking was getting pretty bad. And now he'll be even worse. He'll be in an awful state. He did love me, I know that. With all his faults, he did love me."

Phineas is looking bored now and starting to move off. I offer him another handful of birdseed. I need him to stay.

"Phineas, listen! I don't know what to do. I've pulled myself loose from my rock, but now I'm floating with the tides and I've got no idea where I'll end up. Up north next, I suppose, to talk it over with Vic. But before that I'll have to go back home and fetch my things. The thing is, I can't quite bring myself to do that yet."

I've had time to think, and time to observe. Dan hasn't shown any signs of wanting to get back together with Rhoda, which is a blessed relief. But neither has he shown any interest in me beyond steadfast friendship. I have to face the facts.

I wipe my eyes. "I can't inflict myself on

him much longer, can I? He has his son now."

I stroke Phineas on the head, wishing I had more resolve.

The noise of a car engine startles me. Phineas flees, cawing in alarm. I stand up quickly. There, heading straight toward me in his car, is Clive. My mouth drops open. He slams on the brakes right in front of me. I am rooted to the spot. For him to find me here . . .

Horror hits, and scorching shame, as if he's caught me having rampant sex with Dan. Clive's face is livid. His eyes burn with fury. Even through the windscreen I can see the twitching muscle in his forehead. He swings the car around, avoiding me by an inch. Then spurts forward and roars away, back down the lane.

I'm shaking all over.

He'll see it as confirmation of his worst suspicions. I know he will.

Clive is a proud man, and when he is hurt, he lashes out. With a horrible, jabbing certainty I sense he'll crave revenge. Like he did when Jayne was unfaithful to him all those years ago. He took a hammer and destroyed what she loved the most.

And what I love the most is . . .

Oh God, oh God!

41
DAN

The electric lathe is running and I have my earmuffs on. Ellie comes running in, her face white as a lily, her hands gesticulating, her mouth shaping rapid words.

I stop the lathe and take off my earmuffs. I ask what is wrong.

"Dan!" she cries. "I must go, and I must go now! Clive was here, just now, just a moment ago, and he saw me."

I wonder why Clive was here and if he was here a moment ago, why he isn't still here now. Surely if he was here, then his purpose was either to visit me or visit Ellie, neither of which it seems he's done. And why does Ellie suddenly want to go? Does she mean she wants to go back to him? It is all most worrying and confusing.

I'm not sure which question to ask her first, but before I've managed to ask any of them, Ellie bursts into a fit of coughing. The circles under her eyes are bigger; the white of her face is tinged with green; her eyes are brimming with water. She sinks to the floor.

"Dan, can you bring a bucket? I feel sick," she murmurs.

At that moment all the lights go out. Power cuts are fairly common here at this time of year. I keep a large stash of candles in the workbench drawer ready for this eventuality.

I light several candles and bring her a bucket as quickly as I can. She heaves over it.

I run for a blanket and wrap it round her shoulders. Her skin is icy.

"I have to . . . to get out of here . . ." she insists, struggling to her feet.

I tell her there is only one place she is going and that is bed. Not a bed of cushions and rugs on the floor, a proper bed. My bed.

She retches again over the bucket. I can see in the flickering light that it is filling with saliva and sicky bits, pale brown, smelly.

When she can speak again, what she says is this: "Can you put my bag in my car for me?"

I say on no account will I do that. The thing I will do is to accompany her upstairs and tuck her into the bed and put an extra blanket on.

She leans on me shakily, almost accepting, then stops.

"Dan, he knows I'm here. He'll . . . I don't know. But we must make him think I've gone. He must think I'm somewhere else."

I say that if the idea is to make Clive think she's gone, then there is an easy solution: All we have to do is to hide her car. He will then think she has driven off somewhere else. There is no other evidence as far as I can see.

She wavers. "Where could we hide the car?"

I say that I can drive it down to Thomas's if she likes. He won't mind if I leave it next to his red van, in his driveway.

"And if Clive comes here again, you'll answer the door? And you'll say I've gone away and I'm not coming back?"

I confirm that, if it's what she wants, I will.

"Yes, I do want that. And say it as if it's true, Dan! Promise me!"

She is forcing the words out although it's clearly an effort for her to speak at all.

Lying is difficult for me, but she is adamant. I say I'll promise if she will go to bed now and try to relax.

She lets me take her up to my room and help her into the bed. I light another candle and wedge it into the carved wooden candlestick on the bedside table. While she is getting into her nightclothes I fetch her own rug from the little room for her. She is not well, not at all, and will need to stay warm. I spread it over her and the other bedclothes. In the glimmer her face still looks crumpled and upset.

"Go and move the car now, Dan, please. Quickly. Please!"

So I take her car keys and that is what I do.

Thomas invited me in for a drink, but I said no. I said Ellie the Exmoor Housewife was in my bed and I'd better get back to her as soon as possible. He looked at me with a gleam in his eyes and said: "Well, in that case, mate, you'd certainly better look lively. I can give you a lift back if you like, boyo."

But Thomas's wife Linda, who is a large and fierce woman, said his dinner was now sitting on the table and there was no way she was going to warm it up for him all over again when he got back.

"Sorry, mate," he said to me.

It was lucky I'd remembered to take a flashlight. The roads were very icy now. The snow had stopped, but I could see little lacings and tracings of it along the edges of everything in the flashlight beam. The sky was clear and the stars were very bright, just as they were that night when I discovered that I had a son.

If I tried to count the stars tonight I could probably do a better job of it. The bright band of the Milky Way was draped across the sky over the far pine trees. That would be a good place to start counting. But I decided not to count just now because I wanted to get back quickly and check that Ellie was all right.

The walk back from Thomas's house took me twenty-six minutes.

When I arrived at the barn I stopped to sniff. There was a strong, acrid, chemical smell, not normal in the pure air of the Exmoor night. Then I saw there was a car parked alongside the barn, just where Ellie's had been. I had only just registered this when there came out of the darkness a loud, frantic squawking. Phineas. I rushed round the back to where the noise came from.

I waved the flashlight around, but I couldn't see him anywhere. The squawking had stopped. If he was worried about foxes Phineas might have gone to his second bed in the woodshed. I raced round to the orchard. I was surprised to see a small,

364

round light — the light from another flash-light — shining out from the shed.

"Phineas?" I called. But Phineas does not have a flashlight. I knew that really.

"Is someone there?" I called.

There was a low moan. It did not sound like Phineas. Not at all.

I came closer. I shone my flashlight round the corners of the woodshed.

There was a human figure crouching on a log. It was a man rocking to and fro, his head in his hands. The other flashlight lay on the floor by his feet. I picked it up and shone both flashlights at him. The figure did not move. The head in the hands had a receding hairline that I recognized.

"You are Clive Ellie's husband," I said.

He lifted his head. Then I saw that his face had red scratches across it like claw marks. The man blinked. His eyeballs rolled around a bit, then looked at me.

There was a moment of silence.

Then, all at once, he gave a great howl and lurched toward me, his eyes flaring in the flashlight beam, his fists like giant clubs. I had not been expecting this. It was a shock. I dropped the flashlights and tried to duck out of the way. I felt one of his fists slam down on my shoulder. The pain forced a yelp out of my mouth. I don't know what happened to his other fist, but something crashed loudly. My shoulder stung and the only thing I could see was a patch of light on the ground. I was staggering a bit, but I managed to bend down and pick up a flashlight again. I darted it around quickly.

Clive Ellie's husband was sprawled against a log pile at the end of the shed. His arms and legs were struggling to pull him up. I stared. He heaved himself upright and turned to face the light. The muscles of his forehead were pulsing and his fists were clenched again. I could see that he was about to hurl himself at me a second time. His mouth had turned into a great black cave and from that cave came a dragon's roar. There wasn't time to think so I did what my instinct told me to do. I waited a few seconds until he was almost upon me, then skirted to the side and stuck out a foot. He tripped over it and plowed onto the floor.

That was the end of my fight with Clive Ellie's husband.

What happened next was that I bent over him and asked if he was OK. He was making spluttery noises. They almost sounded like laughter but not quite. He seemed to be trying to get something out of his pocket. At last he managed it, and held the something out toward me.

"You'd better take these," is what he said.

42
ELLIE

I woke up with a throbbing head and stiff limbs, a faint murmur in my ears. I sat up. My nose was blocked, my eyes gummed together. I scraped a hand over my face, forced my eyes open and tried to make out the world around me. No moonlight was visible in the black square of the window, but narrow threads of yellow between the floorboards betrayed some sort of light downstairs. The candle was still burning on the table by the bed.

Dan's bedroom door was open. I wrapped the rug around my shoulders and listened. The background murmur was his voice. Had he brought Thomas home, or was he talking to Phineas, as I did? Curiosity awakened, I hauled myself from the bed. Still slightly nauseous, I went to the door, pulling the rug round myself with one hand, clutching the candle with the other. I passed through the little room. My harp stood there in the glow like a still sentinel. I tottered down the first few steps.

I froze. The rug fell around my feet. There, below me in the workshop, lit by a couple of flashlights on the floor, was my husband. He was seated on one of Dan's chairs in a slumped position. Dan stood in front of him, talking in hushed tones. He was holding something. It looked like one of my sweaters, but it seemed to be sopping wet. He dropped it onto the floor by his feet, where there was a pile of other damp materials that looked familiar. His voice was a steady torrent, but his hands were becoming more and more manic, wriggling and slicing wildly at the air.

The events of the past few hours spun round in my head. I had no idea what to do.

I drew back, breathless. My foot creaked on the stair. At once Dan looked up and saw me. He was wearing his thick brown jacket. He looked extremely alert, but his posture was oddly twisted. His hair stood up in wild sprigs.

Slowly Clive raised his head too. He stared at me. I could hardly bear to look back at him, but neither could I drag my eyes away. Red streaks of blood ranged across his cheeks and forehead. His face was blotched with dust and bruises. His eyes were blood-shot. But more than all of these it was his expression that alarmed me. Instead of the tight rage that I'd witnessed over the past weeks, it was fraught with indescribable horror.

I winced. The candle slipped and fell from my grasp. I was aware of my heart hammering, of Clive's eyes, Dan's upturned face, the crowd of harps, the flame traveling downward. The moment pulsated between us; stark and grim, full of questions.

A bright flare sprouted up from the floor of the room below. It seemed to survey the scene for a second, wave gleefully and then burst upward and outward. Clive catapulted out of his chair and Dan staggered back. The damp heap on the floor exploded into a volcano, hurling out wild tongues of fire. The workshop flashed and flickered before my eyes.

I screamed. I tried to move, but my legs refused to work. I knew I should find a phone, find some water, run, do *something,* but I couldn't. I was a wild animal caught in the headlamps, mesmerized by the doom that was hurtling toward me.

Great amber wings of flame unfurled and spread outward. Fire rushed toward the walls. It swooped and swirled in livid bundles of brightness under the windows. Then it changed direction and lapped back across the floor, a tide of crackling energy. Plumes of smoke rose. The air rippled with heat. Faster and faster the flames multiplied. They skipped hither and thither among the heaps of sawdust. They leaped through the frames of the chairs. They licked up the spines of the harps and danced feverishly among the strings. Everything was engulfed in a seething mass of orange.

The two men below had become black shapes against the glare. It seemed that one was moving toward me, the other away from me, but I couldn't be sure. I could hear creaking, hissing, roaring and a half-musical twanging — a dreadful, eerie sound. I realized, with a sharp twist in my heart, that it was the sound of harps tortured, harps dying. I gawped at the jagged wall of fire before me. It pranced like a swarm of demons performing some bloodthirsty ritual. Heat rolled toward me in waves. The brightness seared. My eyes stung. Clive and Dan were now obscured from my line of sight. The wooden banister had caught and the stairs had vanished behind the blaze. My skin began prickling. I was trapped.

A voice rose above the roar. "Ellie! Ellie! The window! My bedroom window!"

At last my body launched into action. Coughing and sputtering, I stumbled backward into the little room and slammed the door shut behind me. I turned and fled through it to Dan's bedroom in the farthest reaches of the building. I was vaguely aware of the solid wood bed, the books on the bedside table, the diagrams of harps on the walls. I ran to the little hatch of a dormer window. I brushed the collection of pinecones off the sill and threw it open.

Fresh cold air poured in. Scarcely aware of what I was doing, I hoisted my legs over the sill. The edge pressed painfully through the thin fabric of my pajamas. Below me was a slope of slate roof, coated in frost, gleaming under the stars. I perched there for a second. After the heat and glare, the dark iciness shocked my system. I could still hear sounds of wreckage from behind the closed door. Why oh why did I have to drop that candle? How could I have been so stupid? How was it possible that this total devastation could happen so fast? My limbs were shaking uncontrollably.

I squeezed myself through the window frame and clambered out.

All at once everything was slithering downward. My bare feet scudded around, knocking off frozen nodules of moss. My body writhed wildly, but I hung on. And then, finding some sort of balance, the world stilled again.

I breathed. My fingers didn't dare loosen their hold on the window ledge so I lay there, dangling, arms stretched up, cheek flattened against the slates.

Wetness seeped through me. The intense cold was mixing with my body heat and starting to glue me to the roof. If I didn't die from the fire, I would surely die of cold, or die from falling. A sob rose from deep within me. I wasn't ready to die.

Dan, Clive, the harps, the flames, my own dangling body . . . they were all spinning and morphing and becoming a blur. Then, suddenly, my brain short-circuited. I was flung back in time. I was in my bedroom, a mere ten years old, and I'd spilled red paint all over the carpet. My mother's words came right through, strident now as they were then. "Ellie, I despair of you. You always, always mess things up. Always."

I didn't know how to answer her.

Then there was another voice, a more welcome voice: Dan's, winging up to me through the night.

"Ellie! Ivy! To your left."

I turned my head the other way and could just make out a tangled mass of something darker against the darkness. It was within reach. I pulled one hand away from the window ledge and moved my palm over the rough knots of ivy. It felt strong. I grasped it and transferred my weight slowly. The matted stems provided a foothold, then another. I lowered myself over the edge of the roof, knocking off icicles as I went, and arrived at a vertical drop of stone wall. Bit by bit, scrabbling and breaking my nails, I inched my way down the ropes of ivy.

"Ellie, you can jump now. I'm here!"

I trusted. I closed my eyes and jumped. Strong arms caught me. Strong arms held me. Tightly, oh so tightly. There was warmth and there was protection. There was a heart beating against my own heart.

"Ellie, Ellie!"

I let out a wail of relief.

"Are you all right?" It was asked with fierce urgency.

"Yes, I think so," I whispered.

The strong arms levered me gently to the ground and tucked me round with a soft padded jacket that smelled of pinewood.

I don't know how long I lay there before I realized. Three things. First, the barn was still burning. Second, Dan was no longer with me. Third, where was Clive?

43
DAN

After I had made sure my Ellie was all right, I set about saving my harps. I didn't stop to do any thinking. Thinking would have done them no good at all. Thinking uses up far too much time. Desire is quicker. I had one desire and that was enough to make me do what I had to do. This: go back into the barn and get the harps out of there. At once.

Grainy gray clouds were billowing out from the barn door and escaping up into the black sky. Inside everything was a-flicker. I launched myself back through the entrance. I was met with a blast of red and yellow fury, hot, violent, brutal. There was a hissing and a roaring in my face, a belching out of strong odors: scents of smoky pine, oak and beech wood mixed with the reek of hot oil, tar, wax and metal. Fiery tentacles were flailing about everywhere I looked. They wrapped around the drawers where I kept my harp strings. They slid along the surface of my workbench and snatched at my tools. They snaked their way up to the cork notice board. The photos of the harpists curled and blackened one by one, the face of Roe Deer among them. I jolted to a halt for a split second to watch. She was looking angrier and angrier as she disintegrated.

Above the roar I could hear clear drops of sound, notes of desperation and despair. The harps needed me. The harps. The poor harps. I pressed on.

I hoisted my *Harbinger* under my arm and carried it to the doorway. It felt heavy, almost as heavy as my heart. It clung to me, its ribs shuddering against my own. Once the two of us had got outside, there was a wild retching that came from me and a pinging sound that came from a string as it succumbed to the sudden temperature change. I stooped and laid the *Harbinger* on its side on the frozen lane. It would survive. But there were so many more. Thirty-six more.

I plunged back into the inferno that was my home. It was hard to see. Sparks flew at my eyes and flames kept trying to dive down my throat and smoke thrashed and tingled in my nose. I ignored them. Something crashed to my right. Something bit into the flesh of my arm. Something spat in my face. There was a cascade of color at the back of my eyes. I directed myself through the choking fumes to the end of the room where I knew the harps were waiting for me. My outstretched arms banged into a familiar-shaped frame. The wood was red-hot, dry, thirsty. I couldn't tell which harp it was, but it was a large one. I clutched it with blistering fingers and heaved it along with me, back to safety. I laid it on the ground in the darkness next to its companion. The stars shone down. Shadows twisted and leaped across the lane from the rectangle of the doorway: amber, black, amber, black.

There were still thirty-five harps to save.

A third time I rushed in. A third time I fought through the brightness and the darkness and the blindness and the obliterating heat, and my hands found the curved neck of another harp. I pulled it out from the dazzle and into the chill of night. Laying it down, I touched the iced prickle of grass blades and my body longed to collapse and lie there on the ground next to the three harps. All I wanted was to splutter the smoke out of my system and rest there in the cold quietness. But there were still thirty-four harps to save. I straightened up, dizzy, my lungs gasping for air.

Then a shaft of white light fell across my shoulders. It was coming from two round centers, the headlamps of a car. The car door opened. Out of the side of the car came the figure of a man, the man who had sprung out of my armchair when the fire began. The man who had lumbered to the door while I was shouting to Ellie through the flames. Ellie's husband Clive.

"Fire brigade . . . I've called them. On their way!" His words were slow and slurred, like great heavy blocks falling from his mouth. Didn't he understand that nothing could be slow now? Harps were burning. Harps were needing help.

I propelled my clumsy limbs back into the barn. My skin bubbled. The air was full of so many things now it was almost impossible to force myself forward, but I stumbled into another harp. I grabbed it and lumped and bumped it over the floor and outside.

The car headlamps were still on, floodlighting the row of injured harps as they lay on the ground. And now another figure was tumbling toward me, barefoot, wearing my jacket over her pajamas. Her hair was wild, her eyes wide. Ellie the Exmoor Housewife.

I turned away from her and I pulled together all of my reluctant bones and joints and half-melted flesh and I ran back to the entrance of the barn.

"Dan, stop!"

I did not stop. I had thirty-three harps to save.

Her shriek echoed behind me. "Clive! Please! Stop him!"

That was when I was bulldozed for a second time that night by her husband. His full weight knocked me down. I was dragged by my feet backward, facedown, through the sawdust, the dirt, the ash and the ice. I was weak. I could do no more.

44
ELLIE

"One drunk, one burned, one fainted . . ."

The voices ebb and flow. They seem far away, like spirits from a different world. I feel as if I'm hovering on the edge of that world, eavesdropping on someone else's life. I pull back inward and try to focus on myself.

I am lying on my back. But it isn't in my bed at home — no, I've left all that behind, haven't I, at Christmas, after a tearing up of poems? But there's been more destruction since then, I believe, or was it all a horribly vivid nightmare? Weren't there flames? Flames threatening to eat up everything I loved?

I recognize the worn touch of my winter pajamas. Didn't I climb out of a window onto an icy roof? In these very pajamas?

I listen. The voices are blending into a babble. There are background noises too, a siren warbling and an engine. I sense a steady movement. I open my eyes. I am in a confined space filled with medical equipment. There is a body lying beside me, wrapped in bandages.

"How are you feeling?"

A nurse is bending over me. She is the motherly type. Her blue tunic is pristine, her hair is looped neatly on top of her head, her smile is warm and comforting.

"I'm fine now!" I tell her, not that convincingly. It seems I've been awake for hours, but it must only be minutes. I don't want any fuss. "I think it was just shock. I'm ready to go home now."

The words just slipped out.

Home?

I sit up. The world spins, then slowly settles. A band of sunlight is shining into the ward. There's a background hum of machinery. People in white coats are coming and going.

The night's events are seeping back into my consciousness now with hideous clarity. I remember what happened, but I can't be sure of the end results.

"Do you know anything about a man called Dan Hollis? He was with me, at the barn. He — I think he was hurt?"

"Yes, dear," the nurse replies. "I thought

you'd ask. He's in the burn unit."

My heart feels as if it is about to explode. "Will he be . . . ?" I gulp. My throat is so choked up with dread I can't finish the question. All I can do is look at her pleadingly.

"He'll be all right. The flesh on his arms and hands is damaged, but it'll heal in time. Just some scarring."

I could weep with relief.

"Can I see him?"

"Not yet, dear. They're still patching him up."

I'm remembering more and more. A host of harps went up in flames. It must have been nearly all of them. Not to mention the workshop. Everything Dan loved and lived for, reduced to ashes. Because of me.

How the hell am I ever going to live with this?

And also . . .

Oh my God, *Clive.* Another tide of guilt sweeps through me. Clive trusted me and treasured me, but I repaid him with nothing but willfulness and deceit. Yet still he loved me enough to come to the barn to bring me back. And it was Clive who saved the day by calling the fire brigade after my stupid accident with the candle. After I'd nearly destroyed us all. He's done more than that too. In spite of his extreme jealous suspicions he threw himself forward to drag Dan out of the flames. He saved Dan's life.

Clive saved Dan's life. Clive is a hero.

I have misjudged again, made a mess of everything again, just as my mother said I always did. I feel weighted, as though I am being pulled downward, as though I am filled with massive blocks of stone.

The nurse looks at me anxiously. "You've been through a lot. Are you sure you're all right?"

"Yes," I lie.

Clive must be at home now. He'll be recovering from the shock too. If he still loves me he'll come here soon, to pick me up and take me back with him.

Do I want to go home with him? Well, where else can I go? Perhaps Clive and I can sort things out together now. Perhaps things will be different between us. I close my eyes. I can't bear to think of anything anymore.

"Mrs. Jacobs, the doctor's here to see you!"

I open my eyes and try to look a picture of health. The doctor, a short, stumpy, earnest sort of man, peers at me through his glasses and asks the standard questions. Aside from a few bruises I am fine, it transpires, and am free to go.

I wonder exactly how I'm supposed to do that, with no car, no money and no clothes apart from pajamas and Dan's jacket.

"Have you got anyone who can pick you up?" the doctor asks.

Yes, but only one person. He must know I'm here. He must come soon.

I wait for my husband at reception. I wait two hours. During this time I repeatedly ask the woman behind the desk if I can go and see Dan. But he is still in recovery and they won't allow visitors.

I think about ringing Clive. But I want it to be him who makes the effort, him who strives toward a reconciliation.

Is that what I want? Is it? Is it?

45
DAN

"What the hell did you think you were doing?"

My sister's voice is frosty, but I observe quivery little drips of water hanging from her eyes. She brushes them away and furrows up her brow. She is perched on the edge of the hospital bed, where I'm propped against the pillows. A bunch of grapes is on her lap, purple ones, large, in a plastic bag. She pushes the bag toward me.

I don't take one because it is painful to move. Everything is painful. I am bandaged in lots of places.

She selects a grape and puts it in her mouth. She chews it. I wonder when she's going to spit out the pips, but she never does. I surmise they must be seedless grapes.

She repeats her question.

I inform her that what I was doing was saving Ellie from the fire. After that I was saving harps from the fire. I managed to save four harps. It wasn't as many as I'd wanted to save, though, because after that Ellie's husband had taken it upon himself to save *me*.

"Ellie's husband? What the blue blazes was *he* doing there?"

I look down. I'm not sure if it's a good idea for her to know this information. Not at all. She repeats her second question, however, and I know she'll keep on repeating it until I answer, so I tell her.

"Here it is, then," is what I say. "Ellie's husband was in the workshop last night because he had a plan. His plan was this: to set fire to the Harp Barn."

She gapes. "But I thought it was an accident!"

I tell her that it both was and wasn't.

"Please, Dan! Start at the beginning. Tell me everything."

So I do. I tell her how Ellie had asked me to move her car, which I had done, and how I'd come back from Thomas's to the smell of paraffin and the loud cawing of Phineas. How I'd found Ellie's husband Clive in the woodshed and how he'd attacked me. How, after he had been hit twice (not by me, I hastened to add; first with a pile of logs and then with the floor), he had proffered me the box of matches. How he lay there for a long while.

"It was a problem," I tell Jo, remembering. "I had no idea at all what I was supposed to do. To be honest, I don't think he knew what he was supposed to do either. Which surprised me, as he'd struck me as the sort of person who always knows these things. Maybe I got that wrong. I took the matches away from him anyway. And I said he'd better come inside out of the cold."

"You invited him in!"

"He was hurting quite badly and had had enough of fighting. So come in is what he did. There wasn't much else he could do at this point apart from freeze to death."

But after he came in, Ellie's husband Clive had acted most strangely. He had sat in a chair and laughed. He'd told me he *knew*. He knew all about Ellie and me. Even if she wasn't here now, Ellie had been here, he'd seen her, he'd seen the look on her face. But really he'd known for weeks. Ellie had changed, she'd been drifting away from him bit by bit, and it tore him apart and there was nothing he could do about it. And it was all because of me and my romantic sodding beautiful bloody harps.

That was the thought that drove him to it. That filled his head with images. Images of romantic sodding beautiful bloody harps *on fire.* He'd been thinking of burning harps for weeks on end, he said. He said it in a trancelike sort of way, and to be honest I wasn't sure if he was talking to himself or to me, but I listened just in case. He might have been a bit confused because of the bang on the head he'd received from the floor of the woodshed. I can't be sure. Anyway, he went on and on about the burning harps. He said that image had a strange appeal, and the appeal had been growing stronger and stronger every day. All those harps, he said; Ellie probably considered my barn to be like heaven, with all the harps, but he saw it more as hell. At least, he could turn it into hell, with the help of a box of matches. A neat exchange of extremes. He laughed again when he said that. I did not like the fact that he laughed at such a thing.

After he'd seen with his own eyes that Ellie was at the barn, he'd gone home and steeled himself with whiskey. Then he'd soaked rags in paraffin and put them in a bucket, in readiness. He was prepared to wait, but when he came back to the barn he saw that Ellie's car was already gone. He assumed she'd taken fright and whisked me away somewhere, perhaps up north to her sister's. He thought me and Ellie deserved a big surprise when we got back. So he stuffed the rags in all the crevices around the barn and got out the matches.

When he told me this I went round the barn to see if it was true, and it was. I collected up the rags. There were a lot. Some of them looked like Ellie's clothes. The cherry-colored socks and her moss-colored cardigan and her terra-cotta T-shirt. They were very paraffiny and they were everywhere: under the windows, in the letter box and there was one — it looked like her russet-colored sweater — that was beside Phineas's pheasant flap. In fact, Ellie's husband Clive had (he told me) just stooped down to stuff the sweater into the flap prior to lighting a match when Phineas came out of the flap. Phineas is not viciously inclined, but Phineas got a nasty shock when he tried to go out for a midnight stroll and found a man stuffing a paraffin-soaked sweater into his pheasant flap. So bad was the shock of his discovery that he flew into the face of the man.

I pause. "I would say it was self-defense, wouldn't you?"

Jo doesn't answer. She has stopped chewing grapes and is staring at me.

"It was not only a shock for Phineas," I

tell her. "It was also a big shock for Ellie's husband — to have a whirling pheasant in his face just when he was about to set fire to her clothes and the barn and the harps."

Jo continues to gape.

"In fact, the shock was so big that, rather than setting fire to anything, he went and sat in my woodshed instead. Which was where I found him. And where he attacked me."

"Sweet Jesus!" Jo mutters under her breath.

I go on with my narration. "After I'd learned this about Ellie's husband and his intentions I felt alarmed. I started talking and I told him all about what I was thinking. Which is what I am still thinking. Which is this: that Clive is slightly not quite normal in the head."

"Slightly! The man's a psychopath!" cries Jo.

I inform her that Clive the psychopath still didn't know at this point that Ellie was actually lying in my bed feeling queasy. But then Ellie came out of my bedroom and saw him. And she was as surprised as he was and so dropped her candle. And the candle landed slap bang in the middle of the heap of paraffiny clothes that I'd been gathering. Which was a dreadfully unlucky thing and one that had almost cost all our lives.

I am tired with all the talking now and sink back onto the pillows.

Jo's eyes are smoldering and she looks as though she is about to snort a great burst of fire from her nostrils, like a dragon. "God in heaven! That Ellie has a lot to answer for! And I thought Rhoda was bad!"

46
ELLIE

Only a sister would offer to drive three hundred miles for such a cause, when she has a child ill in bed and three others clamoring for her attention.

"But I'm afraid I'll have to drive us straight from the hospital back up to Yorkshire," Vic says, and I hear down the line how much her voice is sagging. "I'd suggest a B and B, but Alan is at work tomorrow and I won't be able to get a babysitter at such short notice."

Six hundred miles, then. It's asking a lot, even of a sister.

If only Christina was here!

I cudgel my brain for other possibilities. Then I tell Vic to stay where she is. There's a phone directory in the booth. I shuffle through the pages. The number is listed.

The phone rings on and on. I'm about to give up when I hear a click and a voice greets me in a singsong Welsh accent.

"Hi, Thomas, it's Ellie Jacobs."

"Ellie Jacobs! Hello, Ellie Jacobs. What a pleasure, indeed! What can I do you for?"

He knows nothing of last night's events, apart from the fact that Dan left my car at his house. I break the news as gently as I can. Thomas bombards me with colorful expletives as I struggle through my description of the fire.

"So our boyo Dan? He's all right, is he, now?"

I assure him that Dan is reasonably all right, here in the hospital too but still being "patched up."

I explain my current problem and ask about my car.

"Yes, it's still here next to the van," Thomas tells me. And yes, Thomas, bless him, is happy to come and pick me up and take me to it. He is also sure — or pretty much sure — his wife won't mind if I borrow some of her clothes.

The drive to Yorkshire is longer than ever. I'm still feeling extremely delicate. And uncomfortable, and itchy. Thomas's wife's skirt is an awful creation, a tubular thing in puce nylon that's three sizes too big for me. The sweater is grotesque too, with flouncy sleeves and a pattern of enormous turquoise

393

and pink roses. I'll return them both to their kind owner at the first possible opportunity. My outfit is the least of my worries, but I've improved it as best I can with Dan's brown jacket. The jacket smells horribly of smoke, but behind that is the scent of pinewood and behind that, possibly, the scent of Dan himself. The scent of a kind, brave harp-making man.

The vision of burning harps haunts me throughout the journey. My driving is erratic, disturbed by memories: the smell, the heat, the sound of roaring flames and breaking strings. Dan will be haunted too, lying in his hospital bed, groaning in pain. Cursing the day he met me.

I only pray he recovers quickly and finds some way of carrying on. Thomas promised he would go and visit as soon as visits were allowed. I wish I could be closer. I'll try ringing the hospital once I arrive at Vic's.

As for my own future, I just don't know. Logic suggests I should go back to Clive if he'll have me. If he had come to collect me from the hospital I'd have gone home to him again like a lamb. After all, he saved Dan's life after my clumsiness with the candle nearly killed him, and how can I ever forget that? Yet I shrink away from the idea of life with Clive again. Perhaps it's because

I've got into the habit of living off dreams. Reality seems a hell of a lot less attractive.

I stop off three times, to fill the tank with petrol and drink awful coffee, at crowded service stations. At one of them I spot a man heading into the car park and I'm sure it's Clive. I can only see his back view, but his height and the sandy color of his hair . . . Could it be that he has followed me, that he is even now planning to take me home? Then he turns and I see that it isn't him at all. I start breathing again.

With a throbbing head and stinging eyes I finally reach the close of redbrick houses where Vic lives and pull up in the driveway. Her children are playing in the garden. They flock round the car and drag me into the house with small, sticky hands.

"Auntie Ellie's here! Auntie Ellie's here!"

I manage a smile.

Vic runs to meet me, her auburn hair streaming behind her, face flushed, arms open. "You're in for a noisy time, I'm afraid!" she cries as she envelops me in a hug. I was cryptic on the phone, but she knows I've been through something and she knows it's big.

"But how . . ." I stammer. ". . . . It can't be true!"

I clamp the receiver to my ear, wondering if it's possible I've misheard. But I know I haven't.

Jo's voice is terse. "I don't think Dan would lie about such a thing! Do you?"

I stare at the six pairs of boots in Vic's hallway as if they can provide the proof I need. I'd rung Jo hoping for news of Dan. But instead she'd assaulted me with a hideous, horrifying revelation. I'd assumed the fire had been all my fault, which was bad enough, but this! My husband, a criminal. My husband, an arsonist.

"I just . . . I can't comprehend how Clive could have wanted to do such a thing," I stammer.

Could he really, really have meant to strike that match? I recall the tang I smelled on his breath the last time we were at home together. I picture all the empty whiskey bottles. The effects of alcohol on an over-strained mind . . .

"I don't get it either," Jo grunts. "What did Dan ever do to him? If — and nobody ever hinted this was the case until now — your reason for leaving your husband was to be with my brother, then that was *your* call and *your* choice. But it's Dan who's lost his livelihood and ended up in horrible pain in the hospital. While you skip off to the comfort of your sister's in Yorkshire."

"Jo, I —"

"How could your husband even *think* of it?" She's getting worked up now. Her voice is screechy. "What kind of a person is he to go to such extremes? What did you do to make him so jealous, so violent? Were you sleeping with my brother?"

"No!"

"Well, clearly something was going on. And now you know the consequences of your actions. I hope you're happy."

She slams the phone down. I don't blame her one bit for her anger. I stand shaking in the hall, trying to take in this new slant on things. The vision of the burning barn is alive in my head. It's so terrifying I can't bear to think of anyone deliberately planning it, let alone my own husband.

Clive, *Clive* — how is this possible? Over the last few hours I've been telling myself he's a hero. I was even contemplating going back to him. But now the message is thundering home: How much heroism did it actually take to call the fire department and to drag an exhausted Dan back from the barn? More to the point, how much malice did it take to plan a scene of destruction like the one I'd witnessed? Malice and sheer, venomous evil.

The world is turning on its head. I think back. Everything is coming into sharper focus. Clive isn't the one who called to me through the flames or guided me down the roof and caught me when I jumped. Or who dashed back into the furnace to save the harps. It isn't Clive who is the hero.

Everything now homes in on Dan, the kindest, bravest, truest man I know. What horror I have brought into his life! How can he ever forgive me? How can I possibly overcome the bitter regret clawing inside me?

47
DAN

My first visitor in the hospital was my sister Jo. My second visitor was Thomas. He was wearing an anorak over his shorts, electric blue. The fringe of his hair was on a jagged slant and pressed flat against his forehead. I guessed he had let his wife Linda give him a haircut again and not liked it again and tried to improve it himself with a pair of nail scissors again. This happens often with Thomas.

Thomas sat in the chair by the bed and expressed his deep concern for my well-being and asked if I was doing all right. I informed him that according to the doctors I was doing miraculously well. He patted me on the shoulder.

"Ouch," I said because my shoulder was tender. Not as badly burned as my arms and hands, but still not good.

"Sorry, mate," he said.

We sat in silence for a while. I thought

about my harps. Thirty-two had been burned. I had managed to save four, and by good fortune Ellie's harp had also survived. The fire brigade had put out the flames before they reached the upstairs room. But thirty-two was a lot of harps to lose.

Thomas said, "I gave Ellie J a lift from the hospital. She drove off up to Yorkshire. Just in case you wanted to know where she is, boyo."

(I already knew where she was, in fact, because Jo had told me. I had asked lots of questions about Ellie when I found out Ellie had been on the phone to Jo, but Jo had said don't you go worrying about Ellie; Ellie's not the one who got severe burns and lost thirty-two harps and her whole livelihood, is she?)

After another pause Thomas said: "I presume you're insured, mate?"

I didn't answer immediately, so he said it again, in different words: "You took out buildings and contents insurance for the barn, didn't you, boyo?"

Buildings and contents insurance is when you give more money than you can possibly afford to a company made up of people you have never met and in exchange they will ask you to fill in a lot of forms packed with questions to which you don't know the answers.

I said no.

"That's not good, boyo," Thomas said. Then he said: "Where are you going to live? How are you going to survive?"

To which I answered that I hadn't the faintest idea.

48
ELLIE

"He could be charming in his way, but I have to admit I always thought you were far too good for him."

"Good?" The word makes no sense.

Vic reaches out and strokes my arm. "I never particularly warmed to Clive, Ellie, but I never dreamed he could do anything like this! Whiskey or no!"

It is late. We are at the kitchen table, with wine. I take a sip from my glass. I need it badly. Telling Vic seems to make what happened even more real. Her husband wanders in.

"Alan, sorry, but Ellie and I are having an important catch-up."

Alan looks apologetic and backs out.

When he's gone again she tops up both our glasses. She keeps shaking her head and making faces. "Do you know, I had this bad feeling about Clive right from the start. I know it's easy to say now, but I never felt he was right for you. He was unbelievably manipulative. He played on your insecurities, Ellie, and he cramped your style. He could put on a good show of kindness, but he knew exactly which buttons to press to get his own way and make you feel bad about yourself. I did try to tell you, but you wouldn't have it — you always sprang to his defense. You just kept giving him the benefit of the doubt. I thought you must have some kind of a blind spot or something."

"Well, my eyes are opened now!"

My mother instilled in me such pitifully low self-esteem I'd always considered myself lucky to have a man like Clive.

Lucky? I laugh bitterly.

"What about this harpmaker?" Vic says, pushing back her hair, searching for a positive. "Is there anything there?"

I look down into my glass. "Vic . . . thirty-two harps . . . *thirty-two*! One would have been tragedy enough, but . . . If you had seen those harps! If you'd seen him working at them day after day, creating such fine, noble creatures out of blocks of wood . . . so carefully and lovingly shaping them . . . Each one a work of wonder, each one totally unique. The smell of them, the touch of them, the exquisite sounds they could make! And because of me, because of stupid,

stupid me, they are all burned to cinders!"

My grief is contagious. We weep together.

A long time later I stand up and go to look at the calendar that's hanging on the wall. "I must visit Mum. How is she?"

"She's got a bit of a cold, but they're looking after her well."

"Can we see her tomorrow?"

"Of course."

At this moment I feel that the sight of my mother will be reassuring. It just goes to show how much life has changed.

"Ellie, Ellie, what's happening!"

I throw back the bedclothes and sit bolt upright, gasping for breath. My heart is jumping about in my rib cage. "What? What?"

Vic is at the door in her dressing gown. "You screamed."

I realize where I am. The panic begins to subside. "Bad dreams," I explain, rubbing my eyes.

"Oh, my poor sis! You were bloodcurdling. You terrified us all. What were you dreaming?"

"Bad stuff. Burning harps, flying pheasants, my husband setting fire to my clothes."

She sits beside me and strokes my hair. I cling to her. The images replay in my head.

My husband was setting fire to my clothes. And I was wearing those clothes.

"Mum, look who's come to see you!" declares Vic as we enter the small, functional, overheated bedroom. Mum is in an armchair, holding a book upside down and viewing it earnestly. A pink paper crown from Christmas is perched on top of her white curls.

"Ah, Mum, look at you, still looking so festive!"

She would never have worn such a thing in the past. I wonder if one of the carers placed it on her head and if she even knows it's there.

"Just a minute, I'm all blocked up," she mutters, turning the book over and over in her hands.

Vic and I exchange glances. We're not sure in which sense she is blocked up or whether she even has any comprehension of the words she's saying. We wait. At last she lays the book on her lap and looks up at me. Her eyes are encrusted with rheum, but signs of recognition slowly spread across her face.

"Ah, you!" she says to me, then turns to Vic. "She looks thinner, doesn't she?"

"Yes, she does, but we're very happy to

405

see her, aren't we, Mum?"

Mum's wrinkles shift slightly. She's never been very good at smiling.

We stay and chat for a while, covering the topics of Christmas at the care home, the weather, memories of our childhood and favorite foods. Mum contributes little, and only fragments are relevant. Vic updates her on the ballet and swimming lessons of her throng of grandchildren. I provide precisely no updates about my own life.

Wherever I am, whatever I'm doing, the thought keeps slamming into my consciousness. I fling it out time and time again, but it comes back like a boomerang. Clive wanted to ruin Dan and mortify me. Clive wanted to burn the harps. I simply cannot comprehend such cruelty.

Neither Dan nor I have reported him to the police. As far as the fire service is concerned, the cause of the fire was a fallen candle, and the rapid spread of flames was due to the quantity of wood shavings and other flammable objects in the barn. Nobody has mentioned a heap of paraffin-soaked clothes, evidence that was wholly destroyed. Was it arson, anyway? Clive (thanks to Phineas) never actually lit a match. We could, I suppose, drag him through the courts, but it would only be traumatic for everyone, most of all for Dan, who can't bear to be in a room with more than five people. But I wonder if Dan could claim compensation. Or if I could somehow help him negotiate an out-of-court settlement with Clive. I've discussed it with Vic and Alan and they think that might still be a possibility.

The thought of ever being in touch with Clive again, however, makes my blood run cold.

They've all left early this morning, Alan and Vic for work and the children for school. I brew myself a strong coffee. The aroma takes me straight back to the Harp Barn. I'm pretty much always there in my thoughts anyway. It has already been a week since the fire, but time has folded into itself and everything seems to refer back to that event. I decide to hoover the house or make myself useful in some other way before the family returns. There's a plastic helicopter on the chair, a one-legged doll on the fridge and a felt owl staring at me from the windowsill. The owl has a reproachful look and sadness in its big purple eyes. I sit down with my coffee, wondering where to start. Then I see it: the letter lying on the kitchen table, addressed to me. Clive's handwriting.

My coffee lurches all over the table. Luckily the tablecloth is childproof and easily wipeable. I find a kitchen sponge and clean the mess. Then I pick up the envelope gingerly, as if it's about to bite me. Sooner or later I'll have to look. I force myself to run a finger under the flap and unfold the paper inside.

Dear Ellie,

I have written to you so many times, but this time I'm going to post it. Words don't come easily, but you and I still have futures and I know I can't get on with mine if I leave this hanging.

I want you to know that I've stopped drinking. I'm tempted often, but all I have to do is remind myself what a monster whiskey makes of me. I know I'll never go near it again. I can never forget your face that night, and never forget what I did and what I was so close to doing.

There is nothing I want more than for you to come home, but I have no right to expect that now. You still have your keys. When you are ready please come back to the house and take whatever is yours. If you don't want to see me, then come during my office hours.

I've transferred a sum to your account, which I hope you will accept. There is enough, I believe, to support you for a good while and to make repairs to the barn if that's what you want to do (and I have a feeling you will). It hasn't escaped my notice that no charges have been pressed against me. Your kindness stands in stark contrast to my own bitter actions.

I am in pieces without you, Ellie. All I can do is hope you'll let me do this much for you.

I can't say anything else at the moment except this. I am — truly — sorry.

Clive

I am dumbfounded. What it must have cost him to write a letter so contrite, so groveling! What has happened to the proud, strong, fierce man I used to know?

I am in pieces without you, Ellie.

All those years I viewed Clive as a rock, myself as his limpet. Now it dawns on me for the first time. All those years it wasn't him who was the rock. It was me.

49
DAN

The third, fourth and fifth people who came to visit me in the hospital were Ed and his grandparents. My ex-girlfriend Roe Deer did not come with them. But Ed's rabbit (who is called Mr. Rabbit and who Ed is very fond of) did. None of them stayed for long because Ed's grandparents had a meeting all about a new traffic layout system that, if it goes ahead, is going to upset all the residents in their part of Taunton. They needed to get back and drop off Ed with the babysitter and have a bite to eat and then make sure they were at the meeting in time to get a seat near the front.

It was good to see Ed, very. He sat close to me on the edge of my bed. Mr. Rabbit sat next to him. Ed was wearing a blue sweater with a red tractor knitted onto the front of it. Mr. Rabbit was wearing a yellow ribbon round his orange neck.

"Is Phineas OK?" was the first thing Ed asked.

I assured him that Phineas was fine. He had made his escape via the pheasant flap long before the fire started and had kept well away from it. Not a feather was singed. And now that I wasn't there to feed him, Thomas was doing that task for me. Thomas, of course, couldn't play the requisite chords on the medieval harp, and even if he could, it would be impossible because the harp had been burned. But he'd promised me he would call Phineas and be sure that he ate his meals, and be sure that he was sleeping all right in his second bed in the woodshed, and be sure to provide him with extra blankets. Thomas had muttered "Bloody bird!" under his breath, but afterward he'd said all right, mate, anything for you, mate.

"Can we go and visit Phineas too?" Ed asked his grandmother.

She shook her head. "I don't think that would be a good idea, Edward."

I said never mind, as soon as I was out of the hospital I would give him a lift in the Land Rover and we would go to visit Phineas together.

Ed's grandfather stuck his chin out and made a humphing noise. "We can discuss

411

that later," he said.

Ed then took a sheet of paper out of his fluorescent yellow backpack and handed it to me. "I drew this for you, Dad."

I studied the paper with great attention, then turned it the other way up and studied it again. It was all rainbow colors, streaky and very fine, but I couldn't make out what the picture was meant to be.

"It's Phineas, Dad!"

I could see now that he'd pointed it out to me that it was indeed Phineas. I said thank you and how proud and delighted I was to have such a picture of such a magnificent and heroic bird. I would put it on the hospital table beside my bed and admire it often.

When I look at past events it seems to me that they are made up of long, wavering strings of ifs. If, for example, I had not given Ellie the cherrywood harp, she would never have come back to the barn to play it. If she hadn't come back, she wouldn't have taken harp lessons with Roe Deer. If she hadn't taken those lessons, she wouldn't have discovered that I had a son Ed. If she hadn't discovered Ed, I wouldn't have known of his existence. He wouldn't have known of mine. A huge great chunk of wonderfulness would have been missing and we wouldn't even have realized it.

And if Ellie hadn't told me about Ed, Roe Deer wouldn't have been cross and spoken to Ellie's husband Clive. Ellie's husband Clive wouldn't have got angry and ripped up Ellie's poems and she wouldn't have left him. He wouldn't have come to the barn to see if she was there and wouldn't have stuffed paraffin rags around. And if we hadn't saved Phineas all those weeks earlier, Phineas wouldn't have been in his bed so he wouldn't have flown into Clive's face and Clive would have set fire to the barn when Ellie was asleep and I was away, then not even one of the harps would have survived and Ellie would not be here anymore and neither of us would be happy about that. That would be a sad thing. Much sadder than just losing thirty-two harps.

Sometimes the ifs work for you and sometimes they work against you. Sometimes you think they are working for you whereas in fact they are working against you, and sometimes you think they are working against you whereas in fact they are working for you. It is only when you look back that you realize, and you don't always realize even then.

Lying in a hospital bed with all the nurses,

doctors, patients, machines and bleeps was disturbing, but I wasn't allowed to leave, so I kept my brain busy by thinking about all the ifs. Another thing about ifs is that they help you understand things. If I hadn't been in a fire, I wouldn't have understood this: that although people as a whole are difficult and I would rather most of them did not exist, there are certain people who are very, very important. Even more important than harps. Ellie Jacobs is one of those people.

My son Ed is another.

If my son Ed had been in the fire . . . but I'm absolutely not going to think about that.

50
ELLIE

I rang Jo again yesterday. Dan is now out of the hospital and staying at her house, although she can scarcely squeeze him in. When she answered the phone Jo was still resentful about the havoc I've wreaked in her brother's life, but she softened when I announced my intention of rebuilding the barn.

"I want it to rise like a phoenix from the ashes," I gushed, all abuzz with new determination.

"Ellie, you are one hell of a crazy cow! But yes, please, *please* do it! I can't cope with Dan here a second longer than I have to, and I've been worried sick about his future."

"Could I possibly have a word with him?"

I sense a stiffness. "No, Ellie, I really don't think that's a good idea right now. Both of you need to sort yourselves out. I'm having a hard enough job getting Dan to relax as it is, without you stirring him up again."

"I'd hardly be stirring him up! I just want to share the good news. I just want to tell him I'll do everything I can to —"

"Look, I've got nothing against you personally and it's great that you want to make amends. But I'd honestly rather you stayed away from Dan. You're involved with a very dangerous man. Dan nearly died, and so did you. Who's to say Clive won't turn nasty again?"

"He won't. I'm sure he won't."

"He may be trying to buy you back. He may take it out on Dan again when it doesn't work. Hell, I don't know! But he's an alcoholic and a psychopath. Sorry, but I'm just not prepared to see my brother getting hurt again. Clear?"

"But . . . Please can't I just speak with Dan?"

"What part of *no* don't you understand?"

I swallowed down my hurt and indignation. I needed Jo on my side.

"Jo, does Dan, um . . . does he ever talk about me? Does he ever mention me?"

A short pause.

"No, actually he doesn't."

There. That puts you in your place, Ellie Jacobs.

"I'll let him know you're going to fix the

barn," said Jo in a more conciliatory voice. "He'll be pleased."

I'd so much rather have told Dan myself.

I ran upstairs and hugged Dan's jacket instead.

I miss Christina and long to tell her everything. Vic and her family are endlessly, unstintingly lovely, but somehow I can't talk things through in the same way. Christina should be back from Thailand by now, but I've left countless messages on her answerphone and she's never got back to me.

The money I now have in my possession is more than I'd ever envisaged spending in a lifetime. I was quite hysterical when I saw the bank statement. All that scrimping and saving, all that moaning about bills, yet Clive had so much hoarded away the whole time! I'd no idea. So generous was the sum I now wondered if I could actually build Dan a whole castle rather than just repair his humble barn.

But it turns out that builders and workmen and harpmaking tools are all way more expensive than I'd imagined. And there are logistical problems with just about everything. Endless phone calls are necessary to make people do what I'm paying them to do and I'm too far away to plead in person.

Workmen simply seem to be allergic to work. It's hard to get hold of anyone because of the holiday season, and when I do they plague me with questions about structural details that I don't understand.

"Please, just make everything exactly how it was before!" I beg. However, in technical terms I am quite incapable of describing how it was before. My lips are bleeding because I've bitten them so much from sheer frustration. Dan would be better at explaining, but I am reluctant to refer the builders to Dan. Dan hates talking to people on the phone — especially people he doesn't know.

I have extracted from him (via Jo) an itemized list of everything that was in the workshop. We'll get a catalog and replace all his tools once the builders and decorators have finished. Jo and I have both agreed we must get Dan back to normal as quickly as we can. I've offered the builders a lavish raise in pay if they hurry up. Which has made a massive difference.

"What would Dad have made of the way I'm spending all this money?" I ask my sister, having blithely parted with another six hundred pounds.

"Hard to say," she answers, shaking her head. "Mum wouldn't have approved —

wouldn't approve — but I don't know about Dad."

"I like to think he'd be pleased. It's all due to him that I'm in this position, after all. Him and his insistence that I follow a dream."

Vic studies my face. "And what of that dream now, Ellie? When you've finished being so manic, what are your plans?"

I can't look that far ahead. But I know I can't stay here forever, trespassing on her kindness, fitting around her family's clutter, acting as though I'm happy and normal.

"What about your harp playing?" she asks. "Will you go back to it?"

Harp playing? Me? Now? That seems as impossible as a browned and withered flower head trying to be a bud again.

The house is silent as though holding its breath, watching to see what I'll do. I let myself in. It is early afternoon. Clive is at work.

I wander around collecting books, CDs, my photo albums, the remainder of my clothes. The look, the touch, the smell of everything is the same, but the place doesn't feel like home anymore. Perhaps it never did. Like the rest of my past, it doesn't really fit me properly.

I am at least pleased to note there are no whiskey or beer bottles around. There are a couple of postcards lying on the windowsill.

Hey, Ellie! Here I am in Thailand. Best non-Christmas Christmas EVER. Get this: palm-fringed beaches, blue, blue sea, me in teeny bikini! Gadding around in sunshine. No sexy beach bums yet, but hope springs eternal. Hope U R well and everything sorted with You-Know-Who.

Love and kisses,
Christina

The second postcard reads:

Hi, Ellie,
Guess what? I've met a lovely Thai family who've offered me food and lodging for another month here in exchange for helping the children with their English. I had to think about it for all of five seconds! The kids are sweet, no hassle and it's great. I won't be back in Exmoor for ages. Hope all good for you and Clive.

C xxx

I smile sadly and tuck the cards into my

bag. Christina and I have some serious catching up to do.

A sudden noise startles me. The front door opening. My heart jumps to my mouth. I swing round.

He's there. Not the monstrous, hateful version I've been picturing over the past weeks, but my husband: real, human, complex. Haggard.

"Clive!"

His hands stretch out toward me.

"Ellie . . . my El . . . I'm so glad you're here."

"I just came to get my things." I nod toward the suitcases. "I thought you'd be at work."

"I know." His head bows in a submissive gesture. His presence feels raw. "I've been finishing early this last week, taking work home instead. A new arrangement."

"Right." I don't know what to say.

"Did you find everything you need?"

"Yes, I think so." I move toward the cases and make as if to go.

He stands in my way, a wall of desperation. "Just a minute! Now that you're here . . . Ellie, listen!" His eyes bore into mine. "I never meant to hurt you. You know that, don't you? I thought you'd gone away that night. I'd no idea you were still at the barn. It kills me thinking about it, about how close it was to . . . I was going crazy, you see, with everything going round and round in my head. Thinking how you'd lied to me, thinking of you with *him,* and missing you, just missing you like hell. And the drinking . . . I wasn't in control. I couldn't help it, El. Can you ever forgive me?"

His words clatter around my brain. I want to escape. I try to answer his question, but a noise like a growl comes out.

"Ellie, honeybun, don't do this to me . . . don't . . ." He swallows, hard. "OK, here it is: I love you. I love you so, so much. Don't you see? I love you and I can't do without you. I want you to come back to me. Please."

I stare at him in disbelief.

"I *need* you," he urges.

"I'm not coming back," I tell him.

"Let's put this behind us, El. This, this madness. Let's go back to how we were. You and me are good together."

That charm of his.

"And I still love you."

The "still." The way he says it, the wounded accusation. By "still" he means in spite of everything *I've* done. In his mind he is being magnanimous in his offer to take me back. He's done with apologizing and

422

transferred the blame right back onto me. I am the guilty party here. I am supposed to feel grateful and submissive.

I shrink from his touch. One word. "No."

"Please, El, I'm begging you!"

"No."

"Haven't I made amends? Haven't I said I'm sorry? I wrote you that letter. I gave you more money than I can possibly afford. I was generous. I was more than generous." There's a whining, waspish edge to his voice.

Thirty-two harps burned, a workshop destroyed, Dan injured, myself nearly killed. And he thinks money can make it right.

"C'mon, El, don't be difficult. This is your home. Your life is here, with me. You *need* me." Willing me with his eyes. He leans in so close I can smell his aftershave, that hint of bergamot and leather I know so well. He isn't drunk now, just greedy. He steps forward to take me in his arms.

I can't help it. My own arm reaches back for an instant to gather force, then slams into him, the flat of my hand across his face. He reels sideways, loses his balance and crumples onto the floor. He clutches an elbow, whimpering in pain. Looks up at me, his face brick red with rage.

I step over him. Sure of my own decisions at last.

"Good-bye, Clive."

51
DAN

Whenever I mention Ellie to my sister Jo, she answers: "Dan, Ellie will be fine." Whenever I mention Ellie she says, "Ellie can sort herself out." Whenever I mention Ellie she says, "*You're* the one we need to worry about now." Whenever I mention Ellie (which is often) she says: "Dan, shut up about Ellie! Enough about Ellie! I don't want to hear about Ellie."

Ever since our parents died, my sister Jo has been very protective over me. I know this because she told me so herself once. "It's great that you're so independent, bro," she said, "but you just don't get that sometimes people take advantage. You've got to believe me, I've got your interests at heart. I'm not being bossy, I'm just giving you some *guidelines.*"

My sister Jo can see things in a way I can't and understand people in a way I can't. I therefore decided long ago that it's a good idea to follow her guidelines.

Maybe now my sister Jo can see this: that whenever I mention Ellie there's a great big mountain of feelings swelling inside me. Some of these feelings are like a thirst; some are like an ache; some are like a flock of bright butterflies. My sister Jo doesn't want me to go through any more pain. My sister Jo knows (as I do now) that I am not cut out for relationships. Not at all. I am made of all the wrong ingredients. Ellie must know this too. Whenever Ellie rings she does not want to talk to me, apparently. She just wants to talk to Jo and arrange stuff about the rebuilding of the barn. I am happy about the rebuilding of the barn, very, but I'm not happy that Ellie doesn't want to speak to me.

Five is the number of harps that were saved. Five includes Ellie's cherrywood harp. The reason Ellie's harp survived is that it was upstairs in the little room at the time of the fire, and Ellie closed the door of the little room behind her when she escaped, and (according to the firemen) because the door was tight-fitting with no gaps round the edge, the flames did not get any farther but concentrated instead on the workshop downstairs. I am glad Ellie's harp survived. Very.

Thirty-two is the number of harps that were burned.

The number of days I spent in the hospital was eleven. The number of days I spent in Jo's bungalow in Bridgwater was thirty-four. The eleven days were not good ones for me, and neither were the thirty-four. In the hospital there were way too many ill people, too many visitors, too many doctors, too many nurses and too many machines that went bleep bleep bleep. In Jo's bungalow there was not enough space, not enough air and not enough things made from wood. Outside her bungalow when I looked out there were not enough trees; only streets and cars and more bungalows.

When you're waiting for something, time has a way of slowing right down. Those weeks I was at my sister Jo's house time went slower than a snail with very bad rheumatism. I wished I could have pressed the fast-forward button on time and got myself back to my Harp Barn, but Jo said I was not well enough and anyway the barn wasn't ready yet, so waiting was my only choice. I did not like waiting. Not at all. I was twitchy.

■ ■ ■

Today, at last, the day has arrived! I am going back to the barn. Jo is driving me. Ed is with us too. He made his grandparents drop him off at Jo's house because he wanted to be part of the celebrations. We have brought coffee and sandwiches (peanut butter and cucumber, rectangular, wholemeal bread). Ed is bouncing around all over the back of the car, saying things like "You're better, Dad!" "You're going home, Dad!" and "You're going to be all happy and harp-making soon, Dad!"

I say yes I am, yes I am, to all of these.

The day is a bright, bold one. The trees are stirring the air with their branches and ragged white clouds are racing each other across the sky. The sun is blasting everything with color: greens ranging from emerald to sage to lime; even the old brown shreds of bracken are rich with auburn and burnished copper. As I watch from the window the landscape becomes wilder and hillier and sheepier. I feel that simultaneously I am becoming *Dannier.* And I realize that Exmoor is more than my home. Much more. Exmoor, in a way, is me. It is where I can do my harpmaking and where I can be my absolute self, and those two things are very bound up in each other.

When we arrive at the top of the lane, the barn is there, as real and solid as ever, with a new door all shiny. Thomas is standing by the doorway holding an enormous bunch of balloons. And there, scratching away in the dirt, his plumage all splendid and his eyes glittering like jewels, is Phineas my pheasant.

"Welcome home, mate," Thomas cries and presents me with the bunch of balloons.

I say thank you and then hand them to Ed because Ed likes balloons more than I do and besides, I completely need to hug Phineas. Phineas saved Ellie's life, after all. He is no ordinary bird. Phineas submits to being hugged and pecks my earlobe lightly in a way that is affectionate and pleasing.

Jo, Thomas, Ed, Phineas and I are all gabbling away at each other, happy and excited to be here again. We unlock the new door, push it open and go inside.

Ed runs around saying, "Look! Look! Look!" which is exactly what I am now doing. The workshop seems very big and empty with only four rather bedraggled harps in the middle and no heaps of sawdust and no bits of lichen, fir cones, feathers and the other things I like to keep around. But the room is fully equipped with a brand-new table, chairs, workbench, band saw, planer, lathe and all the other bits and pieces I need for making harps. Winter sunshine streams through the three big windows onto all the new things. They gleam.

But maybe even better than all the new things is what is up on the walls of my workshop: pictures, stuck up at all sorts of angles, stuck up everywhere. I recognize the style of the artist. The artist is my son Ed. This time I can see clearly the subject matter of the pictures. They are pictures of harps, all different sizes, colored in different-colored crayons. The lines of the strings are thick in some places and thin in others and they go over the sides of the harp frames and the woodwork is scribbly and the straight edges aren't straight, but I think that they're by far the best pictures I've ever seen.

"Do you know how many there are?" Ed cries.

"Yes," I answer, because I've counted already. "There are thirty-two."

"Do you like them?"

I say that I do indeed. Seldom have I liked anything more.

"Ellie said I should do them for you!" he

exclaims, pulling me by the jacket toward the wall to look at them more closely. "Ellie said you'd be missing all the burned harps and she said if I drew some more you'd be cheer-upping much quicker."

"Ellie?" I'd no idea Ed had seen Ellie since the fire. I thought Ellie was up in Yorkshire. That's what Jo had told me. Up in Yorkshire and busy sorting herself out. Not wanting to speak to me on the phone or anything because she was so very busy. That's what Jo had told me.

Jo looks over at Ed with arched eyebrows. Then she turns to me: "Ellie came back here the other day to check that everything was OK. Ed and I came to meet her here because she said she needed to make sure she hadn't forgotten anything important. It was just a flying visit."

"I saw her afterward," Thomas adds. "She called in at my place to drop off Linda's clothes. Just as well or I'd have been in for it. That was Linda's favorite sweater, you know."

That was kind of Ellie to check up on everything so carefully. But I feel a bit odd about her coming all that way and seeing everybody except me.

I wish Ellie was here now. But I expect she'll be back soon. She's bound to be back soon. She'll be wanting to play her harp.

"Have you seen, Dan? The staircase is new too!" Jo points out.

She is right. The staircase is made of oak wood, very handsome. I stroke the banister admiringly. Then I go up the stairs. I count as I go. There are still seventeen steps, a thing that pleases me a lot.

I feel all sorts of things being back here again. Suitable metaphors for the way I feel might be: a singing bird, a dancer's feet, a skipping lamb, a burst of wonderful music. But as I reach the top of the stairs I see a sight that changes everything in an instant. The singing bird suddenly develops a sore throat. The dancer's feet are yucky and smelly. The skipping lamb has landed in the mire. The burst of wonderful music has ended on a jarring chord.

There, in front of me, in the little room, is Ellie's harp. But it is pushed against the wall and draped in a big white sheet. At once I know that the harp is conveying a sorrowful message. A message so sorrowful I can hardly bear to think of it. The harp tells me that it will not be played anymore, perhaps not ever. The harp tells me that Ellie Jacobs is gone.

52
ELLIE

Mum is staring fixedly at a picture of a flock of sheep that's hanging on her wall. I have to tell her now.

"Mum, listen! I'm leaving the country. I'll be away for quite some time . . ."

She says nothing.

"I promise I'll ring you when I can."

"And you still have no idea where?" Vic asks, absently curling a strand of her hair.

"I don't know where I'll end up. The only thing I know is that it will be somewhere totally, totally different from home." My voice sounds alien. Sharp.

My sister sighs. "Oh, Ellie! You will come back, won't you?"

I go to the window and look out. There is only a view of a car park.

"Ellie," Mum says abruptly, as if referring to somebody not in the room. "She always was difficult in that way. Head full of strange ideas. Don't know where she got them from."

I smile darkly. "Mum, take care, won't you?"

"Take care yourself!" she returns, as if it was an insult.

I stoop and kiss her.

I snuggle into Dan's jacket during the flight. I should have left it in the barn for him but didn't. The conversation with Jo reruns in my head.

I asked if Dan was OK. She said yes, he was much better. I asked if he had managed to forgive me for all the trouble I'd unwittingly caused. She replied, "Forgive? Don't be silly! Dan doesn't think in that way." I try to recall her face as she said it, her intonation and her intention, but I can't wring any extra clues from my memory.

Ed clamored to be first in, thrilled to see the barn's transformation. When I made my suggestion about drawing the harps he was all eagerness. He reminded me of his father so much.

I walked around trying to take it all in, not sure if I approved or not of this brand-new version of my fairy-tale place. It was well finished and pristine, but it just seemed so empty.

I asked Jo if it was all right, if I'd forgotten anything. She said: "Looks good to me!" I thought for a moment she was going to hug me, but she didn't. She gave me a little pat on the back instead. "Well done, Ellie. And thank you. And, for what it's worth, I think you've made the right decision."

"About the barn?" I said.

"About everything."

About everything. That clearly included getting out of Dan's life without even a good-bye. Despite my efforts and all the money I'd spent I was seen as a disruptive element. I wasn't welcome anymore. Dan wanted to be free of me. Jo had made that perfectly clear. It was a bitter pill.

The sun is twinkling on the lagoon, making a thousand golden loops and twists on the water's surface. I watch from the balcony of the villa where I'm staying. The old me would have written a poem, but now all I can do is gaze. I am mesmerized by the honey-colored shapes forever dividing and joining in bright, restless patterns. Above them, Venice gleams. Something about the buildings reminds me of antique lace. They are so intricate in their design and so perfect. They stand proud, starched and taut against the blue sky, but their upside-down

435

reflections are a different matter, loosely weaving and wobbling, unsure of themselves.

Here I am, living in a crowded city, but I'm a sad, solitary creature. Even though I jostle with people every day I feel no connection with the rest of humanity. I hardly talk to anyone. It's a relief to be so anonymous. This landscape of palazzi, gondolas, bridges and bell towers provides a picturesque setting, but their beauty fails to resonate the way it should. I spend my days wandering in the myriad twisting backstreets. I get lost often and don't care greatly. I don't eat much: an occasional panino from a bar or a thick hot chocolate to keep me going. Every little thing — brushing my teeth in the morning, putting on clothes, even breathing — seems a massive effort. The future looms ahead of me, dark and empty. Pointless.

The slim, bronzed lady in reception is curious about me.

"Signora Jacobs is always only her, singly, alone. She waits for her man?"

"No," I tell her. "There is no man."

She throws up her hands in horror. "Then she must find one, here in Italia. We have many fine men here!"

"Yes, you do," I acknowledge.

Perhaps that will be a way forward. Perhaps I'll forget my past in the arms of an Italian. The quickest route to forgetfulness — that's what I crave.

My former life won't leave me alone. Memories torture me. Images flick in and out of my mind: Clive watching football, Clive giving me jewelry, Clive kissing my neck. Clive with the newspaper, Clive with the whiskey bottle, Clive with the poker. I try to understand. Did I ever love him? You could say that I did. You could say that he loved me too. Neither of us really questioned it during those long years together. But I see everything in a different light now, a light that is tainted with violent, flickering orange. I see another Clive. He is nothing like the man I thought he was. The qualities I admired were all sham. His violent reactions to everything (which I'd interpreted as strength of character) were plain, childish, self-serving neediness. Clive needed me badly, but in fact I've never needed him. Far from it. I was the rock in the relationship. But this discovery has brought no joy. Rocks are heavy. Rocks sink easily.

More painful still are those other thoughts. Thoughts about my harp and the harpmaker who set in motion all the events that have led me to this spot. Feelings run deep.

Thank God I managed to repair the barn! That helps soften the distress, but it is always present, a dark underground gully of guilt, hurt and sorrow.

"Signora Jacobs will find a handsome Italian man and be happy again!" cries my concerned receptionist.

"Will she?" I answer, not meeting her eye. "We'll see."

53
DAN

Thomas takes a swig of cider. "So, mate, what's going on with your love life?"

I take a swig of mine. "Nothing."

"Nothing?" he asks.

"Nothing," I confirm.

He takes another swig. It glugs noisily in his throat. "Roe Deer?" he asks.

I shake my head.

"Ellie J, the Exmoor Housewife?" he asks.

I shake my head again.

"She's gone, then?"

"Gone," I say.

I hear nothing from her. I don't know what I am supposed to feel or think.

"So you don't have any lovely ladies visiting you anymore?"

I acknowledge that this is the case.

"Well, that's a turnup for the books, boyo!" he says.

I ask him which books he is talking about.

"The books of Grim Despair," he answers,

ensuring both words have capital letters.

We sit and swig in silence for a while until our glasses are empty.

"Women!" says Thomas. He then stands up with a sigh, goes to the bar and asks for another round of ciders. The barmaid with painted-on eyebrows smiles and the barman with the shiny face says, "No worries."

Thomas brings back the ciders and goes on to tell me all about his most recent arguments with his wife.

Thomas and I have a lot of conversations like this.

On the journey to and from the pub I get the back of my neck licked by his dogs.

I need to make harps quickly now and sell them to help pay the bills and to contribute toward Ed's upkeep. I am making four simultaneously. My sister Jo has said we need more publicity. She has made a lot of flyers with pictures of a harp and the website details and the words: *Would you like a harp? Take a look at this!* She originally put three exclamation marks on it, but I said that was too many.

"Do you think so?" she said. "Well, maybe you're right. Less is more."

I pointed out that this was a contradiction in terms and actually less is less whereas more is more. And in my opinion less than three exclamation marks was what we needed. Less than two, even. One would be quite adequate. I wasn't even sure we needed one.

"OK, OK, whatever you want," is what she said.

I am grateful to be back here and pleased to be making harps again. But I am not in the mood for exclamation marks. Not at all.

I walk, I make harps, I feed Phineas, I eat sandwiches, same as usual. I do not eat so many spicy things now and there is not so much variety in my life. However, my sister Jo visits more than she used to. She brings stew and soup and gives me instructions about this and that. My son Ed still comes to visit on Saturdays too.

Our harp is coming on nicely. We spent a long time discussing what sort of a harp it is to be, but now that's settled. It will be made out of walnut wood, because he likes the quality of the graining in the wood and the color, which he says is the right amount of dark. I tell him about the special kind of deep resonance that walnut has. He tells me he does not like to eat walnuts because they taste like bricks, but that he thinks a harp made out of them will be good. We go out

441

for long trips pebble hunting, putting on our wellies and following the path of the stream together.

We have found the right pebble. It is roughly diamond shaped and is very light, almost white, with a dove-gray mottling. There were a few possibilities, but Ed said as soon as we saw it that this was the one. He held it between his finger and thumb and viewed it from every angle. Then he looked at me with his big, round eyes.

"Do you miss her?" he said.

I asked him if he was referring to his mother, Roe Deer.

"No," he said. "I mean the kind woman. The woman with the nice hair and sad eyes. The woman who slid all about everywhere in the snow. Who read us the 'Jabberwocky' poem. Who got me to draw harps. Ellie."

I thought about Ellie Jacobs the Exmoor Housewife. Some people, when you don't see them for a long time, become sort of transparent and blurry round the edges. Ellie Jacobs is not one of these people.

I told him yes.

"I thought so," he said, and his eyes looked straight into mine in a way that made me look everywhere but back at him.

"Is she coming back ever?" he asked.

I said I didn't know. But I thought in all

likelihood she wasn't.

We were silent for a bit. I was aware of Exmoor stretching all around us. The trees were scratchy and sharp against the raw, empty February sky. In the silence I thought more and more about Ellie and why she went away after the fire. I guess it can only be because she loved her husband Clive very much but he had planned to do an awful thing and she knew she couldn't go back to him once she knew about the awful thing but she still felt lost and lonely and sad and probably just wanted things to go back to the way they were before but that was impossible. Love can be very complicated. I should know. I would so much have liked love to be a part of my own life, especially where Ellie Jacobs is concerned, but I am made of all the wrong ingredients. I know that now.

"If Ellie would come back you'd like it, Dad, wouldn't you? You'd be happy if that would happen, much more than now?"

I said I would, I would indeed be happy more than now, hugely more. A flock of feelings like a murmuration of starlings swirled around inside me at such a thought, then disappeared again over the dim horizon. Strange things were happening with my face too, things I couldn't control.

"Can I come and live with you one day, Dad?" is what my son Ed said next.

I bent over and started picking up lots of pebbles very fast without even registering what shape and color they were. I told him that if it was up to me I'd say yes of course, but I didn't think it was up to me. It wasn't even up to him, which isn't very logical at all, but then you have to accept that because lots of things in life aren't. It was up to Roe Deer and Roe Deer's parents and the laws of the land; and probably all three parties would not take kindly to the fact that I was penniless and living out in the wilds and not quite like other people, and also I was not (and never had been) married to Roe Deer, which seemed to make a major difference about how much of a father I was allowed to be. I knew all about it because Jo had given me a briefing just in case the subject should crop up.

I noticed Ed's look of intense concentration while I was telling him this. I said I didn't really expect him to understand and I didn't fully understand it myself. However, if he was sure he wanted to come and live here (and I would love it myself if that happened; in fact, I had begun to feel recently that my life was maybe lacking in some way, which is a thing I had not thought previously, not at all), then it was probably worth mentioning the fact to his grandparents. There was a slight possibility they might consider it was a good idea too. At least, Jo had said so. And who knew what his mother thought? I certainly didn't.

"Shall I ask her what she thinks next time I see her?" he said.

"You could," I said. But I wasn't sure. Sure is a thing I am not feeling much these days.

Ellie's harp sits under its sheet in the little room. Nobody has touched it for months now. It looks lonely there, shrouded in white. The sight of it fills me with feelings as sad as November rain. It is looking as if Ellie's harp will sit there unplayed forever.

54
ELLIE

Water. This is a city of water. Water surrounds me. I am aware of it all the time, everywhere I go. The constant lap and plash, the transparent colors, the moving ripples. Water becomes more and more seductive. It is so golden, so peaceful, so full of light. Like music, like a dreamworld. How would it feel to plunge in, to immerse myself completely, to breathe in that sweet forgetfulness? How many breaths would it take?

The idea is alluring. No more decisions. Present, past, all my problems dissolved and washed away. Beautifully simple.

For the first time I really understand what Christina is talking about when she describes her bouts of depression. It is like huge black weights loaded onto your heart. Beauty and sunshine only serve to make your own darkness darker. While the outside world becomes brighter and busier week by week, I feel I'm sinking ever deeper into hopelessness. I tell myself to get a grip, to move on . . . and the weights only get heavier. I am tired of life.

I watch the water for a while, then retreat from the balcony. I still have a sister. I still have at least one friend.

The most recent letter from Christina is lying on the bed. I bring it out and adjust the wicker chair to be sheltered a little from the Italian heat of the April sunshine. Then I sit and reread.

Christina writes that, despite the disappointing lack of beach bums, the holiday in Thailand worked wonders. Although her tan has now faded she's keeping her spirits up. She even mentions trying to quit smoking. Meow, who still hasn't forgiven her for the prolonged stay in the cattery, is at least glad on this count. Christina's son, the irascible Alex, has been on a visit, bringing the Swiss girlfriend. It seems an announcement was made at the girlfriend's house in Geneva on Christmas Day — an announcement they had tried to relay to Christina but she was unattainable. However, now that they've met, Christina approves of her daughter-in-law-to-be and is excited about the prospect of becoming a grandmother, even though she says she feels far too young for the role.

Christina has sent me a cutting from a local newspaper too. The headline caught my eye straightaway: *Taunton harpist and guitarist tie the knot.* In the photo is a handsome couple: she, immaculate and svelte in a close-fitting, low-cut wedding dress, cleavage on display; he, suited and smiling, the cat that got the cream. I wonder if little Edward was there at the wedding. I am not surprised I wasn't invited.

Everyone else is moving on with their lives, but I can't seem to do that. It has been two months since I left England. As a long-term guest I have a reduced rate at the *pensione,* but my stash of money is dwindling. When the house sale goes through I'll have to get myself sorted, but my mind shuts down every time I attempt any plans for the future.

I stir myself to action. I'll go and visit San Marco. For now I'll satisfy myself by drowning in splendor.

I don't need a jacket, as the April air is warm, but I take one anyway. I'm not sure how long I'll linger. I walk down through the palazzo and out onto the front steps, bidding *buona sera* to the lady at reception. She is listlessly turning the pages of a fashion magazine.

"Buona sera," she returns, lifting her head briefly. Then "Signora Jacobs!" she calls

448

after me as I reach the bottom step. "There is letter for you!"

I come back inside. The letter is from Vic this time. I decide to take it with me and open it on a bench somewhere. I put it in my pocket.

It would be quicker to take a vaporetto down the canals, but I take the long route along the streets and over the bridges because the walk is as important as the destination.

At last I find myself in Piazza San Marco. The paving gleams white in the sunlight. Pigeons swarm and strut hither and thither in a vast bedraggled congregation. The basilica looms in front of me.

I perch on a bench overlooking the water and pull Vic's letter from my pocket. I'm disappointed to see she hasn't written much, but there's a scrawly picture in crayons, evidently drawn by a child. I assume it's from Zoe, the younger of my nieces. I don't pay it much attention but read what Vic has written.

Hi, Ellie. Not much time to write, but will send you a proper letter soon. I was surprised when this arrived in the post yesterday. Jo sent it. She said she was babysitting for Ed the other day and he drew it while she was getting tea. The guy in the picture is Dan, as you might see by the dark eyes and hair. Jo asked Ed if the woman was Rhoda and he said no. Then he told her it was you, the kind woman called Ellie. Jo kept the picture for a while, then decided to send it here, as she still has my address. She said I could forward it to you if I thought it was a good idea. And — well — here it is!

Very much love,
Vic

I take the picture again, touched, but wondering why on earth they'd bothered.

In the background is a big, brown triangle, presumably the Harp Barn. A yellow sun sits in the sky, surrounded by ragged rays. The stick figures are standing close together at the front of the drawing. Dan has huge eyes and I have a mop of scribbled hair. Our spiky fingers are intertwined. Big smiles are on both our faces.

How did Ed get this image in his head? Dan and I have never held hands. Did I let on to Ed in any way that I loved his father? No, I never did — I was careful not to! How could a child so young have gleaned such a thing? I fold the paper up and shove it back in my pocket.

I cross the piazza and step into the vast, vaulted portico. At once I am aware of music, wonderful music like a distant chorus of angels. I push the heavy door and walk into the main body of the basilica. As my eyes adjust to the dim light, I see there's a choir assembled at the far end, some fifty or sixty singers. They have no uniform but are carefully arranged with the women in front and the men behind, tallest in the middle. Their voices rise, echoing and surging through the vaults. A small, sweaty-looking conductor waves a baton at them and leaps about. I stand and listen.

"La musica è bella, no?" says a voice at my shoulder.

"Sì, bella," I answer. It's about as far as my Italian will stretch.

"You are English?" he asks. He is a tall, smartly dressed man with glittering eyes and a curved beak of a nose.

"Yes. Is it that obvious?"

"To me, yes. You have that — how do you say? That certain freshness that is very, very typical."

I presume it's a compliment so I smile politely.

He indicates the choir. "They practice for

a concert tonight. It will be good, don't you think?"

"Yes, it's lovely music."

"Will you come this evening to hear them?"

I shake my head. "I think not."

He is standing too close. "Where are you from? London? Birmingham? Brighton?"

"No," I answer. "Exmoor." As I say the word the singing soars up to an almost impossibly high note.

"Ah, I don't know it," says the man. "You are all alone here in Venezia?"

I wish he would stop talking. I want to listen to the music. I have a feeling it is trying to tell me something.

"You are married or no?" Only an Italian could be so blatant.

"Yes," I say impatiently, although it won't be true for much longer. I don't wear my rings anymore.

I am aware of the man searching my face for signs of encouragement. I don't give him any. I fix my eyes on the choir.

"Your husband, he is a lucky man," he says finally.

"Mm-mm."

At last he is gone. I can give the music my undivided attention.

It is golden and opulent, like its surroundings. Every note is polished and perfected by the joint expertise of the conductor and the choir. The harmonies are a mosaic, full, rich and complex. The effect is dazzling.

I feel a twinge inside me. It will not leave me alone as I stand there in the vastness and listen. I turn my eyes inward and examine the twinge. Finally I recognize what it is. It is a longing to make my own much simpler music. It is a longing to play the harp again.

I have left my harp in Dan's little room in the Harp Barn on Exmoor.

Why did I do that? I could easily have taken it with me. It isn't so very heavy and I don't exactly have much other luggage.

I know the answer. I was clinging to the tiniest, last shred of hope that one day I'd go back. Crazy. It's time to let go of that now. *Let go, Ellie.* I must and I will let go.

My footsteps are heavy as I walk out of the building, through the porch and into the light of the piazza again. Ed's drawing is still in my pocket. I pull it out and take another look. Such a sweet picture. A picture of my own lost dream: so simple, just two figures, me and Dan, together. If only it had been his dream, too . . .

Then I realize there are a few words written on the other side of the paper. Words in

453

a child's large, loopy writing.

If this wud happin my DaD wud be
happi agen.

55
DAN

Spring is here. Catkins blow on the hazels. The birds tweetle loudly in the bushes. Clouds roll across the sky and days come and go. There are new beech leaves everywhere. They are meticulously folded like tiny fans. Once they uncurl themselves they are the palest of emerald greens, pleated and perfect. Their edges are trimmed with fur, downy and white. I look at them and I stroke them. My fingers are too big and rough. I show them to my son Ed. He looks at them and strokes them too. His fingers are more like it.

Phineas disappears for longer and longer. I suspect that now the sap is rising he has decided he needs a lady love and so off he goes, searching for one. Thomas says it is a miracle he didn't end up in a pie. I tell him I will not come out for a drink with him again if he says such things. He says sorry to upset you, mate. Only kidding. He says he has actually gone quite soft himself. He says he has told his wife Linda not to cook any pheasants for dinner anymore. Out of respect. He and his wife had a flaming row about it apparently. Then afterward she said she was sorry and said he did have a heart after all and she was glad of it, then they went to bed together. We toast that and Phineas's health with a fresh round of beers. Thomas says he's sorry it didn't work out for you with Ellie J, boyo. I drink deep of my beer and try not to think about it. But I do think about it. All the time.

The little birch saplings that Ellie and I planted for Ellie's birthday have begun to sprout in the seed tray. They are tiny and vulnerable, so I keep them sheltered. Weeds often grow in among them, so I keep them weeded. They get thirsty on dry days so I keep them watered. They will need to be planted out one day, but they are not ready yet. You can't rush birch trees.

Roe Deer has been to visit. She said she is extremely tired what with trying to organize her harp tour and having to put off the honeymoon and everything. She said her professional life as a harpist does keep her so busy. She said that she has talked it over with her parents and her new guitar man husband and if Ed really wants to come and live here with me, we could try it out for a while. I am, after all, his father. And her parents, although they love Ed very much, are getting rather too old and creaky to cope with his levels of energy. As long as I promise to feed him properly (not just sandwiches) and make sure he gets to school (which is a long way, so we'd have to get up very early and I'd take him in the Land Rover) and do up the little room for him so that it's comfortable for a five-year-old boy (I could certainly make it train-trackable) and other such things, then that's all right with her. But she and her parents still want to see him. Perhaps he could go to their house in Taunton at weekends and stay with me during the week — in fact, exactly the opposite of what it has been up until now. I said this seemed a very good plan to me.

I made the little room train-trackable and Ed moved in the following week. His grandparents brought him and a car stacked high with stuff. It was too much stuff to cram into the little room, so Ed and I made some decisions about how to simplify his life, and he gave his grandparents permission to take half of it away again. He will have an abundance of things when he goes to visit them at weekends, but while he is with me he will have Exmoor trees and fields and streams and pheasants and pebbles and not a lot more. His grandparents tutted and raised their eyebrows at this, but Ed seems to be happy with the idea, and so am I.

We go for lots of walks together now the days are getting longer. There are lady's-smocks growing in the marsh, hundreds of them, white with just the faintest hint of purple. The orange-tip butterflies love them. They flutter around or else sit on the petals, happily sunning their wings. The woods have turned green again. The meadows are studded with bright yellow celandines.

Ed and I climbed the hill the other day and counted sheep. Ed said it would make us fall asleep if we did that, but actually it didn't. We counted two hundred and seventeen.

"Don't you feel even a little bit sleepy?" he asked me on the two hundred and seventeenth.

I told him no.

"Nor me," he said. "Maybe it only works if you're lying down."

I told him we'd have to try that sometime.

As we were coming to the highest part of the hill (the part where there's a row of beech trees growing out of an ancient stone wall), I looked back over the view and what

I saw was this: a woman. She was quite a way down the valley, on the banks of the stream. The woman was stooping down among the young fronds to pick something up. The woman had walnut-colored hair and I knew, even though I could not at all see them from this distance, that she had eyes the color of bracken in October. She was wearing long boots and a cornflower-blue skirt and a white top. She had over one shoulder an enormous bag, canvas.

As soon as I saw her my two feet started running. They couldn't and wouldn't stop. They took me stumbling, tumbling, leaping and bounding, round the gorse bushes, over the rocks and through the bracken. They took me at full speed all the way down the hill. Ed took off too and ran after me.

Ed's legs are quite a bit shorter than mine. Because of this I arrived at the stream a long time before him.

I stopped just before I reached her. "El-lie," I panted. "Ellie."

"Dan," is what she said.

I wasn't entirely sure what I was supposed to do, but she knew exactly what to do. She took three swift paces toward me. She put both her arms around me and hugged tight, like she never wanted to let go. It hurt a bit, but at the same time was nice, very, very,

very and even more verys than that. The stream trickled and giggled beside us.

We only stopped hugging when Ed caught up with us and gave a loud "Ahem!"

"Ed," said Ellie, turning toward him. "I'm so happy to see you again." She stuck out her hand to him. He shook it up and down lots of times.

"Me too," he said.

Then she asked after Phineas and we told her Phineas was well and she said she was glad.

"I can't believe I've found you two," she said next, laughing (she always did have a problem believing things). "I was in Italy this morning. I've just arrived back in Exmoor. I came out here to the stream on impulse. I haven't even been to the Harp Barn yet."

I told her that when she did go she would find her harp waiting for her. But it was not in the little room now because that was Ed's room and full of Ed's bed and other things. Ed likes to run around in his room a lot, knocking everything over. So to keep it safe I had moved the harp into my bedroom.

"Oh," she said. "I see. Ed lives with you now?"

I confirmed that this was indeed the happy case. Ed nodded vigorously and said, "I

460

have my train in there and everything."

"That's wonderful," she said. Then she looked at the wind in the trees, then she looked back at me. "I was hoping to stay on your floor again for a bit, but I expect I could stay with Christina instead."

I told her that on no account must she stay with Christina. She must take whichever bit of my floor would be best and most suited to her needs. Although Ed should really have a room to himself and the kitchen was unpractical and the downstairs was drafty and full of sawdust, so, thinking about it, there weren't that many options. Perhaps, as her harp was now in my bedroom, she would like to sleep on my bedroom floor?

"On your bedroom floor?" she echoed.

I said yes, unless she wanted to use my actual bed. As she already knew, it was in fact a very warm, soft and nice bed.

"That's true," she said.

She turned her head toward Ed, who was now paddling in the stream.

"I almost didn't come back," she murmured, and a tiny noise like a sob came from her throat. "It was so close. If it wasn't for Ed's drawing . . ." She turned her eyes back full on me. They were large, shining like the sea.

I didn't know what drawing she was talking about and I didn't know at all what I was supposed to feel. But I did know what I did feel, and it was strong. Very strong indeed.

The breeze caught a little wisp of her hair and blew it over her face. I reached out and rearranged it beside her cheek, which was where it was before and where it looked best.

"Dan," she said, and the sunlight fell on her face, making it look all pink and blossomy. "I've got a little something for you."

"A something?" I said.

"Yes. I want to give it to you now. Just before you came here I found it in the stream and . . . well, call me sentimental, call me romantic, call me a dreamer, but I couldn't resist. Dan, I . . ." She stopped for a second and shrugged her shoulders. "This says everything. Everything I want to say."

She put the something into the palm of my hand. It was a small, flat pebble, with two rounds at the top and a point at the bottom. It was almost exactly in the shape of a heart.

"Do you understand?" she whispered.

I looked into her eyes.

I was too happy to speak, but yes, I understood.

ACKNOWLEDGMENTS

My huge and heartfelt thanks go to everyone who has helped this book come into existence. Particularly I would like to thank:

My incredible agent, Darley Anderson, along with Mary, Pippa and the whole team. What a wonderful thing that I stumbled across your website when I was at my lowest ebb! How happy I was when you took me on! What a difference you have made in every way imaginable!

My brilliant editor Francesca Best and everyone at Transworld. It is a privilege to work with you. Your dedication, vision and enthusiasm are legendary. I couldn't have dreamed of a better home for my novel.

Danielle Perez and the amazing people at Berkley. Many thanks for all your help, dynamism and inspiration from America.

Sally Bellingham for reading my initial attempts at novel writing and saying lovely things about them. Who knows if I would have continued writing without your encouragement?

Writing Magazine and *Mslexia* for all the writing tips and competitions, which have spurred me on. Special thanks go to *Mslexia* for short-listing an early version of this novel for the Women's Novel Competition in 2015 and inviting me to a rather important party at Foyles.

Literature Works for supporting writers in southwest England.

The Literary Consultancy for the Free Reads Scheme, which gave me my first professional editorial assistance.

Tim Hampson. Thank you, Tim, for answering all my questions about harpmaking and taking time to show me your beautiful harps and your workshop.

My harp. (Is it a little odd to thank my harp? I'll risk it. It was, after all, the primary inspiration for this novel.) Harp playing has enriched my life a hundredfold. Who could not fall in love with such a sound? Music is vital to Dan and Ellie in this story, and because it evokes a spectrum of emotions, lifts lives every day and has been my own motivator, I'd like to thank all music makers — especially my friends from Foxwillow and The Hummingbirds.

Exmoor. (Is it a little odd to thank

Exmoor? I'll risk that too.) Exmoor is at the heart of this book, and I owe so much to my beloved walks — to heather, hawthorns, bracken and beech trees, the streams, the slopes and the sea — that have all somehow filtered their way into the story. Of course I must also pay tribute to Phineas, a visiting pheasant who gave me the idea for a slightly offbeat fictional character.

Swanwick Writers' Summer School and Winchester Writers' Festival. Both have propelled me forward. Many thanks to those hardworking committees for the wealth of opportunities you give to budding writers. It was winning my way to Swanwick in 2014 that made me start writing seriously. Swanwick is a place where magic happens. It will always be special to me.

My fellow scribblers, who have helped me more than I can say. Simon Hall, thank you so much for your guidance, your belief in me and your endless, much-needed encouragement. Thank you also to Nia Williams for your continual cheerleading, to Rebecca Tinnelly for your companionship through numerous ups and downs on the road to publication, and to Richard Hewitt, Val Penny, Sarah Vilensky and Angie Sage for your invaluable support.

Purrsy and Tommy (The Guys), who were

constantly with me — at my side/on my lap/ usurping my writing chair/blocking the computer screen — during the creative process; who have been helpful in all sorts of ways I cannot explain.

My husband and best friend, Jonathan, whose kindness has kept me going through so much. Elephantine quantities of love and thanks for everything. This book would never have been written without you.

ABOUT THE AUTHOR

Hazel Prior is a harpist based in Exmoor, England. Originally from Oxford, she fell in love with the harp as a student and now performs regularly. She's had short stories published in literary magazines, and has won numerous writing competitions in the UK. *Ellie and the Harpmaker* is her first novel and she is working on her second.